WELCOME TO THE WORLD OF THE VANGUARDS

Book One: The Omegas
Only a vampire is man enough to teach werewolves how to fight.

Book Two: The Alpha
Someone is about to get some Spice in his life.

Book Three: The Beta
Three days of hell, in charge, and running out of antacids.

THE VANGUARDS
BOOKS 1 - 3

By
Annie Nicholas

Annie Nicholas

Lyrical Press, Inc.
New York

Lyrical Press, Incorporated

The Vanguards Books 1 - 3
13 ISBN: 9781616503086
Copyright © 2010, Annie Nicholas
Edited by Pamela Tyner
Book design by Lyrical Press, Inc.
Cover Art by Renee Rocco

Lyrical Press, Incorporated
Staten Island, New York 10308
http://www.lyricalpress.com

Published in the United States of America by Lyrical Press, Incorporated

First Lyrical Press, Inc print publication: September 2011

DEDICATION

To Pam and Renee who took a chance with a nobody with a quirky idea.

THE OMEGAS

BOOK ONE

CHAPTER 1

"I found the solution to our problem!" Eric strode into Sugar's living room holding an envelope. He handed it to her and joined the rest of his werewolf pack lounging on her mismatched furniture.

Sugar examined the front, then the back of it. "Pal Robi Incorporated. What's this?"

"It's our salvation." Eric shifted in his seat to lean forward. "Read it to everyone."

She slid her fingernail in a corner, tearing it open. The letter was printed on good quality paper with a huge golden company emblem stamped at the top. An errant blond curl slid in front of her eyes, she shoved it back behind her ear.

To the Omega pack:

I have reviewed the details of your plight. Pal Robi Incorporated deals mostly in security issues, but I find your problem worthy of my personal attention. Enclosed you will find a non-negotiable contract. Please review it closely, and have your signature notarized. The return fax number is listed on the contract so proceedings can begin. Mail the original to my office. Thank you for your business.

Sincerely,

Daedalus Pal Robi

As Sugar scanned the contract a cold surge of intuition clenched her stomach. Shocked confusion exploded inside her mind, robbing her of any coherent thought. "You hired a vampire?" Her shout shattered the silence around them.

The pack responded to her outburst with low growls directed at

Eric.

On days like this she wondered what she'd gotten herself tangled in. She wasn't pack, just a plain vanilla human. The Omegas were her neighbors. They were also her best friends.

Every full moon they became werewolves, each of them outcasts from their old packs. Driven by loneliness, Eric had solicited Sugar to help him search for others like himself. Werewolves with no attitude. Geeks of the underworld. Pansies of the paranormal.

Their friendship spanned years, since high school, when he'd rescued her from a home of drug abuse. Eric had treated her like a little sister, advising her on life in general. When he survived his werewolf attack, both their worlds shattered and their roles reversed.

Eric found four others to join him: Sam, Tyler, Katrina and Robert. No alphas ruled in this pack. They needed each other, so they became a family. All five lived in the apartment next to her.

Eyes wide, Eric held his hands out in front of him. "Mr. Pal Robi is offering to teach us how to fight."

Sugar tilted her head as she surveyed her friend. "Yeah, for a substantial fee. How can you guys afford this?" He always thought with his heart.

Eric looked at his pack, pleading. "Before you make any judgments, let's have Sugar read the contract out loud."

She held it in front of her.

This is an agreement between Pal Robi Incorporated and Eric, Sam, Katrina, Tyler, and Robert, from here forward to be known as the Omegas.

Scope:

1. Pal Robi Inc. will provide to the Omegas, training in defense,

hand-to-hand combat and small weapons use.

2. Training will take place for the duration of the period beginning with the trainer's arrival until the challenge date.

3. Combat training is inherently dangerous. Pal Robi Inc. is not responsible for injury or death sustained during such training.

4. Trainer will not intentionally hurt and-or kill any Omega during the period of this agreement.

Responsibilities of the Omegas:

1. Omegas will provide trainer from Pal Robi with appropriate lodgings.

2. Omegas will provide daylight security of said trainer.

3. Omegas will submit to the direction of the trainer without question for the duration of the training.

Fees:

1. Omegas agree to pay Pal Robi Inc. $8,000 in cash prior to the beginning of training.

2. In addition, Omegas will provide the trainer with fresh, consumable blood upon request.

Penalties:

1. Failure to provide payment renders this agreement null and void.

2. Failure to abide by the terms specified represents a breach of contract which renders the agreement null and void.

3. Breach of contract will result in an immediate investigation. Vengeance will be swift and unmerciful.

Sugar placed the contract on her lap while waiting for their reactions.

Robert held up his hand to speak, like a kid in a classroom.

She sighed. How could this pack of puppies fight a pack of wolves? "Robert, speak up. You don't need to ask permission to talk anymore, remember?"

He grinned sheepishly. "What do they mean 'vengeance will be swift and unmerciful?'"

They turned to Eric, but it was Tyler who answered. "It means if anything happens to the vamp, we can kiss our asses goodbye."

Eric stood to face his pack mates, staring at each one in turn. "How can we not hire him? The Ayumu pack officially challenged us. One of us has to fight and beat one of their alphas in a month. There's no other way."

"We be absorbed again," Katrina whispered in her exotic oriental accent, as she hugged her knees tight against her chest. Being a submissive female in a pack equated to being anyone's meat. Sugar tried to help Katrina open up and come to terms with those old wounds, but they kept her captive, stuck in this phase for life.

Tyler shuffled closer to Katrina, petting her long, black, silken tresses. She shrank from him, fear etched on her delicate features.

He looked at Sugar and shrugged. It made her furious to watch Katrina cringe. Nothing would make her happier than to get some kind of revenge on the pack mates that did this to her dainty friend. How did preying on weaker members equate to strength? She just couldn't understand werewolves.

"Couldn't you run away?" The weight of Sugar's words hung in the air.

Eric crossed his arms. "There will always be another Ayumu pack wherever we go. We're finally happy. We have jobs, friends, and a home. It's all worth fighting   for,   right guys?"

Sugar looked around her disorganized living room at her stray werewolf friends. They nodded to each other, sealing their fates.

There went her quiet life.

A vampire would be moving in next door.

* * * *

Two nights later Sugar heard struggling outside her apartment door. The book in her hand didn't grab her attention like the racket in the hall did. Standing, she left the book behind and tiptoed to the door. She cracked it open to peek outside. Eric, Tyler and Robert were carrying a large, black, shiny coffin past her apartment.

Sugar sighed and rubbed her chin. She'd like to hide in here for a month, not wanting to meet the trainer. It was silly to worry about this stranger, but he meant change.

Vampires had announced their existence years ago, becoming legal citizens. This one apparently ran his own business, which would help her friends. It wasn't like he'd be something from the horror movies that had kept her awake with nightmares when she was a kid. She squared her shoulders. Time she faced her own demons and met this new neighbor.

She padded down the carpeted hall barefoot, to where the boys were trying to wedge the coffin through their doorway.

The thin Weres battled with the box, and she smiled at the sight. "I think you need to turn it sideways and slide it at an angle." The coffin shone like glass. Temptation got the best of her, and she ran a finger along the surface. It felt cool. "Is he in there?"

"No, he's not." A rich, masculine voice drifted over her shoulder.

Sugar spun around, sucked in a hard breath, and stepped back against the coffin. Magazines ran pictures of mainstream vampires. TV even showed a few interviews with them, but nothing prepared her for this particular one.

The deep blue color of his eyes reminded her of the sea. Well-defined cheekbones led to a strong jaw and a slight teasing smile on his full, sensual lips.

A stirring began deep inside her. He wasn't beautiful, more sexy and hot.

Breathless, Sugar experienced an impulsive urge to ask him to rub the smooth, pale skin of his bald head all over her body. A hunger awoke, one she thought lay dormant. It unfurled inside of her and wanted to be fed.

"You're not wolf." He loomed over her. A black tattoo on his well-developed chest peeked out from underneath his partially unbuttoned white dress shirt.

Eric tapped her chin with his finger, silently instructing her to close her mouth. "Sugar is our neighbor." He gestured to the rakish vampire. "This is Mr. Pal Robi."

Heat crept up her cheeks. She stuck out her hand. "Nice to meet you."

His hand engulfed hers while he shook it tenderly. "Is that your real name?" He didn't release his hold.

She dropped her chin. A thrill ran through her. "My parents have a poor sense of humor. I have a twin named Spice."

Amusement creased the skin around his eyes. "Sugar and spice, and everything nice."

The poem annoyed her more every time someone quoted it. "Yes, I've heard the rest. I'm not a little girl anymore." She withdrew her hand from his. Maybe the phenomenal packaging was only skin deep.

A carnal light sparked in his eyes. "Definitely not a little girl. You may call me Daedalus." His gaze traced her face and slipped lower, caressing the curves of her breasts, then down along her hips.

Sugar gasped as this alarming man studied her. She could almost hear the Omegas leering at her response to Daedalus. "I'll get out of your way."

He didn't move as she pressed herself against the wall to squeeze by him. The tips of her breasts brushed his well-muscled arm. They pebbled, pushing through her blouse. Naughty images of him running those large palms over her nipples played in her mind.

Her panties got damp as a flash of desire burned through her. She realized he'd wanted her to brush against him. He was such a cad, and it made her want him even more.

* * * *

Daedalus watched her heart-shaped ass wiggle back down the hall. She was ravishing. He would never mix business with pleasure, but she didn't belong to the pack. Just a neighbor and a bonus.

She reminded him of the 1950's pin-up poster girls, pretty and full of luscious curves. He still kept those posters in storage.

Sugar. His thoughts sprang to the hard caramelized shell on crème brulee. He would like to ignite her sweetness into a passionate inferno.

Daedalus had felt her response to him as she brushed his arm. The flush of color in her face pleased him. He wanted her to turn and look his way one more time before she entered her home.

The Omegas began wrestling with his coffin again. "Can we call you Daedalus?" one of them piped up.

Sugar glanced back at him.

"No." He gave her a shameless wink.

CHAPTER 2

Sugar walked to the Omegas' apartment. Quiet dominated their corner of the building since Mr. Pal Robi's arrival last week. She'd seen them when she went out on her garden balcony to water the plants last night. They jogged with their vampire trainer on the sidewalk. He ran, and they straggled behind. Other than that she hadn't seen any of them. No one came over to visit. Not even Katrina, who had become a permanent fixture in her home.

She stood in front of their door and wiped her sweaty palms on her old, worn jeans. *Maybe I should have changed.*

The thought irritated her. She'd never worried about her looks before he moved in. She'd never lusted after a man like this either. Her past lovers always started as emotional relationships, then grew into something physical. What she experienced with Daedalus seemed more animalistic. If she fucked him and got it over with, then maybe her mind would clear. The memory of his sexy half-smile with a wink haunted her every night. Those blue eyes, broad shoulders, firm body, bald head—

The apartment door swung open, and the demon of her fantasies stood staring at her, shirtless. A thin sheen of sweat covered his pale skin as if he'd been doing some vigorous exercises. It made him shine. The circular tattoo she'd glimpsed through his shirt on their first meeting covered his heart, a black snake eating its tail.

He gave her a crooked smile, melting her to the spot. "Hello, sweetness. I got tired of waiting for you to knock." He stepped back and gestured for her to come in.

As she entered the Omegas' apartment she noticed the place looked cleaner than usual. Five wolves under one roof could make quite a clutter. Daedalus must have them run a tighter ship.

"How did you know I was out in the hall?" A little shaken after his sudden appearance, her concentration slipped and she couldn't remember her reason for being there. His being half-naked didn't help.

"I have a good sense of smell." He closed the door behind her.

"You smelled me? Good to know for future reference."

Fingers ran through her curls as she walked past him. She glanced over her shoulder, but his back faced her while he locked the door. It must have been her imagination. The touch felt real though. Did he move that fast?

He finished with the locks and turned around. "I heard you walk down the hall too. Why were you waiting?"

She didn't know, looking for some courage maybe or a little self-confidence with an internal pep talk. "I was thinking about going back for a book Sam wanted to borrow," she lied. Something unsettling occurred to her. "Can you read minds too?"

He chuckled and leaned in close, his nose almost touching hers. "Possibly. Are you thinking dirty thoughts?"

"No!" Her cheeks burned.

"Then I guess I can't."

Did that mean he was thinking them?

He brushed past her to sit on the worn, beige couch. His touch sent a thrill through her, it unnerved her too. He tapped the cushion next to him.

Out of her element around him and his flirtatious ways, she sat in the armchair across from the couch. His request to sit next to him ignored since she couldn't trust herself to not jump on his lap. Her lack of self-control surprised her. She allowed her eyes to roam his handsome face to his bare chest, each time she jerked them back up to meet his stare, they'd meander back down to those well-defined muscles.

An unfamiliar quiet filled the living room, where laughter and banter normally flooded the space. "Is anyone else home?"

"No." He leaned forward, resting his elbows on his knees. The heat in his gaze grew as he made his interest in her clearer. "We have the place to ourselves. What did you have in mind?"

Not sure what to do with the invitation, she blushed even more as the room became warmer. What she had in mind was to tear her clothes off and let him have his way with her, but the Omegas could walk in at any moment. "Where did they go?" she croaked, her mouth and throat gone dry.

His smile widened as the burning heat in his eyes turned into amusement. "I've sent them on a mission." He snickered to himself. "See..." He gestured around the room. "They don't have a television, and I *really* need to watch football this weekend. I have a division of Pal Robi Security housed not far from here, so I've sent them to steal theirs."

She raised her eyebrows, her anxiety and insecurity combusted in her fury. "You want them to steal for you?" The nerve this vampire displayed, to turn her kind-hearted friends into thieves. It made her blood boil. A mission indeed. She knew hiring him would be a mistake.

He leaned against the couch, his arms along the back. "Is taking stuff from yourself stealing? Technically, I own the television."

She stood up, hands on her hips. "Will your security see it that way?"

"No."

She stepped closer to him. "They'll hurt them, Daedalus. This isn't a joke. Your contract stated they wouldn't get injured."

He stood up, and up, to overshadow her. She felt small and fragile next to him.

The sexy smile faded. "Don't quote my contract to me. A little ass kicking is part of the training. They're werewolves, Sugar, not human. My security can't damage them too much. They can take more of a beating than you think, or for that matter, than they think. If the Omegas don't stop fearing pain they may as well concede the challenge to the Ayumu pack."

"Is that so bad?"

He raised an eyebrow.

"Instead of fighting? I don't want any of them to get hurt. If they can't win, they should concede or run away."

"Who said they can't win?"

His question slapped her across the face. "Win? Eric and Robert are computer programmers. Katrina's a waitress in Chinatown, Tyler's a real estate agent, and Sam delivers pizza. Not exactly warrior material."

"The problem is you see them in only a human perspective. They went against pack instinct to follow their alphas, for whatever reason, and banded together. Do you have any idea how difficult that is or how unique they are? It takes strength of character. They'll win with some guidance."

"What kind of guarantee can you offer them?"

He shook his head. "None."

"They agreed to this?"

"They didn't have a choice, sweetness." His voice became tender as he pushed her hair behind an ear. "I understand you care for them, but coddling them won't help defend their freedom. Do you want them to become the scapegoats of the Ayumu? Where the pack could take their frustrations out on them?"

She shrugged his hand away and looked at her feet. "Of course not." In her book, violence only begot violence. Nothing she did or said would keep the Omegas safe. She hated to admit it, but maybe Daedalus could save them.

His sigh caught her attention, and she brought her head up. He'd sat on the couch again, his arms crossed over his bare chest while he watched her.

She sat on the edge of the armchair, determined not to apologize for her beliefs. "Does it need to be a fight to the death? There has got to be some other way for packs to resolve things."

His expression did not soften with her heartfelt words. "There used to be. The werewolf packs have diminished over the centuries due to infighting and territory wars. Many of the young were left untrained in the ways of honor. After corresponding with Eric, it became clear pack issues are getting worse, with slavery and crime being among them. The Omegas are damaged goods but young and good hearted. It's a sad time when a vampire needs to teach werewolves how to be 'pack.' I'll do my best to instruct them."

"In the 'ways of honor?'"

He chuckled. "No, they're not ready." He grinned and leaned toward her. "Did I pass my interview?"

She couldn't help but laugh. "Yes. I didn't come here to grill you though. I wanted to invite them to dinner tomorrow."

"Their schedule is pretty full. I'll pass the message on." He arched a brow. "What about me?"

"Huh?"

"Am I invited?"

"Oh, of course. I didn't know you could eat."

"I can't, but I'd like the company."

"Sure, you're welcome to come over." What was she doing? She did her best to keep herself isolated, to keep her life quiet and stress free. This struggle became harder when she'd adopted her werewolf neighbors as friends. Now she found herself lusting after a kickass vampire. Had she lost her mind?

She rose to her feet. "I should go." On the way to the door she could sense his presence close behind her.

The visit went better than she'd expected. Not an Omega to be seen, but her conversation with Daedalus cleared a few of her concerns. She didn't think Daedalus would lead them astray.

It wasn't every day she got to spend time conversing with a half-naked, sexy vampire. Maybe she could be friends with him, hopefully more. Why did he have this effect on her? There were a lot of good looking men in the world, but she didn't lust after *them* like a cat in heat.

He undid the locks and opened the door for her.

Something he'd said about the werewolf packs nagged at her. She looked back at him and tried not to get caught up into his dark blue eyes. "When you spoke of the werewolf packs' changes over the centuries, it sounded like you experienced it yourself. You're very old, aren't you?"

He barked a surprised laugh. "What a horrid thing to say."

"I didn't mean... I meant... I'm sorry." She touched his shoulder, then jerked her hand away. A thrill electrified her fingers where they'd touched his skin.

He continued to smile and took her hand. "I would have said 'experienced.'" He pressed his full, lush lips to the back of it, his stare never leaving hers. The kiss felt warm and moist. The gesture sent tingles straight to her pussy, making her wet.

She bit her bottom lip to prevent a moan from escaping. The sensation of his mouth against her skin lingered on her all the way back to her apartment.

What should she do? He represented all the things she feared—adventure, violence and passion. After his kiss, she expected it to be hot, dirty, really great passion. He could easily seduce her, and although excited at the prospect, she worried that he'd steal her heart.

She needed to lock it away to avoid attachment. Falling in love with an immortal being would only lead to sorrow.

She needed to keep this as a fun little fling.

* * * *

Daedalus closed the door, her taste still on his lips. He'd been pleased when he'd first smelled her scent as she stood in the hallway and debated with herself about knocking on his door. Fear and anxiety intertwined in her luscious smell, but so did desire.

Her loyalty to her friends drew him to her even more. He admired such qualities. He also admired the curves of her breasts and the way her worn jeans fit snug to her nice ass.

He needed to stop thinking with his cock when he was around her. At first, he'd thought a late night tryst would be possible, but clearly her relationship with the Omegas involved more than being just a neighbor. When she jumped up in anger at his description of tonight's mission, and the vehemence flashed from her eyes, it took all his restraint to not kiss her. Their simmering attraction could be fanned into an inferno.

He needed to cool off. She represented all the things tender and gentle he lacked in his existence. Since she'd left a hollowness filled his chest. Not a good sign, it meant he'd probably fall hard for her. None of the boys had claimed Sugar when he'd made a pass at her a week ago, and werewolves were pretty territorial when it came to mates. But these boys didn't act like traditional Weres. He'd better clear things up when they got back from their mission.

He needed to determine if he should have her before the challenge or after.

CHAPTER 3

Daedalus knocked once on Sugar's apartment door, and the angel of his fantasies swung it open. The messy chaos of her curls made a halo around her face and would have taken his breath away if he had any. Her gaze slid past him as if checking for someone else, and her wide smile wavered when she saw he was alone. Clearly, she expected the Omegas, and a sharp pang of jealousy surprised him. He wanted to change her disappointed look, make it something more wanton.

"I know I promised they'd be over for dinner tonight, but they're still out running, Sugar. They'll have to come over tomorrow night."

She turned to look out the French doors that led to her patio garden. Rain beat down on the flowers and the wind tore at their leaves. "It's storming."

He raised an eyebrow at her comment, unable to see the problem. The storm front didn't carry any lightning. A bit of cold rain and wind would break the monotony of the Omegas' routine.

Yesterday's raid to steal a television had become a farce. He had found the small pack hogtied on the apartment building's doorstep very late last night. Good thing the other tenants in the building had been asleep. His security team had gone easy on the werewolves in his view. If running in a storm got Sugar upset, he'd best keep this hilarious story to himself. He couldn't remember the last time he'd laughed so hard.

Tyler and Robert had yet to speak to him since the incident. Katrina never did talk to him much. Eric and Sam showed promise though. They were "manning-up" to the situation and laughed with him.

Sauntering in, he pushed past Sugar to examine the small apartment. The smells of dinner warmed the tidy little kitchen to the right. Books lay scattered and stacked on every available surface in the living room on his left. Layers of thick rugs covered the floors under a collection of comfortable, mismatched love seats. They faced the French doors overlooking her green garden retreat, setting the mood for tranquility. She didn't decorate by style but by texture.

He loved it.

Except something was missing. He sighed and shook his head. "You don't have a television either. Guess I won't be watching the football game tonight." His frustration tied a knot in his gut. First, his lack of assessing the Omegas' situation better, then Sugar's tempting presence, and now he couldn't take pleasure in his one hobby.

She giggled.

The quiet, melodious sound made him smirk and shake his head. He twisted to glare at her. Not for laughing but for being so damn adorable. They had the apartment to themselves, the cubs were out chasing raindrops, and he'd run out of things to distract him from his lustful thoughts. It looked like he would surrender to her charms sooner than later.

She'd clapped her hands over her rosebud mouth. The gesture made her tight pink blouse rise enough to reveal a peek of creamy, soft flesh. The buttons strained between her firm, full breasts. He wanted to rip the top open and let those buttons fly.

"I guess they didn't succeed in getting the television," she mumbled behind her hands before letting them fall to her sides, lowering her shirt. "There's a sports bar down the street, you can catch the game there."

"I don't like sport bars." He could imagine the trouble his presence would cause at such a place. Their business came from selling food and drink. What could he possibly purchase to watch the game? A waitress? Vampires were legal citizens, yet still not well liked.

Sugar shifted back a few steps, stifling another nervous laugh.

If he focused his hearing, he could hear her heart race. She smelled of lavender and cinnamon. A tinge of fear tainted her scent. He didn't want her to be afraid. "Do I frighten you?"

"Frighten?" She stopped her backward motion. "No, not really, more like intimidate." She gave him a shy smile, but the way her eyes traveled over his body spoke of unashamed interest.

His cock grew thick at her heated gaze. "Intimidate I can accept. That's my job." He grinned and advanced on his tempting prey. "You have nothing to fear though. I don't bite, not unless you want me to." The delightful way her eyes widened at his comment undid him.

* * * *

Sugar retreated further until she bumped against the cool metal of her fridge. She'd been disappointed to find only Daedalus at her door but didn't regret his presence one bit now. His tight, black t-shirt outlined every hard, scrumptious detail of his chest. Lust awakened. An urge to splay her hands on his delicious body, kneading those hard muscles, gripped her.

With each sinuous step he closed in on her until she found herself cornered. His body inspired all kinds of naughty ideas. She'd love to pour massage oil on his smooth head and let it drip down his naked body, so she could rub it all over him.

"I've been thinking about you." His husky voice brushed along her skin. Caged between his arms against the fridge, she felt trapped. Her heart raced with expectation, and she tried to moisten her suddenly dry lips by pressing them together.

He leaned in until his face almost touched hers. Yearning replaced his mischievous grin. His eyes feasted on her as they traced along her face to focus on her mouth.

"You have?" She wanted to drown in his half-lidded gaze.

"Haven't you thought of me, Sugar?"

The way he spoke her name, like it tasted good, sent a thrill down her spine. Every single night   he   invaded her thoughts, starring in all her fantasies, but she couldn't admit that to him. Even though he'd openly admired her, the desire he now displayed amazed her. She was a librarian, not some porn star, though his actions made her feel like one. "You've been on my mind once or twice."

Almost touching her, he denied her a kiss. Their lips were close enough for her to sense their movement when he spoke. "What will I do to entertain myself while your friends are gone?"

The wait for his embrace made her burn with feral passion. It grew too much. She laid a gentle kiss on his mouth in sweet surrender. A bare touch.

"I could think of a few things." Who was this bold woman using her voice? Her curiosity for him made her brave enough to lose all her discretion.

His eyes widened, amusement crinkling their edges. His tongue traced his lips where she kissed him, like he could taste her.

Mesmerized, she watched, tingles rippling along her own mouth as if he licked her lips instead. Anticipation fluttered in her stomach.

"So can I." Avid desire still shone in his eyes when he glanced down at her. His responding kiss crushed her to the fridge as he cupped her ass to lift her from the floor.

Her arms entwined around his strong neck, and her legs circled his narrow hips. All the strength of his body wrapped in her limbs made her wetter. Such savage hunger for a man was a new experience. She wanted him to ride her hard and make her scream for mercy.

Daedalus pressed against her. Even with their jeans between them, she could feel his length, hard and firm, bulging against his zipper.

His kiss became an easy, practiced slide of his mouth against hers, gently demanding. She expected skill but not the ravenous appetite he displayed. His tongue toyed with her bottom lip, then entered her mouth in a slow, sinuous stroke. He tasted of something faintly metallic, like blood.

Her stomach knotted at the slight taint, but it dissolved when his hand cupped her breast, found her hard, throbbing nipple and rolled it between his fingers. She wriggled beneath his touch, grinding herself against his hard cock.

He moaned and pulled away. "Damn, you're driving me crazy."

She reached up for another taste, craving him.

A sinful smile tugged his mouth. He undid the buttons of her blouse one at a time until he exposed her thin, white lace bra.

She bit at her bottom lip as she watched. Her head spun with need. She wanted Daedalus badly. There had been enough fantasizing about him, now it would come true. Finally.

He slipped the bra strap from her shoulder to allow one of her nipples to escape its confines, and boosted her to give his mouth access to it. The pleasure he produced, as he sucked, shot straight to her clit.

She wriggled and couldn't control the small noises of pleasure she made. The heat of his mouth and the touch of his tongue drove her wild. "Ah... Yes." She raged with fever, and he was the cure.

Daedalus rained kisses along her exposed neck while lowering her to rest against his hips again. She couldn't stop her gasp when he nipped and tasted her flesh. Those sharp fangs teased but never broke skin. She felt his lips smile at her reaction. He pinched the hard nipple under his hand and ground the growing bulge in his jeans against her groin.

Short of breath, she clung to him. "Stop teasing me." Her pussy steadily grew creamier with each grinding thrust.

His laughter rumbled deep within his chest. Demanding her mouth, he pressed his tongue inside, probing and greedy, leaving nothing unexplored. He released her breast to undo her jeans and yank them low enough to give him access. His other hand supported her weight against the fridge while he slid his fingers in her panties. They brushed between her outer labia. An enticing stroke along sensitive flesh.

She gripped his t-shirt when he plunged inside her. Pinned between his hard body and the fridge, with his fingers deep inside, she didn't have much room to move.

He pressed his thumb to her clit, making circular motions, steadily pumping his fingers inside of her. His tongue traced along her ear. "You're very wet."

Grasping his shoulders, she groaned and tried to rock her hips to his rhythm. She'd forgotten how good a man's touch could be. Pleasure throbbed and built. "Please, Daedalus...please." The pressure released in an explosion of sinful delight, sending cascades of ecstasy through to her core.

She writhed under his hand and bucked against the fridge, trapped while this passion rode her, sending thrills of bliss down her limbs. Her legs clenched him closer, her sex grinding on his fingers. The pleasure seemed to know no end.

A sigh escaped her as the passion released her from its grip. She rested her head back against the cool fridge. Sweat trickled down her neck and between her breasts. Her blouse stuck to her skin and her curls to her face. Satiated, she closed her eyes to rest. Daedalus had other ideas.

Still thunder-struck, she didn't understand when Daedalus whirled her to stand in front of the kitchen island, until he yanked her jeans and panties to her ankles.

He didn't pull off his own jeans but tugged them down enough to expose his long, thick cock. "It's my turn." His voice, rough with heat, brushed her ear as he spun her to face the island.

His cock slid against her ass. The angle was all wrong, so he lifted her to lay face down across the counter, then grasped her hips.

He ran his hard length along her ripe opening. It nudged her, proceeding achingly slow as he stroked himself into her. The agonizing stretch of her sex caused some discomfort, almost to the point of pain. He continued his gentle entry until he was sheathed deep inside of her.

He stayed there, running his hands over her ass while spasms of tenderness and excitement surged through her, squeezing around him.

"Sugar... You're so tight." Hands trembling, he pumped slow deliberate strokes, each one accompanied by a small groan.

She struggled for breath, panting as his rhythm grew rougher.

He pounded, pressed, and plunged deep inside of her. Hot and hard, faster and faster, stoking the fire growing in her core.

The pleasure made her back arch, tightening her muscles around him, feeling every thick inch. His noises grew louder and wilder as he thrust himself in. And in. And in.

The orgasm coursed through her, suddenly loosed by his merciless onslaught. She bucked once more to the ecstasy while he held on and rode her. Mindless in its power, she cried out, unable to stop.

He joined her in duet and cried out, rejoicing in his conquest when he spilled himself into her yielding sex.

* * * *

They tumbled to the floor in a tangle of limbs. Daedalus rolled onto his back, off Sugar, still panting from the astounding sex. He scooped her up to cuddle against his chest. She fit perfectly in his arms, as if she'd always belonged there.

The smell of lavender drifted from her silken, wavy blond hair as she murmured quiet, satisfied noises.

He grinned and couldn't help feeling smug. That response rocked him, he'd expected something meeker from her. The passion she unleashed on him! He loved being surprised. After such a long existence, not many things astonished him anymore. More than a sweet temptation, this small, gentle neighbor symbolized a tornado of spun sugar. Now that he'd tasted it, he hungered for more. He was addicted.

To think he'd only been looking for a television tonight. He heaved up onto an elbow. "Let's go to the bedroom."

Looking up at him, her eyes widened. "More?"

He kissed the tip of her nose. "Of course." He pulled up his pants, then helped her stand. Her knees buckled when she got to her feet. His smug grin returned as he carried her to the bedroom.

The thumps of feet entering the building caught his attention. He sighed in disappointment. The Omegas were back. He'd hoped to get through one more round before they returned. No football and now no more sex.

Their progress should have pleased him. They'd cut their running time significantly. The rain helped, as he'd guessed.

He laid Sugar down on the blankets, taking in her honest, open face. She wanted him, he could smell it. Too bad their time for tonight was up.

He pushed a lock of hair from her face. "Your friends are back. They'll be hungry. Do you still want them to come over?"

Eyes wide she looked down at her half-naked body, panic clearly on her face.

He placed a gentle hand on her shoulder. "They'll be soaked from the storm and will have to dry off first. When they're done, I'll send them over." He chuckled. "You have time to clean up, and they can have the rest of the night off."

"What about you? I want you to stay."

Those five words made him happier than they should have. He would have loved to jump in her warm bed and make love all night, but he'd put something off for far too long. She cared for the Omegas. If they were to survive he needed to get this done.

"Another night. I have to go meet someone." He kissed her, savoring her warmth, then left before the Omegas made their way up the three flights of stairs.

While they ate, he planned on checking out the alpha of the Ayumu pack. Damn, he hated rain.

CHAPTER 4

Sugar struggled through the door with a bag of groceries, surprised to find the Omegas in her living room, flipping through her books. A flood of joy poured over her and proved how much she missed them. Without the Omegas, she felt alone.

She took a breath to settle her startled nerves and closed the door. Once in the apartment, she noted there were only three of them: Tyler, Katrina and Robert. She stomped on the small spike of disappointment when she didn't spot her vampire stud among them. They hadn't hired him to entertain her, after all.

Boxes of Chinese take-out sat on the kitchen island. Every time she looked at the island a thrill ran through her. No one had ever taken her with such raw desire. Daedalus was a skilled and scrumptious beast.

The time she'd spent with him had made her feel so alive and sexy. A small part of her wished it hadn't happened, because now she thought of nothing else. Men like him didn't want relationships, and she could accept that, but a break-the-box-springs, bring-the-ceiling-down affair would be a splendid change in her life.

A week had passed—who was she kidding, ten days and thirteen hours—since their fun in the kitchen. His strong body and careful restraint made her feel secure. He could have easily broken her, instead he'd ignited her. Her poor, abused fridge sat tilted to the left, it would never be the same. Since their glorious evening, time sped and left them only passing kisses to tease her awakened libido. Her frustration mounted.

"No training tonight?" Her voice sounded too high.

Tyler grinned ear to ear and spun his chopsticks to point at their group. "No training for us anymore."

Katrina sat close to him, looking more at ease with herself than

Sugar could remember. What a mismatched couple. Katrina's somber, beautiful oriental features countered his crazy red curls and goofy antics.

"What happened?" Sugar held up her hand. "Wait. Where are Eric and Sam?"

Robert towered over her as he took the grocery bag and started putting things away. "Eric is the answer to your first question."

She blinked. "What?"

Robert continued from behind the fridge door, "The night of the big storm, your *boyfriend* went and checked out the alpha of the Ayumu pack. I don't think he was happy with what he saw. Since then he's mainly been training Eric."

The reference to Daedalus as her boyfriend caused heat to rise in her face. She turned to Tyler. "You've been out training all week with them, though."

He twirled his chopsticks around his ear. "Something about keeping us as back-up in case Eric wimps out, but I'm not worried, he's doing great. Turning into a werewolf ninja. We're off the hook now."

"And Sam?"

Robert finished with the groceries and ran his hand through his short, scruffy, brown hair. "Back at our place moping. He wants to be the one to fight. Did you know your fridge is listing to the left?" He bent down to adjust a wheel under the fridge.

Katrina fluidly rose from the floor and fixed Sugar a plate of take-out.

"Why does Sam want to fight? Could he win?" Sugar accepted the plate Katrina offered. "Thank you."

Robert stood. "*Mr. Pal Robi* doesn't think so, and he's the expert."

Katrina touched Sugar's arm. "Sam want protect Eric." Her

exotic, heavy accent played with her words. She lifted a box from behind the take-out. "Let play Scrabble."

Eric would fight for the Omegas. Sugar smiled to herself, imagining a ninja werewolf taking on all the wrongs of the world. He'd always wanted to be a superhero. She hoped it didn't get him killed.

The idea of Sam fuming by himself didn't sit well with her. "Set up the board, I'll get Sam." She walked down the hall to their apartment and knocked on the door.

This meant the others could get on with life. Robert and Eric worked out of their apartment on whatever computer project the company gave them, the others took time off, and Sam lost his job.

No one answered the door, so she knocked again. "Sam, it's Sugar. I know you're in there, open up."

The door cracked open and Sam peeked out with his pale gray, red-rimmed eyes.

"We're going to play Scrabble. Tyler has the dictionary memorized, and I need you to help me beat him." She smiled, but he stepped back.

"I'm not in the mood."

"Sam, what's wrong?" The sound of heavy footsteps echoed up the stair well. She could hear Daedalus chuckle at something Eric said.

"Ask Mr. Pal Robi." He closed the door in her face.

Hands on hips, she swiveled on her lover and best friend as they arrived in the hall.

"Oh, oh." Eric turned around.

"Stay where you are, ninja wolf. The three of us need to have words."

"Words?" Daedalus glanced at Eric behind him. "Is that a modern way to say ménage?"

Sugar approached him and slapped his hard abs with the back of her hand. She thought it probably hurt her more than him.

His eyes flared. "Hey."

"Words, means she's pissed." Eric peered over Daedalus's shoulder.

"If Sam still wants to train he should be allowed to."

"This is why you're angry? They don't all have to fight, just one. *I* need to be able to focus on Eric, and *you* need to mind your own business."

A flash of red blinded her for a moment. She ground her teeth and attempted to form a coherent response. "My business?"

Daedalus stepped back as she came forward with her finger pointed in his face.

"You demon loving, zombie breeder. They signed a contract and paid for training. Sam lost his job because they only wanted him to work nights. The others are happy to be off the hook, but Sam still wants in. You need to keep your end of the deal." His dark blue eyes bored into hers, and she remembered who she was confronting—a very strong and deadly vampire. She swallowed, then retreated a step.

"Eric, get your sparring partner."

He grinned while he brushed past Sugar and went to his apartment to get Sam. As soon as the door closed, Daedalus picked her up and pressed her to the wall. His mouth found hers in a savage kiss.

She shoved at his shoulders, but she may as well have tried to push a mountain. One of his hands found her breast and pinched her nipple until it pebbled at the attention.

Her struggles didn't last long before she surrendered to him and rubbed her hands along his smooth scalp. All her anger evaporated, its heat turned to passion.

He kissed along her jaw until his fangs rested on her jugular, firm enough to prick.

Her heart raced, and her blood went cold with terror. Trapped in his arms, she fought to get away. A scream built in her throat, but before it came out he let her go.

"I didn't mean to scare you. I thought you wouldn't mind."

She steadied herself with a hand on the wall. "You thought wrong. I never considered letting you feed off me. It surprised me."

"Next time I'll ask first."

"Yes, please do." She went up on tiptoe and kissed his cheek to take the sting out of her reaction. A door opened and closed behind her.

Eric and Sam walked down the hall. Daedalus nodded at them and went down the stairs followed by Sam. No words were exchanged.

Sugar rolled her eyes. Men.

Eric stopped beside her before descending. "You okay, sugarbear? You're pale."

"Yeah, fine." He hadn't called her that since high school.

"Looks like Daedalus is helping you grow a backbone too." He leaned down and kissed her forehead. "He's good for you." Then he left to catch up to the others.

She returned to her apartment with new determination to beat Tyler at Scrabble.

* * * *

The next morning Sugar basked in the pale morning light among her cherished plants on the patio. She noticed Katrina peeking around the patio door. Sugar never locked her apartment since the Omegas moved in, one of the perks with having werewolves as neighbors.

She patted the space next to her on the bench while she twirled a single red rose under her nose.

Katrina sat by her and pointed to the flower. "Is it from Daedalus?"

Sugar smiled and continued admiring the Chicago skyline. The sweet scent of the rose filled her senses. "Yes, I found it by my pillow when I woke up. It came with this poem." She offered the handwritten note for Katrina to read.

Her soft giggle, a rare precious thing, shook their shared bench. "Is nice."

Sugar took the note. She folded it carefully and placed in her robe pocket. "Who knew he could rhyme?" Their laughter sweetened the morning air. What a romantic gesture. A fire-breathing dragon sleeping in her bed wouldn't have surprised her as much as Daedalus's tender gift. She wished he'd woken her up, though.

"Things serious between you?" Katrina's question broke her reverie.

"I would've said 'no' until I read the poem." Sugar sighed, leaned her chin on her hand, and stared back at Chicago. It seemed he might want a relationship after all. The poem said he thought of her through the nights when they were apart and couldn't wait to get back to her. Maybe she read too much in his words and he meant only the sex.

She turned to Katrina. "How can I be in a relationship with someone who can't grow old with me?"

Katrina blinked, then chuckled. "You asking wrong person. Tyler is the romantic."

"Speaking of twisted relationships, you snuggled up close to him last night while playing Scrabble. Are you his mate?"

Katrina lowered her gaze.

Sugar could almost see her friend physically shrinking back inside herself. She reached out to touch her knee. "You're my friend, Katrina. Whatever happened in the past is over. Don't build walls between yourself and those who care about you. Build them between yourself and the past."

Katrina let out a shaky breath. "I know. I lucky to have such good friends. It take time. Tyler will wait, he say." She looked back at Sugar with a fragile smile. "You take some of you own advice."

"What?"

"You need build wall to you past. Daedalus strong vampire, gentle heart." She tapped her chest with this proclamation.

"Gentle heart?"

"See?" She craned her neck around, then showed her wrists. "No bite me, never touch me or feed. He no ask me but somehow know my pain. Gentle heart. Is good man."

Sugar caressed the folded piece of paper in her pocket with new insight. A tough exterior and a soft heart. It didn't change the fact she was human and he a vampire.

Katrina touched her knee. "Daedalus good for you. I see change in you."

"What change?"

"You walk different."

"Well...he's kind of big, and I did get sore..."

"Eww! Not that!" Katrina giggled while slapping playfully at Sugar. "You walk more free."

Sugar lifted an eyebrow and tilted her head. She loved Katrina with all her heart, sometimes the language barrier made things difficult though.

Katrina sighed with frustration and got up. "I..." She pointed at herself. "Am you." She pointed at Sugar, then started walking around the patio, swinging her hips as she took great strides with her short legs.

Sugar's mouth dropped open. "I do *not* walk like Betty Boop." She laughed at Katrina. Tyler's sense of humor had rubbed off on her. Sugar would do anything to have things work out for them.

Laughing, Katrina came to sit by her again. They watched as the clouds floated by the city and the planes made trails marring the sky.

"I noticed a full moon two nights ago. Where did you and the boys go for the change?"

Katrina bounced on the bench. "Daedalus take us out to woods. No tame city park but far into the wild places." She said 'wild' with awe and wonder. "You know Nosferatu clan and werewolf share the hunt in old times?"

"No. What clan?"

"Daedalus's clan, Nosferatu. He is upset we know nothing of it. He angry the packs lose the way with old law. He teach us."

The pride in Katrina's voice surprised Sugar. She'd never heard it before. Daedalus must have inspired it. Her vampire warrior with the soft heart.

CHAPTER 5

The window stuck as he tried to slide it open. Silence was of the essence on his mission, so he couldn't force it with his strength. Footsteps echoed in the alley below, so he became one with the brick building as he hung upside down, held by fingertips and toes.

A human male strolled by while whistling *Dixie* under his breath. The man rummaged through the trash cans as if shopping at the market.

Silently, the monster on the wall banged his forehead against the brick. His sweet, juicy target slept on the other side of the glass. Close enough to smell.

Lavender mixed with clean cotton.

On any other night he would have had the patience to wait out the homeless man. Not tonight. He built a low growl in his chest and let it vibrate through the alley. The rattle of a lid crashing to the ground was the first response, the pitter-patter of running the second.

He grinned. Mission accomplished, it was about time. With a little applied pressure to the frame, the window opened enough to slip inside.

Sugar slept soundly, cocooned in her soft, thick blankets. Probably tired after an evening spent in laughter with her friends. Quiet snores escaped her blissful repose. Unaware of the shadow that slid into her room and stalked around her bed. Ignorant of the monster who wished to feed on her sweet, yielding body.

Delicious.

He removed his underwear, one of only two things he wore, and tossed it in a corner. With preternatural quiet he untucked the covers from the mattress. The blanket flowed off her in a smooth slow motion, lest she be woken too early. She laid spread across the white cotton sheets. An undersized, blue t-shirt barely covered her generous round bosom, her midriff exposed above a pair of white panties clinging to her hips.

A beautiful midnight snack.

* * * *

The bed quivered as someone crawled over her. Sugar woke, startled, and tried to sit up, but something heavy kept her pinned and held her hands to the bed. Her heart raced. She struggled against the solid mass and kicked out. A scream tore from her throat.

"Hey, sweet thing." A husky male voice cut through her terror.

"Daedalus?" Stunned, she stopped her tussle. "You scared me!" A mix of annoyance with anticipation swept away her adrenaline rush.

The weight of his delicious body pressed her to the bed. Her irritation dissolved when he gave her a moist, deep kiss while laughter rumbled in his chest. Still pinned, she kissed him back, eager for pleasure, and joined in with her giggles.

Their embrace grew longer and deeper, the laughter forgotten.

She explored his mouth, touching both delicate, sharp fangs with the tip of her tongue, careful not to prick herself. His lips were soft, such a contrast to the rest of him. This time he tasted of…mint.

He released her hands and tangled his fingers in her curls. He kissed her like he was drowning and could only find breath in her mouth. At that moment she would have let him devour her.

She ran her palms down his powerful, sturdy shoulders, along his bare, solid back, to his round, hard ass. The taut skin covering his well-defined muscles registered in her consciousness. She pulled from his kiss. "You're naked."

"And you're not." Amusement filled his voice. Sitting up, he straddled her hips, and efficiently tugged off her shirt. He wrapped his fingers around her panties, and with a quick snap of his wrist, tore them from her hips.

She gasped at the rough treatment but didn't care. Her attention was focused on Daedalus. The nightlight on her wall gave enough illumination for her to finally see him nude. Every sculpted muscle moved visibly under his pale, translucent skin as he undressed her, his gestures fluid and precise.

The black snake eating its tail tattoo over his heart was the symbol of eternal life. She'd googled it at work and found it fit him. Her gaze trailed down to what she had only felt but not seen. His cock stood huge and erect against his hard abdomen.

When he saw the object of her curiosity he gave her a smug smile. He stroked his cock while his gaze traveled along her body. "You're so luscious, Sugar."

She wanted to taste him. Suck him hard and deep until he begged for mercy. Something silky hanging around his neck distracted her. "Are you wearing a white scarf?"

"I'm in the mood to play." He pulled it off, and then snapped it between his hands.

She jumped at the sharp pop. "How?"

A wicked grin exposed a little fang while he tied her wrists to the headboard.

She tugged futilely at her bonds out of reflex, not fear. The silk, smooth and cool, held tight. Scandalous delight coursed through her. She'd never done anything like this before.

The slow, easy way he stroked her skin sent a chill down her spine.

"Let's discuss the rules."

She dragged her eyes from those magical hands touching her. "Rules?"

His grin returned. "Can I feed?"

Sugar blinked and glanced at her bonds. What had she gotten herself into?

"You said I didn't frighten you." He lay next to her and brushed his fingertips along the edges of her belly button.

She watched him admiring her breasts. "I lied." She hated the quiver in her voice. "It's not you, I'm worried about what you are. Won't I become a vampire if you bite me?"

His gaze didn't leave her breasts. "No, the world would be over populated with us if it were so simple."

"Will it hurt?"

"I'd never hurt you, Sugar," he whispered. She could hear the ache of disappointment in his voice.

The light breath he blew across her nipples made them pebble, sending a potent snap of sensual awareness to her core. No one had ever made her feel so wanted.

He continued examining her body with heated interest as he listed the rules. "No biting, then." He glanced up at her and grinned. "No kneeing."

She nodded. "No kneeing."

"If I do something you don't like, you shout…touchdown."

"You've got to be kidding. I'm not saying that."

He chuckled. "If you don't, I won't stop."

She tugged at the scarf again and sighed. "Touchdown." Then she nodded in agreement.

With a vicious growl, his lush mouth claimed her over-stimulated nipple and made her spine arch, stretching her body along the length of his. His hand slid up to fondle her other nipple. He rolled it. Pinched it. Pulled at it.

She couldn't help but cry out. Over the past ten days, she'd yearned for his touch.

He licked, tasted, and nibbled her skin. Waves of delight made her shudder as he paused at her navel to lap around it. She hoped he would do this to her clit, and just the thought made her writhe.

His hand brushed the curly, pale hair covering her sex. He stroked down between her outer labia, to her inner, and then slipped a finger deep inside her core. Sliding it in and out, his finger petted her slick sex.

A moan escaped her at the torturous slow rhythm.

"More?" His voice sounded husky with need.

"Yes...oh yes."

He wedged his broad shoulders between her thighs and spread them wide to display her like a banquet.

Still wrapped in the silk bonds, she remained vulnerable to his every desire.

She lifted her head to gaze at him, only to meet his half-lidded, intense stare. He held her attention as his head lowered to reach his tongue down, licking between her labia. She squirmed helplessly, gasping when he lapped, then flicked her clit with his marvelous tongue. He did devious things with his mouth, and her arousal intensified, blowing any coherent thoughts from her mind.

"Daedalus!"

He raised his face to lean his chin on her pubis. "Do you need me to stop?" She could hear the amusement in his voice. One day there would be payback.

"No, please, no!"

Her pleas elicited a crooked smile from him before he dipped down to plunge his tongue inside of her. He tasted her with a satisfied rumble.

It was all she could do to catch her breath. The pleasure built and filled her core, overwhelming her consciousness. She lifted her hips to grind against his mouth as bliss assaulted her senses. It blazed through her like wildfire.

She bucked and Daedalus held her to him so he could suck harder to increase her orgasm. Only when her voice became hoarse did she hear her own cries, fading with her climax.

As she lay dazed from her near out-of-body experience, he crawled up her sweat-soaked body. Pressed against her, he kept her pinned, then slid his firm cock to the entrance of her core.

"Do you want this?" His voice had deepened.

She searched his face, looking for something familiar and found nothing but need. It went beyond lust. He allowed her a glimpse of his loneliness. "Yes."

He thrust himself inside her, even with her wetness, he needed to work himself in. A gasp at the tormenting ecstasy fled her lips when he filled her. The feel of him, stiff and hard, pushing inside, made her thrash and pull at her restraints. The tips of her breasts jiggled with her movements. The hard nubs rubbed against the firm flesh of his chest, eliciting another gasp from her.

"Let...let me go." She wanted to touch him. No, who was she kidding? She wanted to grab him and fuck him hard.

He ignored her plea while he pushed back in. Thrusting gently at first, he built a rhythm that got deeper and harder with each stroke. Out of control, she needed to feel the solidness of him to ground herself. "Please...please... I need..." She couldn't remember the word he'd told her to shout.

He lifted himself off her, releasing her lower half to move with him. She met each pump with her hips, trying to grind against him, but he wouldn't allow it.

The sound of her ragged breathing filled the room. He lowered himself, pushing up close to her face to catch her mouth in a consuming kiss. She returned it with as much heat and passion as he gave. Any touch he offered, she'd take with enthusiasm.

His rhythm grew more erratic, more demanding. It fueled her fire, and her orgasm bowed her in a spine-cracking onslaught. Her cries mixed in with his roars while he released himself inside of her, arching his back so the faint light painted dark shadows across his face.

He collapsed beside her, resting his head on her heaving chest. "Damn, I didn't last long again. You know how to hit all the right buttons, Sugar." He reached up to release the knots binding her, then gathered her in his arms.

* * * *

Sugar snuggled against his chest. She fit perfectly in his arms, curvaceous and tender. It had taken the entirety of his restraint to keep from sinking his teeth into her as she begged beneath him. He really liked the begging.

She ran a finger aimlessly down his body.

He sighed. He hated mixing business with pleasure, but Sugar was intertwined with the Omegas. No way could he choose between the two. Not now. Somehow he'd let his guard down and she snared his heart. He couldn't remember the last time he loved a mortal. "You care a lot about the Omegas." He felt a twinge of jealousy at having to share her, and it annoyed him.

"Yes."

Funny how such a small word could seal their fates. "The Ayumu pack has claim over Chicago. It's a large one, and their leader is powerful." He stroked her hair, to comfort himself more than anything. "He won't bother to fight Eric himself. The Omegas are too small. He'll send a lieutenant."

"Does Eric have a chance?" She twisted to look at his face. Her red rosebud lips were swollen from the crush of his mouth.

He nibbled them. She closed her eyes and gave herself to him. Oh, how he liked it.

Not once since their kitchen encounter had she complained about the lack of his attention. He'd expected it, most women he knew would have. It made him think she'd lost interest. After tonight, he knew different. She'd been waiting for him and understood his duty. It made her more precious to him.

He brushed one of her feather-soft curls from her emerald green eyes. "Eric has an excellent chance. If he wins they'll send another, then another until he has to face the pack leader."

"Why? Why do they want the Omegas so bad?" she cried.

Her distress stabbed him like an arrow. He cupped her upset face, suddenly aware her anguish became his. "The Ayumu gave Eric permission to live here, not to start his own tiny pack." He stroked her cheek. "Taking in Katrina, a fertile attractive female, crossed the line. If the Ayumu don't retaliate, they'll look weak."

"Then the Omegas are doomed."

He laughed. "Hardly. I'm here, Sugar." He continued tracing his thumb along her jaw. Her skin was satiny. Her eyes tore through a tender part of him long ago buried. She needed to learn to trust him. Have faith in him. "I'll take care of you."

"It's not me I'm worried about." She ignored his invitation. It hurt, but maybe she didn't understand what he offered.

"They make you happy?"

"Of course."

"So I'll take care of them too." Her sudden direct stare made him feel shy for a moment, like a human. He chuckled at himself. "I like the Omegas, Sugar. They cling to their humanity, like they should. Eric knows what to do. I'm teaching him well."

"In one month?"

"It doesn't take much to make a king, Sugar."

CHAPTER 6

Daedalus reached across the rug and set one of Sugar's books on top of a pile. Another romance. He didn't know what triggered this need to organize the mess of books in her apartment. A disgraceful habit for a librarian, but a cute idiosyncrasy.

Boredom drove him to continue. The pre-dawn was always a lonely time. The Omegas and Sugar slept. She needed to work in the morning, and the small pack rarely stayed up this late. He usually did his own training when alone, yet tonight he needed to be close to her.

She read a lot of fiction. No history or philosophy, nothing of his taste. Books with aliens, fairies, or wizards sat in the second largest stack, since the romance stuff dominated the books.

He shook his head. Whatever demon created him must be laughing his ass off right now. He'd fallen in love with a gentle, loving dreamer. At least he could admit it to himself.

She, on the other hand, still had issues. He saw her cringe every time he or one of the Omegas experienced a paranormal situation. He doubted she knew about this habit. Heck, she didn't even let him feed, one of the most intimate acts a couple could share. Instead she made him turn to the Omega males for sustenance. Technically, he could use Katrina. His stomach turned at the idea. She smelled too much like abuse for his taste. He didn't need to hear her story to know what she'd suffered at the hands of her old pack.

If Sugar conquered her prejudice their relationship could bloom. Since they'd met he'd become aware of how tired he was of his present life, of being the leader, the provider, and the warrior to his people. With her he'd become the lover, the protector, and the teacher. If she agreed to it, he'd turn her to vampire, then take her as a wife.

His wife.

It had been a very long time since he'd wanted one or even thought of having one. He sighed and placed a poetry book on a small stack by his leg. At least they held one thing in common, except she liked the modern poets.

He'd leave Pal Robi Corporation in capable hands, move to Chicago, maybe into this cozy apartment. Eric could use his advice to tread Were politics and keep from drowning in it. They could make a difference, bring the Ayumu under control, teach them the old ways, the right ways. Then hopefully, with some guidance, it would spread.

Who was the dreamer now? Maybe he and Sugar shared more in common than he admitted to himself. He laughed.

"I don't see the comedy in Frank Herbert's *Dune*."

Daedalus fumbled the book, trying to catch it before it hit the floor. It slipped between his fingers to land back in the unsorted pile.

Sugar leaned her luscious body against his back and wrapped her arms around his shoulders. "I didn't mean to startle you."

He glanced over his shoulder into her crystal clear, green eyes. Even this early in the morning they sparkled with clarity. "You didn't startle me. I heard you coming. The book slipped." He must be off center to get surprised by a small human female. He deserved to get staked if he allowed his defenses to drop.

"Sure, I always grease them up when I'm done." She kissed the back of his neck.

He sighed at the light, feathery touch of her lips. "That explains why they're always scattered everywhere."

She giggled. The gesture made her breasts bounce a little against his shoulders. He was tempted to tear her tight t-shirt open and set them free.

"Why were you thinking so hard?" she whispered close to his ear.

"Worried about tonight's challenge." The lie didn't hurt as much as the truth. Eric would do fine tonight, their plans were set solid. His plans for Sugar made him worry.

"Daedalus? You said they would be okay."

He'd chosen the wrong thing to say. She'd made him a bumbling idiot. "It will be all right. Doesn't mean I won't be thinking about it." He reached back and pulled her to face him. An idea formed to help him with his real problem. "You should come."

She shook her head. "I don't like fighting, and I don't want to watch anyone get hurt. There will be plenty of both tonight."

He ran his hand through her tangle of messy curls. Their color reminded him of spun sunlight, something he'd only seen when he was human, a very long time ago. "The Omegas could use your support."

"They have you." She rubbed her face on the palm of his hand.

The silky touch of her skin stirred his hunger. He wanted to taste the tender flesh in his mouth, feel his teeth puncture her white, milky hide.

He exhaled in frustration.

She glanced up at him. "What?"

How could he explain his need without scaring her away? He smiled, careful to hide his fangs. "Maybe I want you at the challenge." He allowed enough of his hunger in his voice to convince her of his desire. She needed to face her fears. To get over being surrounded by sentient beings other than humans, who developed different ways of surviving. The challenge would be a perfect place.

"I'm scared, I'm not ashamed to admit it." She stared down at his chest.

He lifted her chin and kissed her. She looked vulnerable, resistance was impossible with his sweet Sugar. Her eager response to him ignited his cock to a full salute, but the dawn's approach tugged at the unconscious clock built in his make-up. He groaned as he pushed her away. "We don't have time, the sun is almost here. Come tonight, for me."

She met his stare, her eyes clouded with worry, and nodded. "For you."

CHAPTER 7

The abandoned warehouse stood outside of town. No one in their right mind would be out there at night, including the police. What did that make them? Nuts? Sugar scanned the secluded area, left for nature to reclaim. Nobody would hear their screams if things went wrong.

"I heard the mob uses this place to get rid of the trash," Tyler whispered to her.

She elbowed him to be quiet. He didn't need to add to her vivid imagination or feed her fears. The crunch of gravel under her boots sounded loud as they drew closer to the warehouse. She would have felt better if Daedalus had come with them instead of with Eric. They needed to arrive later, so he sent the rest of them to represent the pack.

Eric begged her to come with them to the challenge when she started to doubt her earlier decision. He'd said, "I *need* you to be there. I won't be able to concentrate if I don't think the others are safe. If you're there they'll be too busy protecting you to get into trouble. Especially Sam."

Sam draped his arm over Sugar's shoulders, waking her from the memory. He gave her a squeeze. "Don't worry, Sugar. Daedalus sent me to protect you."

She sighed. He didn't stand much taller than her, but the training had added some bulk to his body. Even though Daedalus released the others from training, Sam insisted on continuing. Eric told her they didn't mind. He needed a sparring partner and appreciated his company.

The warehouse door slid open, and bright lights spilled out, blinding them.

"Who are you?" An outline of a burly man glowed in the doorway. As her eyes adjusted she saw he stood with his legs apart and his arms crossed over his muscled chest. The sleeves of his shirt were torn off to make space for his bulging biceps.

Sam stepped in front of their group. "We're witnesses for the Omegas."

The guard moved forward and sniffed the air, others gathered behind him. He pointed at Sugar. "She doesn't carry our blood." His eyes traveled up her body. "She stays here with us." A few snickers came from the men behind him..

Sugar stepped back, colliding with Katrina. Small hands steadied her and rubbed her arms. Her stomach cramped as she imagined exactly what kind of 'stay' she'd have to endure with them.

"Sugar's with us." Sam glanced at his pack mates, a devilish twinkle in his eye. "She's almost pack. She's Eric's mate."

The guard continued to examine her. "Not for long." He laughed and stepped back to allow them access to the warehouse. More perverse laughter followed them in.

Werewolves from different walks of life milled around. They chatted and got reacquainted. It felt like they were crashing an Ayumu party. They had even brought bleachers.

Sugar latched onto Sam's arm. "Did they sell tickets to this?"

Sam made a slight gesture, toward a stage between the bleachers, with his chin. "The Ayumu Lead Alpha is the one sitting in the throne on the dais. His name is Michael." His chuckle carried a nervous tremor. "Eric invited him to bear witness to this challenge. He also invited neighboring packs." Sam led them away.

"Why?"

He shrugged and tried to stare down curious onlookers. "Daedalus kicked my ass when I tried talking Eric out of it. Something about bystanders keeping the Ayumu honest."

It made sense to her. She'd wondered what would prevent the

Ayumu from attacking them if they actually won. Daedalus's forethought impressed her.

A voice boomed, "Are these the Omegas' witnesses?" A hush settled over the room and the crowd parted like the Red Sea, exposing the Alpha to their view.

Sugar dug her nails into Sam's arm. "We should have all come together." Katrina, Tyler, and Robert hovered close behind them.

"I'm starting to agree with you," Sam said through gritted teeth.

Michael motioned for them to come closer.

Sugar felt helpless surrounded by preternaturally strong and deadly werewolves. She was a small woman who wanted a semi-normal quiet life. "What do we do when we get there? Bow?" she whispered as the four of them shuffled together.

Sam shrugged.

Great.

They approached the dais. Michael sat on his throne and leaned forward with his elbows on his knees, his hands clasped between them. He assessed Katrina and Sugar with an indecent smirk. "How does such a pitiful pack of dogs attract such beautiful women?" He brushed a lock of his black hair over his shoulder. The inner glow of his amber eyes became more apparent.

Sam placed a hand over Sugar's, where her nails still dug in, and he patted it. His eyes pleaded with her to keep her mouth shut.

Michael watched with interest. He gestured to a bench next to him. "I've arranged special seating for you." His intense stare ensnared Sugar, and she found it difficult to break it. Where Daedalus made her feel risqué, Michael made her feel like prey.

Sam's gentle tug pulled her toward the bench with the others.

"No, not her." Michael motioned at Sugar. "Eric's mate has a seat of honor next to me." He patted a stool beside his throne.

Anger boiled inside of her, ready to pour out of her ears. "Sam," she growled. Why did she let them talk her into coming? This shouldn't be part of her life. She took the two steps to get to the stool on heavy feet.

Michael offered his hand and assisted her to the seat.

She watched the Omegas sit on the bench next to the dais.

"Sugar, is it?"

She twisted to face Michael; she'd never told him her name. The dryness in her throat made her swallow reflexively. Word from the front door guards traveled fast to their leader.

She nodded and gazed out at the crowd of Weres, trying to think positive thoughts. It was difficult since her host continued eying her like candy.

He reached out to run a finger through her curls. She flinched before she could control it. "If I knew Eric kept such a pretty mate, I would have challenged him much sooner."

She glanced at him and raised an eyebrow.

A lecherous grin spread across his face. "It means when he loses, you'll be mine."

She gulped the ball of fear that rose in her throat. "I'm not his mate, just his friend." Her heart hadn't stopped racing since she'd climbed out of the car. Now it beat double time.

"I have witnesses who heard otherwise."

A trace of sweat trickled down her neck. "I'm not a Were."

He leaned closer to whisper in her ear. "Not yet." His voice burned with hunger. "I can't *wait* to turn you."

A cold shiver froze her to the spot. She shouldn't have come, the thought kept repeating itself. Never did she desire to change, not to Were, nor to vampire, nor anything else.

Daedalus and Eric had stuck her in the middle of this situation.

Had they even thought of this scenario? It took one bite, witnesses or no, she'd still become a werewolf.

Michael leaned back in his chair, never taking those fiery amber eyes from her. If they got out of this unharmed, she was going to kick Sam's werewolf ass.

CHAPTER 8

A commotion at the front of the warehouse caught both Sugar's and Michael's attention. She stood to get a better view, but his hand clamped down on her forearm, yanking her back onto the stool.

"Your lover's here."

Confusion clouded her thoughts, then she realized he meant Eric, not Daedalus.

Michael released her arm, and his face transformed from anger to regal calm before her eyes. He glared at the arrival of the Omegas' challenger.

An air of expectation silenced the hum of conversation.

Eric stalked with a predatory grace to the dais where they sat. The Weres who had been guarding the door surrounded him and Daedalus.

Sugar barely recognized her best friend. They'd only seen each other a few times since Daedalus had arrived. She couldn't tear her eyes away from the obvious changes. Confidence radiated around him like a beacon, and everyone in the warehouse drew closer to him.

A leather kilt hung from his lean hips, the rest of him naked. The healthy sheen of sweat covering his skin reflected the neon lights, defining his lean, newly acquired muscles. She noticed, like Daedalus, he also bore a black circular tattoo over his heart. Except his was of the full moon.

He looked like a gladiator.

Daedalus stood a step behind. His usual black jeans and muscle shirt contrasted with his pale, translucent skin. The light gleamed off his head and caused his deep blue eyes to look soulless. It made it impossible for him to hide his vampire origins. The cold, menacing expression on his face sent a shiver down her spine. Thankfully, he was on their side.

Eric's gaze flicked over to her, and she shrugged. Nothing he did at this point could help her. He needed to win. She wished Daedalus would glance her way to offer some reassurance.

Michael rose. "The Ayumu pack recognizes you, Eric of the Omegas. Who is this vampire accompanying you?"

Eric's voice rang through the warehouse. "Daedalus is my appointed advisor."

"This isn't a place for advice." He faced Daedalus. "You shouldn't be involved in this."

"The Accords state I can be present during a challenge." His expression and stance never changed.

Hushed voices hummed over the crowd at this statement. Michael's face lost its amused expression. "The Accords? No one follows those ancient laws anymore."

Eric turned to address the crowd. "That's because most of us don't even know of their existence. We've forgotten them." He returned his attention to the Lead Alpha. "We've lost our way."

Eric climbed the stairs to the dais, causing a stir among the guards. Michael held up his hand to forestall them.

"You knew about the Accords," Eric whispered. Only Sugar and the Alpha could hear him.

Michael lowered his face within inches of Eric's. "Of course, every Lead Alpha does. No one cares."

"I care. They define us as a people, Michael. Without it..." Eric diverted his gaze to the floor. He paused and swallowed, then sucked in his breath. When he looked back up, his eyes matched Michael's, amber wolf. "We're nothing but animals."

Sugar had never seen one of the Omegas this close to losing control of their beast. She found herself scooting back on her stool.

Eric noticed her and gave a small, encouraging nod. The amber glow of his eyes grew. He returned to the floor to announce, "I challenge Michael, Lead Alpha of the Ayumu pack, for the right of his throne."

The outcries from the pack startled Sugar. She feared they'd run out and tear her men to shreds.

Michael waited until the noise died down before he responded with a smirk. "You have to work your way up the pack to get that kind of challenge, Eric."

"No, I don't, Michael. I am Lead Alpha to the Omegas pack. Leader to Leader challenge. We'll absorb the Ayumu. At least one Accord law is still followed."

Sugar looked to Daedalus. He grinned and gave her a shameless wink.

The arena was set in the center of the warehouse. Sugar attempted to join the Omegas on the bench when Michael left the dais, but his thugs blocked her way. The muscled brute who had wanted to keep her at the door pushed her back onto the stool. He didn't leave her side. She looked around him to her friends. Tyler held Katrina, Robert and Sam watched the preparations.

The brute explained to her most dominance fights were to the first draw of blood, but this kind of challenge went to the death. He bent closer to Sugar. "When Michael's done with you, he'll give ya to me." His teeth were stained brown from chewing tobacco, and the smell curled her toes.

"You ever heard of a toothbrush?"

The brute choked on his words while he sputtered, his eyes dilated before he grabbed her by the hair. He pulled her head back as he drew his fist to punch her. Fury burned in his dead eyes.

She raised her arms to protect herself when he stopped mid-swing.

Sam held his arm in his   grip,   then pulled him away. It caused them both to tumble off the dais. Sugar wasn't sure who let the first punch go, but the brawl didn't last long. A piercing whistle made most of the Weres cover their sensitive ears, including Sam and his fist buddy.

Daedalus removed his fingers from his mouth. "Break it up, boys! The fight's between these two." He gestured to the Lead Alphas of the opposing packs.

Sam pushed himself off the floor, nodded at Sugar, and sat back with his pack. The brute returned to the dais, murder in his eyes as he watched her.

Michael stripped completely. He paced the floor, unconscious of his nudity. His eyes never left Eric while he stared daggers at him.

They approached each other in the center of the cleared area. The surrounding crowd cheered. The Alphas began their change.

Sugar didn't want to look, but couldn't make herself turn away. She'd never watched a transformation before, her stare remained glued to the horror. Their skin flowed like water while fur took its place. They groaned when bones and joints popped, reshaping themselves into what looked like half-wolf and half-man. Claws grew from their fingers and toes. Lastly, they stood on their hind legs and howled as their jaws elongated, exposing the long, sharp canines.

She sensed Daedalus's presence before turning to see him beside her.

"You're pale, Sugar. Are you okay?" He lifted her chin with a knuckle.

She glanced back at the werewolf wearing a leather kilt. "I'm managing. Eric seems to be the same size as Michael in his beast form. If he didn't keep the kilt on, I'd have trouble telling them apart."

A pleased look briefly touched her lover's face. "Exercise strengthens the human body, but it's the soul which strengthens the beast." He caressed her face,   then returned to his charge by the arena.

It dawned on Sugar what Daedalus had truly been doing this last month. He taught Eric to fight and built his confidence to give him pride so he could lead. He grew Eric's beast. It must have been his plan from the start, and she loved him for it.

Eric matched Michael in size. Maybe he could win if he could match him in skill.

The Alphas circled each other, testing their reflexes and speed by feigned attacks. Michael sprang at Eric, knocking them both into the bystanders. People screamed under the crush of two huge monsters as the struggle for dominance began.

They fought like the animals they'd become. Fang and claw, bite and tear, a gruesome display of strength and agility. Eric's kilt lay on the ground, torn off during the battle. Sugar couldn't tell who was who now.

The beast under assault placed his feet against the other's abdomen and shoved with great power. The assailant flew across the warehouse, landing with a hard thud on the concrete floor.

The spectators scattered, gathering around the dais. Sugar needed to stand on the stool to watch. Both Alphas raced at each other to collide in a storm of fury.

Sam waved his arm to catch Sugar's attention. "We can't see! Who's winning?" He tried to get up on the dais, but the guards pushed him back.

She stamped her foot on the stool. "I can't tell! They both look alike."

She glimpsed Daedalus. He stood alone by the front door, absorbed in the fight. Occasionally he'd shout something. *At least he can tell which one is Eric.*

One beast stood over the other, its jaw clenched around the other's throat, shaking its head with vigor. In a spray of blood, the dominant werewolf almost decapitated the other when he ripped out most of its throat and swallowed the flesh. He crossed his arms, then faced the crowd around the dais. Bloody gore dripped from its maw.

Sugar's head spun at the sight.

"You are all Omegas now." Its rough voice rolled over them. Sugar twisted to look at the Omegas. They jumped up and down in unbridled joy. She stared as the beast approached them.

Eric had won.

Sugar jumped off the dais and rushed over to the celebrating Omegas. This would be a new era. No more "Wimps of the Underworld" or "Pansies of the Paranormal." They'd be part of the Ayumu. *No*, the Ayumu would be part of them.

The Omegas owned Chicago.

That thought, the enormity of what had transpired, stopped her in her tracks. Things would change, maybe not for the best. Her simple lifestyle wouldn't survive. The Omegas' time would be consumed in maintaining dominance over their new members and worse, they thought she belonged to Eric as his mate.

Daedalus saved her friends, yet at the same time destroyed her quiet, happy life.

The touch of a hand at her elbow startled her. She frowned, expecting her lover, but instead came face to face with the muscled, rude brute. His grip tightened around her arm. Before she could cry for help, he dragged her through the crowd to a small side exit.

The cool air outside snapped her from the shock. Her lungs, stiff with fear, couldn't seem to get enough air. She tried to scream. His steel grasp prevented any escape, no matter how hard she fought and tore at his hand.

He pulled her without effort toward the surrounding woods. His eyes glowed with amber light   in the dark when he glanced over his shoulder. "I'm going to fuck ya." He grinned, exposing long, sharp canines. "Then I'm going to eat ya."

She froze. None of her limbs functioned. The Omegas were too busy celebrating to notice her absence, she was on her own against this creature.

Daedalus strolled out of the woods.

Her heart skipped a beat. Relief flooded her and loosened her knees.

"Nice night to take a walk. Who do you have there, wolf?"

The brute stopped moving forward when he saw Daedalus. "None of your business, blood sucker." He squeezed Sugar's arm harder, making her cry out.

Quick as a blink, Daedalus stood a breath away with his hand on the brute's wrist. With a quick snap, he broke it. "You're hurting my Sugar." The words came from behind clenched teeth.

The werewolf cried out in pain, releasing her arm. His cries grew louder when Daedalus twisted his injured joint.

"Stay here, Sugar, this won't take long." He dragged the brute into the forest, where his pleading screams ended abruptly.

She lay in the dirt and cringed with each of the brute's cries. Something innocent died within her when those shrieks stopped. Tears burned behind her eyes.

Daedalus returned, wiping the blood on his chin with a handkerchief. He crouched in front of Sugar, a small satisfied smile on his face.

Before he could say anything, she pushed him, knocking him on his ass. "Get away!"

"Hey." His stunned response echoed off the warehouse.

She crabbed back from him, then stood. "Sorry, it's... Well..." She gestured to the woods. "You ate him?"

He remained on the ground. "Sugar, I'm a vampire. The world won't miss the likes of him."

"I know. It's just with focusing on the challenge and my own quiet..." She looked at her feet. "I'm starting to realize how naive I've been."

The side exit door opened. "I'm telling you, Katrina, I smell her this way." Tyler and his girlfriend hurried out to find their quarry. "Hey, I thought you were in trouble."

Sugar spun, thankful for the interruption. "Not anymore. Daedalus saved me." How could she explain to Daedalus she'd never thought of him as a monster until tonight? And now he terrified her?

He stood, brushing the dirt off his jeans. "Can you take Sugar home, Tyler?" He looked at her and sighed. "I think she's had enough supernatural excitement for one night."

"Yeah, sure."

Daedalus walked up to Sugar as if approaching a frightened fawn. He lowered his face to hers, expecting a kiss. His lips lingered, soft and velvety. Eyes closed, he murmured her name.

"I'm sorry," she whispered back.

CHAPTER 9

Sugar woke with a start early the next morning. Nightmares had plagued her sleep; something chased her through a dark forest threatening to eat her. Sometimes the hunter wore Daedalus's face. What a horrible night.

She rolled out of bed and rubbed her eyes. Her arm ached where the brute had squeezed it. A purple handprint was her souvenir from the challenge. When Tyler and Katrina dropped her off last night, they saw the marks on her arm and knew something had happened, but she didn't want to discuss it. She needed time alone.

On her way to the kitchen, she found Eric on a chair in her patio garden. He gave her a little smile and a weak wave. There were dark circles under his eyes. Looked like she wasn't the only one who hadn't slept well. She signaled for him to wait, then set the coffee maker to start brewing.

The crisp morning air showed signs of an early fall. She pulled her robe closed and tied it tight. The clear, blue sky brought light to everything around them.

Eric sat bent over in the chair, leaning his arms on his knees. He lifted his weary head. "Hope you don't mind my breaking in. I love sitting here. It's like a small island of solitude."

She pulled a chair next to him and looked closer at his face. It seemed he'd aged overnight. The worry lines between his brows were new. She reached out to smooth them away. "You look like crap."

He jerked in his chair with a surprised chuckle. "I got into a fight last night."

She smiled in return, finally recognizing some of the old Eric. "Really?" She allowed her voice to drip with sarcasm. "I heard it was a doozy. Did you at least win?"

His smile faded, and he leaned back to stare at her with sad eyes. "Yeah."

It tore her heart apart to see her childhood hero upset. Maybe joking about it wasn't the best way to cheer him up. He should have been celebrating. The Omegas were safe, and he ruled the Ayumu. He'd accomplished the impossible. She reached out for his hand to find it trembled under her touch.

He released a heavy sigh. "I didn't think killing Michael would affect me much. We hunt in the woods and kill regularly. I thought it would feel the same, but it doesn't." He looked away.

Helpless, she watched him suffer. His kind and gentle nature took a worse beating than his body did. It would make him a great leader. She squeezed his hand and tucked away her own selfish misgivings in relation to werewolves and vampires. Her best friend, even if he had swallowed someone's throat, needed a shoulder to lean on.

"I'm glad you feel bad."

His head snapped up to face her. "What?"

She smiled, hoping it would soften her words. "Hold on to this feeling. It's right to suffer after you've killed someone, Eric."

His eyes widened, a flash of anger reflected in them.

"You killed a monster last night. That was a good thing to do, I'm glad you didn't enjoy it though. I think Michael would have loved killing you, and I think the majority of his pack would have loved watching him destroy you. It'll prevent *you* from turning into a monster like Michael." She tilted her head and pleaded with her eyes for him to understand.

He stared at her a moment as the anger melted away, then he nodded. "My suffering protects what I have left of my humanity."

"I don't know much in regards to pack life, but after what I witnessed last night, I'd say what the Ayumu have left of their humanity needs to be saved." She released his hand. "Tell me about the Accords."

A light of interest sparked in his saddened face. "The Accords were developed centuries ago by paranormal creatures, even the ones who refused to 'come out' with the declaration of citizenry. They're laws to protect humans, to protect our identities, and to protect against one individual gaining too much power." He grinned at her. "Let's face it, you humans outnumber us. In a war you'd win. Also, without humans there wouldn't be Weres, vampires, or merpeople."

"Merpeople?" Delight twinkled through her, making her want to do a dance. She always wanted to be a mermaid as a little girl. Some dreams don't die. "They really do exist?"

He threw back his head with a belly laugh. "I thought you'd like to know. Don't be running off to a beach yet, they secluded themselves long ago." His face split with the usual goofy grin. "Thanks."

"My therapeutic garden is always open to your pack."

"The pack's grown."

She blinked. "I guess I'll have to start charging." They shared an easy laugh.

His nose flared. "Coffee's ready."

She got up and fixed them each a big mug, then returned with the steaming hot brew. She handed him one with the logo 'Got Blood?' on the side.

He read it. "Daedalus give you this?"

She nodded.

He took a careful sip. "He's pretty sweet on you." He watched the city, and she looked at her plants.

She hated talking relationships with Eric. He knew her too well and thought she guarded her heart too much. She could never just give it away, especially after last night. She started wondering if she truly knew anyone in her life.

She could fall in love with Daedalus easily, but she wanted him to be human. Tears swelled in her eyes.

"He's a good guy, as vampires go. I don't think he'd lead you astray."

Like she predicted, Eric defended the guy. "Why?"

"'Cause he doesn't have to. He's got all the time in the world." He sighed. "He could have moved out last night, Sugar. Our contract is complete. Instead he's resting in my cramped, crappy apartment. He didn't say much, except he scared you. That's got to mean something." He sipped his hot coffee.

"We don't fit. It was supposed to be a fling. He turned it into more and expects me to..." She found herself at a loss for words.

"Accept him for what he is?"

She nodded and stared at her mug, fighting the tears.

"You have a chance at a relationship, even if it lasts a day, a month, or a year. Who cares? It's better to have experienced happiness in life, even with a vampire, than through those stupid romance books."

She wiped her eyes and smacked his arm lightly, it spilled some of his hot coffee from his mug onto his hand. "I didn't buy those books, Casanova. Now I feel worse, thanks."

He shook his fingers and splattered coffee in her direction. "Payback's a bitch." He grinned at her.

CHAPTER 10

Sugar placed a fuzzy, pink throw blanket over Eric's sleeping form. He'd curled up on one of the love seats after she filled him with scrambled eggs and bacon. Then he asked her to read him to sleep.

They'd done this before. Initially after he'd been turned into a Were, he hated to sleep. The nightmares stalked him until she found him secluded in his apartment half-crazed. She shuddered at the memory. This reading ritual began then. The sound of her voice soothed him, and the stories distracted his tortured soul. They did this for months until he met Robert and founded the Omegas.

Sugar closed the book sitting on her lap. Everyone assumed she was the romance junkie, but the books all belonged to him.

The Omegas probably still slept and Daedalus, well, he became unconscious or something with the daylight. She couldn't help the shiver which ran down her spine at the thought.

Her arm throbbed in time with her heartbeat as the muscles in her back knotted like pretzels. A hot bubble bath sounded like nirvana. The world would hold itself together while she soaked and reflected on her own troubles.

She filled the tub with near scalding water until the bubbles threatened to overflow, then eased in, enjoying every heated moment. The suds engulfed her, allowing enough space to breathe. She struggled to clear her mind of the lust, unease, discomfort, and happiness thoughts of Daedalus created. The last wistful one being, *I wish he was human.*

The small pops of bubbles hummed in her ears, mesmerizing her, and brought her to a languid meditative state. A thump in the next room startled her. Eric had probably rolled off the love seat and fell on the floor. She concentrated on thinking of nothing once more. Even though under water, she distinctly heard a yell. She pulled herself out and threw on a robe.

When she reached her living room, chaos was underway. Two men grappled with Eric on her rugs. She stared at the unbelievable scene, shock freezing her to the spot until one of the men noticed her. His eyes glowed with an inner amber light. *Not men, Weres.*

He jumped for her, but Eric grabbed his ankle and pulled him away. "Get the Omegas!" Eric's voice cracked at her like a whip. She raced through the kitchen, out the apartment door, only to get tugged back in.

One of the Weres held the back of her robe and dragged her through to the kitchen. Eric knocked his Were off, strode across the room, and kicked her attacker in the knee. It sent him howling to the floor. Unfortunately the Were pulled her robe with him.

She ran out of the apartment and down the hall to Daedalus, in her birthday suit. With the racket in her apartment, the Omegas should have come to check it out by now. Except their door looked busted in.

She peeked around the corner. The chaos in her apartment couldn't compete with the havoc in this one. Tyler and a stranger were the only ones in the room still in human form. They fought one another on the far side of the kitchen. Beasts struggled against each other within the tight confines of the kitchen and hallway leading to the bedrooms. The clash of cutlery with dishes as they shattered on the kitchen floor made her cringe.

Daedalus's closed, shiny, black coffin lay on the floor by the outside wall.

Sugar spotted a portable phone on the floor between her and the coffin. They needed help, she hoped the police could handle this. She crawled toward the phone, staying close to the floor to avoid attention.

One of the Weres approached Daedalus's coffin. She gasped when she saw he held a stake and mallet.

Katrina's high-pitched scream from the bedrooms made Sugar twist away. She saw Tyler snap his assailant's neck and leap over the others blocking the hallway to reach the bedrooms where Katrina fought.

The sound of hammering drew Sugar's attention back to the coffin. The beast banged on the stake, driving it through her sexy, sweet love. His screech froze her blood. It must have done the same to his attacker since he paused in his assault.

Daedalus needed her. Without thinking, she threw the portable phone with all her strength at the beast. It bounced off the back of his head and he stumbled forward, close enough for Daedalus to knock him out with a punch.

The Were's leg wobbled like licorice before he toppled over.

She hurried to Daedalus's side, her breaths coming in short gasps. *Please, let him be all right.* She'd never told him how she felt about him, the paranormal, or their future. Now that creature had taken away her chance to tell him. She knelt by the coffin. A boulder dropped in her stomach.

Daedalus looked at her with wide, unfocused eyes. They were dilated to black bottomless pits. The stake still protruded out of his chest. As he attempted to sit, a small stain of blood appeared on his pale blue t-shirt around the wound. He lay back down, closed his eyes, and his body went limp.

She wanted to pull the stake out but didn't know if she should. She didn't know what vampires did when they died. Maybe his reaction was a reflex of some sort. She checked for a pulse at the base of his neck. *Stupid, he never had a pulse!*

A crash behind her made her duck. When she turned she saw Katrina's limp body tumble to the floor, leaving a small dent in the wall. Someone had thrown her across the room.

Hands clasped to her mouth, Sugar watched her world fall apart.

All she could hear was her blood rushing past her ears like a freight train. She struggled for breath around a sob that racked her chest. Trembling, she crawled to Katrina's listless body. *Weres heal fast.* She kept repeating this to herself like a mantra over and over in her head. This kept her urge to scream under control. If she started, she'd never stop.

A huge werewolf stomped through the Omegas' apartment door from the hallway. It paused to contemplate them, then examined the coffin before it leaped onto the remaining beasts wrestling in the hallway.

Sugar rolled Katrina over and checked her breathing. Her chest rose in a strong, steady rhythm. Sugar sobbed again, this time in relief. Her friend's right eye swelled and her lip bled. Those were the only visible injuries.

The noise of the fight faded behind her. She glanced over her shoulder to see three battered beasts come out of the bedrooms. Tyler pushed his way past them to get to Katrina. His freckles stood out on his pale skin.

Sugar touched him gently as he knelt beside her. "I think she'll be all right."

He nodded, but examined Katrina anyway.

The remaining beasts changed back to human form. It was Eric who had passed them earlier in his wolf form. He slumped to the floor by the hallway while Robert and Sam rustled through the fridge getting what looked like food and drinks.

Her sense of incredulity must have shown on her face since Eric explained, "I've changed twice in one day, Sugar. I need the calories to recuperate and so do they." He turned his gaze to the living room. "Tyler, how's Katrina?"

"She's hurt, but I can smell her injuries healing." He glanced at Sugar. "Why are you naked?"

She looked down at herself, horrified. Flames of embarrassment burned her cheeks. "Give me your shirt." She helped pull it off his back, then slipped it over her head. The t-shirt reached her mid-thigh and acted as a small dress. "They tore my robe off."

She stepped over the unconscious Ayumu Were lying by the coffin. "He staked him, Eric." Her chest tightened around another scream. A tear spilled from her eye, tracing its way down to her chin.

Eric attempted to stand, but his legs buckled, causing him to stumble to his knees. "Is he dust?"

She shook her head.

"They're supposed to turn to dust when they're staked. The Were must not have hammered it all the way through."

She ran her fingers along Daedalus's face and paused to trace his lush lips. Her tears dripped silently from her chin, splattering one by one on his shoulder. The passion, the violence, and the sorrow, she couldn't handle anymore.

Something brushed her ankle. When she tried to swipe it off with her other foot she met resistance. Cold terror gripped her chest when the touch tightened. She glanced down to make eye contact with a pair of amber glowing eyes.

The Were who had staked Daedalus pulled her leg, and she fell to the floor. It crawled on top of her. The screams she'd held back came out as a herald of anguish and fear.

Tyler wrapped his arms around her aggressor's chest, but the Were back-handed him away like a fly, while its long fingers wrapped around her throat. "At least I'll get your mate, Eric."

She gasped for air, nothing passed through her throat. Her vision tunneled while she grappled with his hand. All she could see were his hate-filled wolf eyes.

This was the last thing she'd experience? Getting killed over werewolf politics?

Suddenly, the Were's weight jerked off of her.

Daedalus grasped the back of its shirt and lifted the Were in the air. Her neck remained clenched in the creature's hand when it yanked her off the floor. The angle of the Were's grasp, as she dangled, gave her enough room to wheeze in a breath. Relief swam over her. Daedalus would save her, he'd protect her, like he'd promised her.

She kicked and twisted mid-air until the Were's grasp broke loose. Crashing to the floor, she gulped for air.

Daedalus pulled the stake from his chest, and in one swift move, jammed it through the Were's head.

A spatter of blood landed on Sugar's cheek. She watched in horror as he dropped the corpse, then staggered to his coffin. Sam and Robert appeared at his side to assist him.

She pushed between them and grasped his hand. "Please don't die." Her voice sounded hoarse.

He tried to touch her face, but his hand fell back to his chest. "Tell Eric to call my office." His eyes closed, and his body became limp once more.

She stumbled back a step to look at Sam and Robert. They only offered her a shrug.

She found the portable phone by the coffin and handed it to Eric. "Call."

CHAPTER 11

Sugar watched them carry him away in his coffin.

Eric had called Daedalus's office, informing them of the attack and of his injuries. They sent their local men. The same ones, according to Robert, who had caught them stealing their television and hogtied them. Even though they looked human, she knew they couldn't be.

They reverently angled the coffin over the stair rails. Who was Daedalus Pal Robi? Someone who traveled with security yet housed them somewhere else. Someone who's company removed seven dead werewolves without question and told them not to worry about it. Someone who taught underdogs to stand up for themselves and stole her heart.

She stared at nothing now, they were gone with him.

She felt empty inside, wrung out, and nauseous.

Katrina moaned behind her, and Sugar returned to the others.

The last of Daedalus's men removed a blood pressure cuff from Katrina's arm. She rested on a couch the boys had righted back up, an ice pack over her right eye. "She probably has a concussion, nothing her immunity can't handle. She'll be healed up by tomorrow. Tylenol for the headache, no anti-inflammatories."

Sugar stood by the security guy, he glanced her way, and his eyes scanned her face. "Daedalus has survived worse." He handed her a business card and closed the apartment door as he left.

The card showed a toll-free number with the Pal Robi logo. She snorted. Un-freaking-believable, her life belonged on *Tales from the Crypt*. Next thing she'd know, one of the merpeople would swim out of her toilet. Did she want this kind of life?

Most women her age had found a stable, charming husband, bought a house with a picket fence, and started having their 2.5

children. She'd dreamed that dream once but placed it on hold to help Eric out.

He'd found his place and didn't need her anymore. The Omegas would be his life, he would make a great Alpha. Maybe he'd settle down with a mate, then they could have puppies. A giggle escaped her, and it held an edge of hysteria.

The subject of her amusement stared at her. "Are you okay?" The frown and hard glint in Eric's eyes told Sugar there would be hell to pay among the disgruntled Ayumu turned Omega. Life would be difficult until they accepted him, which meant more fighting.

She lied and nodded. Thanks to Sam, the Ayumu thought her to be Eric's mate, and it painted a bull's eye on her back. More violence. She'd need to hire Daedalus for combat training to survive being their neighbor. Daedalus. Her thoughts circled back to him.

The situation could be turned into an opportunity to begin fresh, a clean break from the paranormal and its kind, a chance to explore her own future. Maybe find her American dream.

"I'm going home." She planted a gentle kiss on Katrina's forehead. "Take care."

Eric followed her out of his apartment. "I'll stay with you."

She shook her head. "I need to be alone. Just give me some time to absorb what happened." She glanced at her feet, unable to meet his piercing gaze.

"You heard the guy. Daedalus will pull through."

She sighed. "I know. I don't doubt it, not after watching him fight in daylight with a stake in his heart." He was everything she'd ever wanted in a man, except actually being a man. "I don't know if I'll pull through." A sob applied pressure to her chest but she held it. "You need to give me space. Everyone. For a little while."

"Sugar," he whispered. "Please don't shut me out of your life.

You're my best friend."

She walked down the hall with him and entered her apartment. "Give me time." Then she closed the door. The bolt stuck as she struggled to twist the knob, but it finally locked. This was the first time since the Omegas moved in next door she'd needed it.

CHAPTER 12

Daedalus sat in his study and contemplated the roaring fire in the hearth. No matter how much he fueled the flames, his heart remained cold. Centuries old but still stupid enough to fall for a pretty girl. He held the poem he'd written to her and threw it in the fire. She'd returned the others unopened as well.

He needed to reminisce on happier times, it sometimes eased the loneliness. His thoughts always betrayed him, eventually leading to her. The only good times he wished to remember involved Sugar, and they were a painful reminder she wanted nothing to do with him.

It drove him mad. He *knew* she cared. He *saw* her tears when they tried to stake him. Yet, she refused his calls and his letters. She refused him.

How many times over the last two months had he caught himself making plans to steal her away from her new home? He shook his head and rested it on the back of his favorite worn leather chair. Too many. It would be a mistake. Holding her prisoner would make her hate him more, not to mention kidnapping was illegal.

His chest ached, but not from the wound.

The CB mike on his cellphone beeped. He glanced down at it, annoyed. He'd told them not to disturb him. It beeped again. He sighed and unattached it. "What?"

"Did you order a pretty blonde for dinner, sir?"

What? He unfolded himself from the chair and went to the computer to access the camera outputs. A woman with blond curls got out of a cab, then came to stand by the guardhouse at the gate. His heart beat. One sharp, painful squeeze.

It was her.

"Bring her to my study." Now she accepts his invitation? Two months later?

He tried to hook the phone back to his belt but missed, and it clattered to the floor. "Fuck." It skittered under the desk as he tried to grab it. He straightened and brushed any wrinkles in his pants. *Get it together, man.* Whether she stayed or went, at least it would be resolved.

He strolled to the mantle where he would greet her. The dark granite under his hands offered a sense of solidness, a reflection of what he'd like to appear when she walked in, cool and strong.

An ember popped to land on his shoe. He scuffed it out and leaned against the stone, his eyes focused on the door. A faint mumble of greetings floated from the foyer.

This was nonsense.

He strode to the study's exit so he could greet her in the foyer, then stopped. That would seem too eager.

He paced the room, running his hand over his smooth head, and wondered how to receive her. It would land him in jail or worse if he did what he wanted to do—tear her clothes off, confine her to his bedroom, and never let her go.

When had he become so insecure? Not even a minute in his home and she reduced him, Daedalus Pal Robi, a prime of the Nosferatu clan, to a teenager. A small growl rumbled deep inside a well of frustration that had gathered over the last weeks.

The knob turned.

He faced the door and crossed his arms over his chest. She needed to accept him for what he was, no compromises, no apologies.

The door opened, and the sight of the breath-taking enigma gliding into the study nailed his feet to the floor.

Their relationship started in an unconventional way. They didn't have a chance to go out on dates or mingle socially. It remained confined to wonderful moments at her apartment, in between their busy schedules. Never an occasion to dress up.

She cleaned up nice. He'd always thought her beautiful, now she made him take the saying "eye-candy" literally. The black, knee length, spaghetti strapped dress flowed along her lush curves. It contrasted with her milky white skin and enhanced its smooth softness. Her pale blond hair fell in big, bouncy curls around her face like silken threads.

"Sugar," he breathed.

Her stilettos clicked on the hardwood floor.

The gloss of her dark red lipstick drew his attention with visions of them wrapped around his cock. He mentally slapped himself. *Think with the big bald head, not the little one.*

Smiling, she approached him. "I'm happy to see you've recovered."

He touched his chest where the stake had penetrated him. "It didn't go all the way through. If I'd been a younger vampire, it would have been the end of me." He resisted the urge to twirl the wayward curl on her cheek.

She tilted her face up to him. "We never talked after the attack." The tips of her fingers brushed his shirt over his wound, and it softened his resolve to be stoic. "It surprised me you could wake in the day, let alone fight and save me."

Those crystal green eyes weakened his knees. They were the most honest eyes he'd ever seen, nothing hid in them. "Most can't."

She stepped closer, her intense stare making him nervous. "Only the oldest of your kind have those abilities."

He swallowed, she knew. "Where are my manners?" He gestured to the chairs. "Please, sit with me."

With a hand on his chest she stopped him as he began to move toward them. "How old are you?"

"You came across the country to ask me that?"

She gnawed at her lower lip. "No. It's just..." She sighed and let her hand fall, then made her way to the chairs.

He pulled his in front of hers so their knees almost touched. Leaning forward, he answered the question he always hated. "I lost count after eleven hundred years."

She sat up straighter. "Wow."

He caressed her knee. "Does it matter, Sugar?" He couldn't resist slipping his hand under the hem of her dress to touch her skin. "I-I'd do anyth—"

She placed her fingertips to his lips to silence him. "I love you, Daedalus. That's never been the issue."

He sat back. His fingers still tingled from the touch of her skin. "I wondered. It's nice to hear." They were about to have the conversation he'd wanted since he healed enough to rise to consciousness. His courage dwindled for a moment, but why would she travel across the continent to blow him off?

Her grin faded. "I needed time to figure things out. Where did I want my life to head? If I stayed with you and the Omegas, life would be..."

"Difficult?"

"Out of the ordinary."

He stared at her. "And your verdict?"

She stood, then sat on his lap. "I'm here." Her hands ran over his scalp.

As her supple fingers caressed his head he closed his eyes, afraid she'd see the tears that threatened to spill. "I noticed." The urge to ignite this spark she'd planted made him on edge. He didn't want to initiate anything. *She* came to *him*.

"I moved," she whispered in his ear.

He raised an eyebrow, and his mouth twisted in a smile. Like he didn't already know this. "Eric informed me."

She stretched herself along him. "I spoke with him."

"It's about time. They've been concerned about you." The warmth of her body seeped into his.

"He has control of the Ayumu now. I know he asked Robert and Sam to follow me. I told him to stop. He needs them more than I do."

Daedalus told Eric to stop for the same reason. His security had protected Sugar since the day of the attack, keeping her safe from any other retaliation.

The overwhelming emotions which almost drowned him receded. He opened his eyes to a wonderful sight. Exposed generous, round breasts almost spilled out of Sugar's dress as she stretched forward. "Officially, I'm still his advisor," he stated. They were very close to falling out. He couldn't help but silently cheer them on.

She took a deep breath. "It must be hard to advise when you don't even live close to Chicago."

"Yeah." Maybe if he pulled on the fabric.

She traced her fingers along her collarbone, then around her cleavage. "I bought a house."

"Uh-huh." His eyes followed the patterns she drew on herself. The Sahara settled in his mouth, and everything he thirsted for sat on his lap. He licked his lips. She had no idea how she affected him. The hunger she produced.

One of the dress straps slid off her shoulder and exposed more tender flesh. "The original Omegas are moving in while I'm here visiting."

"Yeah?" She wasn't wearing a bra.

"There's room for one more."

He tore his attention from her flesh and lifted his face to meet her eyes. "You want me to move in with you and live with the Omegas again?"

She nodded, eyes wide and earnest. "I've missed you. After the attack I was afraid. I didn't know what to do, where I belonged, or how to stay safe."

"So you left." It came out harsher than he intended.

She straightened and pulled up the dress strap. If he could have taken those words back, he would have.

"Yes, I needed space."

He chuckled at himself. The thought of living with the Omegas again caused him a little trepidation. It had gotten crowded in their slight apartment, yet he'd enjoyed their company and had some fun. Boundaries would have to be set. They wouldn't be allowed to use his coffin as a coffee table again, and there would be a television. A big one. But he'd have his Sugar.

He wrapped his hands around her waist and pulled her to him. With a brush of his lips on hers all was forgiven. None of it mattered, adjustments could be made, his existence would continue on a happier path. He'd given much of his time to his people over the centuries, Sugar would be his reward.

She moaned after she retreated from his kiss. "Is that a yes?"

"Yes."

Bouncing on his lap, she hugged him and pressed against his hard-on. "I'm glad this hasn't changed," she whispered as she ground her ass on him. She glanced over her shoulder at the white fur rug spread in front of the hearth. "Nice rug. What kind of animal is it?"

"Polar bear."

She glanced at him, eyebrows raised.

He shrugged. "I'm a natural predator and a competitive man."

"A predator of predators?"

"Not so much anymore." He couldn't stop watching Sugar as she removed her shoes and ran her toes through the thick, pale fur of his rug.

"It's soft." She slid off his lap to walk to the middle of it. "I've missed you." She reached back and unzipped her dress, baring her skin an inch at a time. "I want to show you how much." The heated gaze she offered him over her shoulder melted him to the chair. The dress pooled at her feet. Naked, she dropped to her knees and crawled across the fur.

The flames in the hearth created the only light in the room. It reflected off her smooth skin, highlighting every luscious curve. She stretched her abdomen along the fur. It barely brushed her taught stomach and ripe nipples.

The blood rushed from Daedalus's head straight to his cock, turning his erection painful with need. He'd denied himself any kind of release since they'd last been together two months ago. It took every ounce of his will power to control the urge to bury himself to the balls in her. Instead, he undid enough buttons to be able to pull his shirt over his head, then struggled out of his pants.

When he approached to stand in front of her, she came to her knees to receive him, touching the length of his legs with her hands. The gentle contact of her kisses as they traveled up his thighs made him quiver in anticipation. She knew what he needed, what he wanted. She lapped at his balls with the tip of her tongue and ran her hands over his hard ass. Torture seemed to be her game. Wanting a better view, he pushed her sunlight spun hair from her face.

Boldly she ran her tongue up his cock, like a lollipop.

He gasped and threw his head back, catching himself when he stumbled since his knees turned to jell-o. The onslaught of pleasure almost caused him to lose control. Almost. He tangled his fingers in her hair.

She gazed up at him. Her breath came in heated puffs over his tip.

The hunger in her eyes matched his.

"Sugar." Her name came out as a groan from the pit of his stomach. She would grant his earlier wish.

Her sumptuous, glossy red lips covered him. She took her time to slide all the way to his base. Dewy, moist, warm. She angled back so he could watch himself slip out while she pulled away.

A sound of ecstasy rolled off his lips before she started to suck him in and out. And in and out. An intense fast rhythm, taking him deeper and deeper with each stroke.

His breath grew ragged with the pace. He twined his fingers in her curls to thrust himself with her rhythm. Passion surged through his body, and the depth of it staggered him. Control slipping, he concentrated to slake off some of this intense desire.

It wasn't working.

"Sugar... I can't... Oh...yes..."

She slowed the rhythm and swallowed him deep, then sucked hard as she withdrew.

He breathed in short, sharp gasps as she repeated this over and over, drawing animalistic grunts and groans from him. Unable to hold back any longer, he slid himself down her eager throat to feel her swallow his seed.

Her hands slid around his ass, clasping him there until he was spent.

He slipped out of her mouth as he came down hard on his knees, then wrapped her in his arms tight. "Sweet, sweet, Sugar," he whispered. Laying her onto the white fur, he looked over the body of the woman who'd haunted him. Round, voluptuous breasts with their pink, ripe nipples, smooth creamy skin, and pale yellow curls damp with her dew. So many choices he couldn't decide where to start.

"Feed on me."

"I plan to." The decision made for him, he spread her legs.

"Not that. Bite me."

"Really?" A thrill of malevolent delight ran up his spine. Sex was great but with blood it became mind-blowing.

A slight tremor shook her. "I want you."

He could smell her fear building. It would make her delicious, yet he'd learned by past mistakes fear was stronger than love. It would destroy anything between them.

"You don't have to do this. You had me when you stepped out of the cab." He added as much reassurance to his smile as he could.

She returned it, and the scent of fear vanished. "Be gentle, you're my first."

He crawled up her body in one fluid motion and stared deep into her clear green eyes. This experience was important to him. If he screwed up, she'd never let him do it again. How long could he stay with her without it?

He caught her mind like all his prey, then willed her to feel no pain, to relax and enjoy the feel of his body against hers. She wrapped him in her arms and legs, a low moan whispered in his ear. He was surprised to feel his cock responding already.

She turned her head to the side.

As he kissed down her throat, he could hear the drumming beat of her heart. It intoxicated him. He fondled her breast, teasing the nipple, eliciting a moan when she arched against him. His sharp fangs closed over her neck to pierce her tender, salty skin.

The initial spill of blood flowed down his throat. He wanted to savor it and remember this taste forever. He let it trickle out on its own, trying not to be greedy, not wanting to take too much. Later it would be harder to control this hunger.

She writhed under him and made mewing noises.

It drove him crazy. He released her breast to slide his fingers along her wet slit. Her scent drifted up to him, adding to his excitement. His fingers slid inside her to touch the silky cushion of her sex. The nub of her clit brushed his thumb and caused her to cry out. He ground it in circular motions.

She scratched his shoulders when her nails bit in his skin. "Oh... That's...that's good..."

His cock throbbed with fullness. He positioned himself so he could have her both ways, with his cock and his mouth. He pressed his tip to the entrance of her sex to tease her opening.

She groaned and raised her hips, inviting him in.

He clamped down firmer onto her neck as he began pressing himself into her tight, soaked pussy. The hunger drove him and grew stronger; he became a creature more of sensation than of reason. He drank deeply while pumping harder.

Her incomprehensible cries grew louder, more labored. She clawed at his back, grinding her hips with his rhythm, panting with each deep, hard stroke.

She felt wet and velvety. Her blood tasted sweet and tangy.

He pinned her down so she wouldn't tear herself on his fangs.

She struggled.

This prey behavior excited him, but he had to be careful to not draw too much blood, not to scare her. The demon housed in his soul wanted to be released. Not this time, never again. Instead, he focused on her hot, wet opening as it convulsed around him.

She squeezed him when her climax crested. His guards out by the gate probably could hear her cries.

He pumped as deep as he could until he came inside of her, then withdrew the bite to roar his own finish.

* * * *

Sugar rested in Daedalus's arms on the polar bear rug in front of the fire, thrilled she'd made the right decision in coming here. The move and the house didn't solve her problems.

Daedalus did.

She loved the expression on his face when she'd walked into the study. Never had she been with any man who made her feel so beautiful, sexy, and safe. Who cared if her best friends were werewolves and her lover a vampire?

She flushed away those hang-ups once she'd been on her own. Danger lurked everywhere, not only from paranormal beings. Humans were violent and unpredictable too. She could isolate herself more but for what? To survive? She wanted to live and to be with the man she loved.

None of her human friends worried about her, sent guards to try and secretly follow her, or wrote her atrocious poetry.

Daedalus whispered in her ear.

"That was a very moving poem."

"It's a limerick. I'm a treasure trove of dirty limericks." He leered at her and wiggled his eyebrows, then leaned in to whisper another.

She giggled. "More."

He whispered again.

"That's the best one of all. I love you too."

THE ALPHA

BOOK TWO

CHAPTER 1

No one could call Spice Monroe weak, at least not to her face, yet she returned to Chicago with nothing but the clothes on her back. If only the strong survived, then why did she feel like such a loser?

Narrow, box-like homes lined the street as she peered at the addresses in the dark. The bus driver dropped her off a block away with directions. Cold winter wind blew through her thin trench coat. She pulled it closer, but her teeth started to chatter anyway. If she didn't find it soon, she'd turn into a Spicesicle

She must have taken a wrong turn. Maybe she was supposed to take a left instead of a right? The wealthy, established neighborhood screamed of money and when she abandoned Sugar neither of them had any.

The street sign matched what she looked for and the number on the house appeared right. She gazed up at the three-story building and swallowed around a hard lump in her throat.

Her sister lived here? She pulled an envelope from her pocket and checked the return address once more. It was correct. Maybe Sugar rented, Spice doubted a librarian's salary was enough to afford a house in the northwest side of Chicago.

The dark brick brownstone sat close to the curb. A wide set of granite stairs led to the front door. Christmas lights still hung from the window and around a tiny evergreen tree struggling to live in the small front yard.

She could relate to it.

It was February. Sugar should have brought those decorations in a while ago.

Spice sighed and stared at her feet. They hadn't spoken in years. Things in Vegas went from bad to worse for her during that time. She never wanted her twin sister to know but now she didn't have anywhere else to go.

She knocked. The wind picked up, and she shuffled her sneaker clad feet to keep numbness at bay. No one answered, but she could see a light in the window.

Bad idea. Sugar shouldn't care about her. Not after the way they parted. Spice hadn't written or called once since she left, and her little sister never had any way to contact her, yet managed to figure out where to send this letter. The envelope crinkled in her hand. Inside, the note didn't say much except Sugar missed her.

She spun around and took a step away from the house. Tears threatened to spill from her eyes. She couldn't remember the last time she'd cried, but shame burned bright in her soul.

Warm yellow light streamed from behind her. "Forget your keys, Sugar?" a male voice asked from the doorway.

She stopped and glanced over her shoulder but saw only his silhouette.

"Oh my God, you cut your hair. Daedalus is going to freak." The laughter in his comforting voice disappeared and he moved closer. "Don't cry." He wiped a tear from her face. "It looks great." With a grin, he ruffled her short blond curls.

She couldn't help but smile back.

He thought she was Sugar, her twin sister. Something in his voice sounded familiar. The face didn't ring a bell though, but shaggy brown hair fell around most of it. He had a nice, easy-going smile. It would be wonderful to come home to a smile like that every night, but it belonged to her sister.

Her grin faded.

He wrapped his strong, thick arm around her shoulders and pulled her inside. Laughter drifted from the living room where three men and an oriental woman were   setting up a board game.

One of the men, who had short cropped red hair, looked up. "Where's the food? You were supposed to grab some grub on the way home from work."

"We'll order pizza." The guy next to her squeezed one more time before walking into the next room, a huge kitchen.

"You cut your hair." The woman spoke with a thick accent and sprung across the room to run her fingers through her hair.

Spice retreated and bumped against the entrance wall. This game of pretending to be Sugar used to be fun as kids but not anymore. With her hands raised, she kept the strangers at bay as they surrounded her like a pack of wolves. None of them looked dangerous, but what were they doing in her sister's house while she was at work?

The way they grinned at her and each other, she concluded they were all good friends.

Sugar had everything she wanted; a loving man, friends, and a home.

"Daedalus let you cut your hair?" A short man built like a bodybuilder approached her.

The awe in his voice snapped Spice out of her self-pity and the protector inside reared its head. This was the second reference to someone allowing her little sister to do something. "What do you mean 'let me'?"

What kind of relationship did Sugar have? She needed permission to cut her hair? Maybe destiny brought her back to Chicago to save her little sister from some monster. Again. All those bad things happening to drive her here couldn't be coincidental.

She crossed her arms over her chest. "Where is my sister, and what are you doing in her house?"

They glanced at each other, confusion apparent on their faces.

"What?"

The man in the kitchen stuck his head out of the door, chocolate brown eyes wide as he stared at her. "Spice?" The smile he'd given to her when he thought she was Sugar returned but wider.

Her heart skipped a beat. In the light his face seemed familiar as well. "I know you."

"You should, we were only neighbors forever as kids."

"Eric!" He had grown. *Stupid, of course he's changed.* But she never expected that the skinny, lanky bottle-cap-glasses-wearing nerd would develop into a charming, handsome I-wanna-snuggle-you-on-a-cold-night kind of man. "Hi." The jobs as a hostess, a bartender, and the most recent, a stripper taught her how to talk to men the way they liked. But with him grinning at her like a happy puppy, her mind went blank.

He swept her into his arms in a bone-cracking hug.

"Wow, I'd forgotten Sugar had a twin." The redhead scratched his chin. "You look exactly alike, except your hair is short."

Eric set her back on her feet. "Let me take your coat." He tugged on the belt and untied it. To her surprise, the small action sparked warmth between her thighs. Not like he took off her clothes but she began to wonder what it would feel like if he did.

Their eyes met. His pupils dilated, the chocolate brown faded to amber, and something feral peeked at her.

She gasped and stepped back.

The pretty oriental girl took her arm and dragged her into the living room. She chattered about making tea, but Spice's attention riveted on Eric as he stood with the men surrounding him.

What the heck? She'd seen need in men's eyes before but this was darker, deeper, and so much more alluring.

The redhead tried to take Eric's arm, but he shook it off and stomped out of sight.

Spice sat on the overstuffed couch. "What did you say your name was?"

"Katrina."

A dainty, petite girl with long black hair to her knees, yet she gave Spice the impression of great strength. Life in Vegas taught her to be an excellent judge of character. Too bad it had taken her so long to learn.

"I'll be back in a minute. You stay while I make tea." Katrina slipped away to the kitchen.

Every flat surface in the living room held a book. Soft cover, hard cover, tattered, or new, Sugar loved her books. The walls were lined with shelves filled with them. Spice picked up the closest one and smelled it. The scent of paper always reminded her of her twin.

The large, square coffee table in front of her held the game Risk. Different colored pieces lay scattered on the thick blue carpet.

Game night at Sugar's house. She glanced at the hallway. With Eric. Many questions formulated in her head. What happened to her reclusive sister over the past two years? When did she get friends? *Probably when her only one, me, left town.* Did she hook up with Eric?

Hope sprung in Spice's heart. Her attraction to him was out of character. She usually loved them tough and bad. Maybe he could be the new beginning she'd come home for.

* * * *

Tyler followed Eric into the kitchen with Robert and Sam in tow. "What's wrong with you, Eric? You almost lost control of your beast."

Running his fingers through his hair, he tried to hide the blush heating his cheeks. *Spice is home.* He'd lost hope of ever seeing her again. The desire in her eyes when he loosened her jacket and the smell from her pussy set his beast-side on a craze.

I, Eric Turner, the geek next door, turned her on. The sexiest, most confident girl he'd ever met, his high school obsession.

"Sorry, she took me off guard." He looked at Robert, his calm, overly serious second in command of the pack, who shook his head at him. "Damn, I almost changed in front of her. What a disaster." Eric's mouth went dry.

Sam handed him a glass of water. If anyone understood losing control of his beast, it was him. Ever since the Omegas conquered the Ayumu werewolf pack, their females kept knocking on the door. The bodybuilder had trouble refusing them, and his beast liked the attention. He didn't completely transform mid-intercourse anymore but they heard his howls.

Eric needed to stop thinking of the pack as Ayumu. They were all Omegas now and he their alpha. The sip of water he tried to swallow went down the wrong way and blocked his windpipe. Nothing came out, not a cough and not a breath.

"Eric?" Sam asked.

Katrina scurried into the kitchen. "I make tea. You want some?" She stopped. "What is wrong with Eric?"

He coughed out a manly squeak and pointed to his throat.

Redheaded Tyler pushed pass Sam and pounded on his back.

Not a moment later Spice sashayed into the room. Even in his distress, her presence drew him like a magnet to iron.

A solid smack on his back set off a cough. He expelled the water from his throat, and it landed on her generous, rounded chest.

She stood with arms out at her sides, and her mouth hung open.

"Smooth, real smooth." Sam patted him on the shoulder and exited the room. The others followed in silence but a few seconds later, Eric heard their restrained laughter from the direction of the living room.

He grabbed a dish towel from the rack by the sink and raced over to her. "I'm sorry." Without a coherent thought in his scrambled brain, he dried her tight, white sweater.

Tension in her shoulders as he bent over to stroke around her curves clued him in that he'd done another boneheaded maneuver.

Her intense stare weakened his knees as he glanced up with her breast cupped in his hand. The urge to fondle it sent a shiver up his spine, but the ingrained gentleman inside of him beat down the beast, who wanted more than just a touch.

He jerked his hand away. "Sorry." Alphas shouldn't apologize that much. Daedalus would kick his ass if he heard him.

Eric straightened and swept the annoying hair out of his eyes. Why did he decide to let it grow? Who cared if all those guys in romance books had long freaking hair?

"Don't be." She gave him a small, seductive smile.

He kept waiting for this wet dream to end.

"Who's Daedalus?"

Nothing more deflating to a man's ego than to ask about the resident stud vampire. "Sugar's boyfriend."

"The one she has to ask permission to cut her hair. Then you're not together?"

"No." That question showed how much she paid attention to them as kids. He and Sugar had been best friends since sixth grade. Dating her would be like dating a sister. Even though they were identical twins, Spice got placed in a different category from Sugar. She topped the list for the five-finger-knuckle-shuffle when he needed it.

She leaned closer and ran her finger down his chest. It left a trail of heat along his skin. "What's happened since I left two years ago?" Gesturing around the room, she raised an eyebrow. "New house, new boyfriend, new friends, and..." She stepped to press against his body and gazed at him with green sparkling eyes. "New Eric."

Where did he start? *We hired a Nosferatu vampire to teach us how to fight about a year ago, who by the way, is banging your twin sister. Oh yeah, all of us are werewolves, except Sugar, and I defeated the local alpha in a fight to the death so it made me top wolf in Chicago.*

"Nothing much. We pay rent to Sugar and live here." The old Eric she referred to still resided inside of him. He still liked *Star Trek*, 'live long and prosper,' worked from home for a computer software company, and read as much as Sugar.

His heart twisted a little. She didn't like *him*; she liked the changes the beast made inside of him. After the werewolf attack, his eyesight returned to twenty-twenty. He got stronger and faster, which meant leaner and more muscular.

She moved back and placed her hands on her hips. "Six of you live under this roof?"

"Seven. Daedalus lives here too."

Shaking her head, she grinned and looked at the floor. "Unbelievable."

He heard the front door open and close. "I've got Thai." Sugar's voice, higher and more musical than Spice's, called out.

"What's going on?" Daedalus must have given her a ride from work. "Why are you guys so serious?"

CHAPTER 2

The expression on Sugar's face made Spice's long, smelly bus trip from Las Vegas worth the effort. Her little sister squealed, shoved the bags of food at her male companion, and hugged her. "Spice, I can't believe you're here." Sugar's reaction melted a little of the ice she'd formed around her heart.

A tall, bald man approached them, juggling the extra bags of Thai in his arms. Upon a closer look, she noticed the slight up-turn of his ears into points, the pale skin, and when he smiled at her, the sharp fangs.

Dread clenched her heart. Without having to ask, she knew who this must be. Daedalus. Her innocent, stupid twin shacked up with a vampire.

Sugar released her. "Daedalus, this is my sister."

He nodded in her direction. "I've heard so much about you. This is a pleasant surprise."

"I wish I could say the same."

"Spice!" Sugar's eyebrows rose as her eyes went wide.

"What the hell do you expect from me? You hooked up with a bloodsucker?" She'd dealt with her fair share of these creeps. They might be legal citizens but it didn't keep them from being monsters.

Sugar stepped between them, then started shoving her down a hallway. Once out of sight, she grabbed Spice's arm and led her into the master bedroom.

As the door closed she heard Daedalus comment, "I want to be the red pieces." She insulted him in public and he worried about a board game?

"Spice Clara Monroe, you'd better behave in *my* house. Do you understand me?" Her little sister stood with one hand on her hip and shook her finger an inch from her face. "I love that vampire. He's the best thing to ever happen to me."

All she could do was stare at her. She'd grown into a strong woman. Even though they shared the same birthday, Sugar always seemed much younger than her. Frail and sweet, so easily hurt and so easy to love. "You've grown a back bone."

"I've had to, you left me." Her voice hiccupped on the last word. "Where have you been?"

Spice glanced at her shoes. "Around." The worn sneakers would be terrible in the Chicago winter. "I need a place to crash." She shrugged. "The house seems full though. Could I crash on the couch until morning?" After that, she didn't have a clue what to do. She'd sold her backpack and clothes at a thrift shop to get the cash for the bus here.

A touch on her hand drew her attention back to Sugar. "You stay as long as you need. Sisters stick together, right?" She used to always say that to Sugar when they were kids. When their parents would leave them alone and scared at night so they could go out to parties, she'd snuggle with her twin and speak those words.

Spice nodded. "Yeah—" She tried to choke back the sob but it won the battle and came out. Turning her back to Sugar, she covered her face with her hands and swallowed back the other sobs that threatened to burst from her. Tears were for weaklings.

Arms wrapped around her from behind and hugged her close. Her sister leaned her head against hers. "I've missed you so much. Don't leave me again."

A pressure built inside her chest. If she spoke, the dam would break. It hurt.

"Spicy?" Sugar's voice carried an echo of the little girl she used to be.

"I won't." She spun around as the tears poured from her and grabbed onto her twin. "Never. I've missed you too." Oh, how she had. She'd let shame get between them but wouldn't let it ever happen again.

She wiped her face on her sleeve as Sugar hurried to retrieve a box of tissues from the bedside table. The king-sized bed took up most of the room and a set of crossed swords adorned the wall above it. "What's with the decor?" Spice took the offered box and used one to blow her nose. "Thanks."

"Daedalus made those ages ago. They're...special."

She quirked an eyebrow at the weapons. "How?"

Sugar stared at her. "He told me in confidence. You should ask him, I'm sure he'd tell you."

The door creaked open, and the vampire stuck his head in the room. "Tell her what?"

Her twin's face bloomed into a beautiful smile as she spotted him. He grinned back like a love struck fool and walked to stand next to her. She wrapped her hands around his arm. "She was asking about your swords."

No doubt they were in love. It made things worse.

"Tell her," Sugar coaxed.

"Umm..." He glanced at Spice. She could see a touch of animosity toward her on his face and knew it must be because she'd voiced her opinions in front of everyone. "A long time ago I preyed on any kind of human that crossed my path." He rubbed the back of his neck, then his scalp. "There came a point when I made a decision to stop. I created these swords to defend the innocent and atone for my past. They've become a symbol for my clan and those who follow my teachings."

"Who do you prey upon now?" She crossed her arms over her chest. How old was he that he   used swords?

"The willing." He gestured to Sugar. "The occasional evil doers, there are always plenty of those."

Great, not only handsome but he had a conscience. "Who decides whose evil?"

His eyes narrowed as he glared at her. It made her soul shrivel up and hide in a corner. "I do."

She swallowed with a mouth gone dry. "Oh."

"Stop it. Both of you." The command in her little sister's voice snapped them both to attention. "I'm not a child, Spice. Being with Daedalus is my choice. I love him."

The anger in his gaze dissolved when Sugar spoke those words. Any hope to save her sister disappeared with it.

"I know you're both in love. That's the problem. He's going to ask you to cross over, to become vampire." The way she jerked her hand on his arm told Spice she'd hit the bull's-eye. He'd already asked her.

"I-I haven't accepted his offer." She stepped closer to him. "Yet. I need to think about the consequences first, but it will be my decision. Not his *and* not yours." Her twin faced Daedalus. "Spice is staying for a while. We'll need to shuffle people around." She didn't ask him, she told him.

Pride swelled in Spice's chest. Maybe she worried for nothing.

* * * *

Eric chuckled to himself as he watched Sugar push her sister to her bedroom. Spice was in for a surprise. Her twin had changed since she'd left.

"I want the red pieces." Daedalus handed the bags of food to a hungry Tyler who hurried to the kitchen with it.

Katrina followed him. "Do not gobble all the noodles this time."

"What color do you want to be?" Daedalus asked.

"I don't think I'm going to play." Eric sat on the couch next to Robert and rested his right ankle on his left knee. If Spice freaked out over a vampire, how would she act once she found out he was a werewolf?

Daedalus smiled and rubbed his hands together. "I love Risk and anything to do with world domination."

Sam sat by the board game and set some pieces for play. "Eric's got other things on his mind." He pointedly stared at Sugar's bedroom door.

"Really?" Daedalus stopped placing his game markers. "There something to like in that woman besides looking like my fiancée?"

The question irked Eric. No one should judge Spice by her prickly exterior. She'd had a hard life. He knew since he'd witnessed most of it. Leaning forward, he faced the Nosferatu vampire. "I don't think you're qualified to make any judgments about her."

His eyes widened at Eric's pointed remark. He tilted his head as if seeing the Alpha for the first time. "Maybe not."

"Don't mind him, Daedalus. He's been acting weird since she walked through the door, almost lost control of his inner beast when he helped to take off her jacket."

Daedalus remained quiet until Sam finished setting the game. Then he glanced at Eric. "You need to get laid."

Eric chuckled. "That's your answer for everything."

"It usually works. If you would just choose a mate from the pack you wouldn't be having so much trouble."

Robert, who sat next to him, nodded.

"You're agreeing with him?" Eric twisted to face him.

"Not that sex cures everything, but the Ayumu pack is so unhealthy because Michael refused to take a mate. You shouldn't follow the same path. The pack needs an alpha female to help you lead."

"We need to stop thinking of them as Ayumu. They're just as much as Omega as we are. I haven't met anyone in the pack I could love."

Daedalus groaned. "Sometimes you have to take one for the team. People marry for politics. This is the same thing. Your one year grace period is over. No matter how much you patrol, you won't be able to stop dominance challenges among the females of the pack. Once they're done, they'll expect you to mate the winner."

"Don't tell me they're still challenging. They promised to wait until the full moon."

"I interrupted one on the way to get Sugar." Daedalus shrugged. "You've stalled for a year. Time's up." He glanced at the master bedroom door, then winked at him. "I'll go check on the girls." With preternatural grace he stood in one smooth motion and left the living room.

Katrina and Tyler carried small cardboard boxes of food to the game table.

"Cashew chicken." She handed him one of the boxes with chopsticks. "Red curry beef." Robert reached for it as she named it. Katrina's voice faded into the background with the others as they ate.

Crazy urges stampeded through Eric's head. He wanted to barge into the master bedroom and see what they were doing. The king-sized bed would easily accommodate the twins and Daedalus. Women threw themselves at the vampire all the time. Why wouldn't Spice? He didn't need to be telepathic to read Daedalus's mind when he saw the sisters hugging—identical twin ménage.

"If Eric has to mate within the pack that means Spice should be free game." Sam's words interrupted his thoughts as if slapped by a wet glove.

He grabbed the thick, muscled, short man by the scruff and pinned him to the floor. Moo Shu Gai-Pan spilled onto the carpet. "No one touches her. She's mine." He stared at each of his original pack mates, then released Sam.

"Yes, Alpha."

To hear them address him by his title hurt. What was wrong with him? Twice in one night he'd lost control.

"I'm sorry, Sam. Here, have my dinner. I've lost my appetite." He stood to leave. All he wanted was solitude to pick at these new emotions tearing him apart.

The bedroom door opened, and Daedalus stepped out. A tick in his temple twitched. "Spice will be staying with us for a while. We need to play musical beds until we can figure out a better solution."

"She can have my room." Eric nodded to her as she leaned out of the doorway. "It's across the hall from you. I don't mind sleeping on the couch."

"Thank you." Her soft words made his heart soar.

CHAPTER 3

Spice snuggled into Eric's pillow and tugged the blankets over her.

Her sister led a pretty nice life. Daedalus slept all day someplace in the basement so Sugar could use part of that time for herself. She worked an occasional shift in the evening at the city library, and her friends lived under her roof. No one seemed to be sponging off of her like Spice worried.

Yesterday afternoon, Katrina took her shopping and bought her some clothes, the basics: jeans, socks, underwear, sweaters, and a thicker jacket.

"I'll pay you back as soon as I can, Katrina. It's very thoughtful of you." For once, when she spoke those words, she meant them.

"No need. When I came to Chicago to live with Eric, Sugar did this for me. It is like a circle. One day you will do the same for someone else."

At a loss for words, Spice hugged her. This wasn't a con or a handout but something a *real* friend did. "Thank you, and I will." The promise rung with truth and lightened her heavy heart, but something Katrina said echoed in her head. "You came to Chicago to live with *Eric*? Not Tyler?" Doubt and dread tangled themselves with her shredded confidence as she waited for the answer. If Katrina and Eric had a past, she didn't want to complicate her life more by getting involved.

"Both. They lived together next to Sugar. It was strange to be in an apartment with only boys, so I stayed at her place a lot." Katrina's pager went off and she glanced at the message. "Sorry, have to go. My office needs me."

"Sure, ah, what do you do for a living?"

"I'm a Chinese interpreter and work for many of the companies in the area who deal with China. Daedalus helped me set up a small company."

Food for thought.

Katrina owned a business and the vampire was involved. Again.

The others had been nothing but kind to her as well. Spice had questioned each one about their lives, and they shared similar stories. All struggling to get by until Daedalus came into their lives. She wondered if any of them realized how much he helped, guiding each of them on the right career path that matched their personalities. Social working vampire? She kind of hoped he would act as her compass and send her in the proper direction too. The choices she'd made sucked, and she couldn't trust her desires anymore.

She pulled the blankets closer around her ears and squeezed her eyes shut. The soft bed squeaked a little as she rolled over. Enough thinking, she needed to sleep. Tomorrow she had a job interview at local bookstore. Sugar set it up for her.

The flannel blankets smelled like Eric. At first, she wanted to toss them in the wash but the scent offered comfort, a reminder of his gentle, contagious smile. Last night she fantasized they were his arms wrapped around her body.

He was the only one she hadn't questioned. Whenever they got a moment alone any coherent thoughts went south, straight to her crotch. Thank goodness the last few nights he'd been out. She didn't want to screw up her chances by crawling under his covers the first night. Impulse control worked better when the temptation wasn't available.

At first, she thought he went to see a girlfriend and she moped around the house, but Sam cleared all that up for her today. He told her they patrolled the neighborhood, like a volunteer watch, and this week was Eric's turn.

If he got any better she'd have to file a patent on him as the perfect man. Warm, melting-chocolate brown eyes, strong prominent cheekbones, and thick just-tumbled-out-of-bed hair inflamed her whenever she thought about him.

Like now.

Sliding her hand inside her panties, she located her throbbing clit and tried to imagine it was Eric's fingers that massaged the spot, but she'd never been very good at pretend. He would probably be real gentle and tease the area until it made her crazy.

All she managed to do with her thoughts was get more hot and bothered. She stuck two fingers in her pussy and pumped as she reached under the tight t-shirt. Her nipples hardened at her touch, and she clenched her thighs around her hand. His fingers would be longer and thicker than hers. He wouldn't need to stroke so hard to make her come. Breaths coming faster, she got closer to the light at the end of the tunnel but she couldn't finish the deed. Not when the focus of her fantasy slept on the couch at the end of the hall.

* * * *

The smell woke him. Creamy and sweet, the intoxication of it would have made him swoon if he wasn't already lying down. Every woman carried their own unique scent, this one didn't belong to Sugar or Katrina. It could only be Spice, in *his* room, tucked into *his* sheets, and on *his* bed.

Did she have someone in there with her making her so heated? He sat upright and yanked the blankets off. His hard-on tented the boxers he wore. Inhaling deeply, he realized no other smells joined hers, she must be alone. He closed his eyes and leaned his head on the back of the couch.

They had this floor to themselves. Daedalus had taken Sugar out for the night. They wouldn't be home until much later.

Spice probably lay naked on his bed, touching her body, running her hands along her smooth white skin, nipples perked and ready for tasting. He stroked his cock. Nothing would please him more than to offer to help her out with those needs, but he wanted more than a quick hump. It frightened him how vulnerable she seemed. In high school, she intimidated the crap out of him. Now, he wanted to scoop her up in his arms and tell her everything would be all right, that he'd take care of her if she'd let him.

The smell faded and he slowed his stroking, she must have climaxed without him. He sighed and opened his eyes.

She leaned against the wall, watching him.

His cock went soft, and he snatched his hand out of his boxers.

"Hey there, big guy. Don't stop on my account."

He stared at her for a moment, unsure what she meant. She wasn't angry? No, she still smelled turned on. His heart raced. Could he masturbate in front of her? He did a few experimental tugs but the shock of finding her in the room with him traumatized it.

"Need some help?"

His mouth went dry. Several different comeback lines twirled in his head, but he couldn't decide what to use. "I wouldn't mind." He tried to make it sound sexy, but it came out more like a croak. His fantasy was turning into a nightmare.

"I've been thinking about you." She stepped across the living room, then pulled her t-shirt over her head, standing in front of him with her round, firm breasts exposed. Her nipples peaked, giving them little up-turned tips. Only a tiny pair of pink panties kept her from being naked.

He loved pink.

His cock got over its issues and returned with a roaring standing ovation. It ached with lust. He took off his shorts while sitting and continued where he'd left off. Things had gone from bad to great in seconds. He would have been happy to just look at her, but then she knelt in front of him and   spread his legs so she could fit in between them and rested her breasts on his thighs.

With a held breath, he gave silent thanks to God for not letting him come right there and then. He suspected what she wanted to do, and it could be a big mistake to let her. She felt alone, he understood this, but using him to fill the emptiness would just hurt them both. They deserved better and needed to take things slow.

She replaced his hand with her own.

His beast roared inside his head and shattered any thoughts from processing. Taste, smell, and desire ruled him.

Her small, delicate fingers tightened and caressed his cock with a slow, steady pace. How could he stop now? The beast's reaction to her shocked him. It never seemed interested in mating with anyone, only fighting, until Spice walked back into his life. Every time she touched him it wanted to surface, as if needing to touch her as well.

No matter how much he tried to distract his mind from the onslaught of pleasure, he felt on the edge of exploding. *Not yet, please not yet.*

Her head of short, blond curls moved forward. The rosebud shape of her mouth opened and approached the tip of his cock. Moist and warm, her tongue swirled around and around. Her lips so close to wrapping around him.

Panting, he flung back his head. Torment couldn't be any sweeter.

She washed his shaft with long sure strokes of her tongue, then posed her pursed lips on his tender tip. Cool air brushed the scorching skin as she blew a gentle breath.

Urgent yearning swelled between his thighs. With a slight thrust of his hips, he pressed against her lips, silently pleading to let him in.

She parted them but didn't consume him like he wanted.

He delved deeper in her mouth and was rewarded with her hungry moan. The scent of her excitement surrounded them. It was too much. He didn't have a lot of experience with women so his willpower's reserves were depleted.

Advancing further with each heave of his hips, he reached the back of her throat. She took all of him. His fingers and toes tingled while his breaths came hard and fast.

With voracious appetite, she began to suck and slid his cock in and out of her lush, moist mouth.

Oh my God, oh my God, oh my God. Clenching his hands along the back of the couch, afraid to grab and distract her, he was so close to blowing.

"Spice." Her name came out sounding deep, as if from the bottom of his gut. "Yes—" he croaked. "Oh, baby. I-I'm going to come."

She didn't hesitate or stop but continued at a more demanding pace until he poured his seed down her throat. Clinging to his thighs, she held onto him and swallowed. The ceiling spun for a moment while he tried to catch his breath. A week ago, if someone told him he'd be getting a blow-job by Spice Monroe he'd have laughed in their face.

All those wishes he'd thought wasted on her finally came true.

The brush of her nipples on his thigh caught his attention. She crawled onto his lap. Flawless, milky white skin covered her voluptuous curves.

He pulled her close. During that whole time he hadn't touched her once. She wouldn't get away without him getting at least a taste. He trailed his fingers from her shoulder to her collarbone, then down her breasts to her nipples.

She arched her back as he touched her.

"You're so beautiful." Life started to return to his cock, not a full hard-on but it definitely filled.

He laid her on the bedding and bent to take the hard nub in his mouth. The small mewling moans she made rekindled his passion. Her other breast jiggled as she wiggled under him. He massaged the soft globe in his hand; he could spend the rest of the night just playing with them, but she had other ideas.

The pink panties came off and she flung them to floor. "Fuck me."

Those two words acted like a bucket of ice-cold water dumped on his crotch.

She must have noticed his hesitation. "What's wrong? If you don't have a condom, I've got one in my purse."

Of course, she would. He sighed. His beast wanted to but he'd let it have its way already tonight. "I don't think that would be a good idea."

Her hands gripped his shoulders. "What?" The question snapped like a whip, but he knew she hid her hurt behind the anger.

How did he explain himself without pushing her away forever? With no experience to draw from, he decided to stick to the truth, even if it embarrassed him.

She started to slide out from under him, but he gripped her ass and yanked her back. "I want to…but…but we need to take things slowly. If you're just looking for someone to fool around with, you're better off with Sam. I'm not a one-night stand kind of guy."

She blinked at him for a moment, then a shy smile replaced the angry frown. "How much more do you want from me, Eric?"

The way his name slipped off her tongue sent a shiver up his spine. "I want it all, baby. Body, heart, and soul—forever." She tensed in his hands. "Spice, I know people have hurt you but I don't play games. If anyone is going to end up with a broken heart, I'm afraid it's going to be me."

She took his face between her hands. "I'm scared." With a light touch of her swollen mouth,   she   gave him a small tender kiss. It meant more to him than the blow-job ever could. "You're offering me everything I've been looking for and I'm going to screw it up. I always do." She glanced around him at the hallway. "Maybe we should talk about this in your bedroom."

He chuckled. "No. I want our first time to be special."

"How?"

"I don't know. When you're sure about us, then I guess we'll figure it out."

She grinned. "Then I'm sure about us. Let's go."

"Spice, I'm a virgin." It wiped the smile off her face.

"Was-was that your first BJ?"

He pressed his body on hers and returned the tender kiss, hoping to relieve some of the anxiety in her eyes. "No, but it was the best."

"So, you fool around?"

He nodded as he nibbled on her ear lobe. "But I don't go all the way." A quiver made her tremble in his hands as he whispered in her ear. He liked it.

"I want to be the one, Eric." Her voice shook.

Lifting his head from kissing her neck, he stared down at her. "I don't want to fuck, I want to make love. Do you love me?"

She chuckled. "I just met you."

"No, you've known me most of your life. Maybe you should try to remember that."

The vulnerable girl hiding inside the angry woman peeked out through her eyes. "I will." She sighed and tried to wiggle out from under him.

"Where are you going?"

"Well, I'm not going to steal your virtue tonight. I may as well try to get some sleep so I'm fresh for my job interview."

"But I'm not done." He forged his fingers between her folds. "Let me at least repay the favor."

She gasped as he slid inside her tight pussy. Being a virgin didn't mean he lacked the skill to make a woman beg for mercy. Becoming an alpha had its perks, but the novelty of fooling around with the willing females of the pack wore away quick, especially when one of them got angry for not going all the way.

With each thrust, her hips met his hands. She whispered dirty encouragements in his ear, and it surprised him how much he liked it. "Harder," she pleaded.

Oh, how he wanted to replace his fingers with his cock. For once, his morals pissed him off.

He twirled his fingers inside her, searching for that magical spot. The way she cried out told him exactly where it lay, and he worked it until Spice became a mass of thrashing limbs.

Her cries probably woke the others downstairs and maybe the neighbors. Smug with her satisfaction, he hugged her close and waited to wake up.

CHAPTER 4

A noise in the hallway outside of Eric's bedroom alerted Spice. She shoved the half-wrapped present under the blankets of her unmade bed and spun around.

Her sister stepped through the doorway.

"Jesus H. Christ, Sugar. You about gave me a heart attack." Her heart slowed with relief now that she knew it wasn't Eric. She wanted to surprise him with a gift. The realization amazed her. When was the last time she cared to give something to anyone?

"What are you hiding?" Her twin peeked under the blankets. "A book? Is it for me?" She grinned with a wicked glint in her eyes. The vampire's personality had rubbed off on her.

"No." Spice pulled it out and exposed the cover. It had taken some work to get Eric to admit the box of romance books under his bed belonged to him, but they'd both enjoyed her methods of persuading his confession. She smiled, remembering the last three nights. He still refused to join her in his bed but didn't protest if she searched him out during the wee hours of the morning and joined him on the couch.

His virginity tortured her. At first, she believed it was the reason for her infatuation but after three days she realized what she felt meant more. Like a moth to flame, his kindness drew her. She hoped she didn't get burned.

"That's Eric's favorite author. How'd you know?"

"It wasn't hard to figure out. I went through his books and she had the most titles. Look." Inside the cover was the author's signature. "She did a signing at the book store yesterday. Do you think he'll like it?"

Sugar gripped her arm and laughed. "He'll love it. How's the new job?"

"I never thought I'd like working with books. It's…peaceful." She finished wrapping the gift in bright shiny blue paper and taped the edges, then took a navy blue ribbon to tie around it. Her sister placed a finger over the knot to hold it while she tied a bow. "It's the best job I've had in a long time."

Sugar's smile faded as she stepped closer. "If you ever need to talk, I'm here for you."

Without meeting her stare, Spice nodded. "I know." Her voice cracked, and she cleared her throat. "That part of my life is over. It's in the past." Taking a deep breath she glanced at her little sister, whose concern painted her face, then smiled. "I'm ready to start fresh."

"Eric is part of it?" Spice realized then the concern on Sugar's face wasn't only for her but for Eric, her best friend, as well.

"I think so."

Her twin hugged her suddenly. "Nothing would make me happier than if the two of you fell in love."

Spice couldn't return the gesture and stepped away, waiting to hear the "but" part of the speech. Whenever something concerned her, the use of that word went with it. *You're smart, but you can't handle the responsibility* or her favorite *you're beautiful but don't have enough talent.* She could write a memoir filled with these kinds of statements.

"But I don't want Eric getting hurt."

Even though she was familiar with such expectations, didn't mean it stopped hurting. "Hmm…" It was the only sound she could make. If she opened her mouth, she might tell Sugar where to shove her worries. What about *her* heart? Would anybody be troubled if *he* hurt *her*?

"Don't give those eyes, Spice."

"What?"

"The eat-shit-and-die glare you give people when pissed." Sugar placed her hands on her hips. "You don't have a good track record when it comes to men. Use 'em and lose 'em, isn't that your motto?"

"It used to be. Until I became the one used." She set the present on the dresser. Eric would be home soon. He'd gone out with Sam and Robert to check on some friends but promised that after he returned he'd take her to a late dinner. She didn't want to wreck the night by carrying a bunch of emotional crap around. "I won't hurt him."

She was about to embark on the most risky endeavor she'd ever been part of—a relationship. Tonight, she'd give him everything, her trust, her dreams, and her heart. No one, except her twin, had deserved such trust. The book symbolized these gifts. She touched it.

"He means something to you." The awe in Sugar's voice should have been insulting, but Spice laughed at it. They knew each other too well.

"Yep, for the first time, I'm in love."

A squeal of joy escaped her little sister just before she jumped on her and knocked them both to the floor. Sugar landed on top of her, the air whooshed from her lungs, and stars pirouetted in front of her eyes. Her sister yelled, "Yes, yes, yes!"

"What's going on in here—oh, my."

Spice glanced over Sugar's shoulder. Daedalus stood in the doorway, his eyes wide and his mouth hanging open. She'd seen that look on other men before once they'd met her twin. The ménage fantasy stare. Not on his life. She'd had her share of cold-blooded life-suckers.

With a twist of her hips, she dumped Sugar to the floor. She appreciated her enthusiasm, but it still stung that she doubted the sincerity of her intentions toward Eric. If anyone understood her, it should be her sister. The emptiness in her soul grew a little larger. She hoped Eric believed in her. They weren't teenagers anymore, and she'd been through enough crap to recognize the real thing when she felt it.

Daedalus lost his dreamy expression and replaced it with a crooked grin. "I thought I was the only one who could make you scream like that." He leaned against the doorframe and folded his arms over his chest.

"Daedalus." Sugar sounded so scandalized Spiced had to chuckle. The girl shared her bed with a vampire yet still managed to keep some of her innocence. It amazed her. Why couldn't Spice retain any?

The sound of the front door closing carried to the bedroom, followed by Eric's call. "Honey, I'm home."

Dang, she wasn't ready for their first official date.

Sugar grabbed onto the dresser as she stood, then sashayed past Daedalus. With the tip of her fingernail, she traced a line down his bulging bicep. Her stare never left his as she led him to their room and closed the door.

Spice wanted to give her sister a mental high five. The way the vampire's expression softened when he watched her spoke volumes. She had worried about who controlled who in their relationship, but after this little display she wouldn't anymore. Yet, she still had to force herself not to shiver at the thought of what they'd be doing in there. If she was going to be part of her twin's life again, she needed to learn to accept the bloodsucker.

Eric poked his head around the doorway. "Are you okay?"

She smiled at him from her place on the floor. "Yeah, I got waylaid by a squealing sister. You know, if you close the door, we could just spend the evening in here." She popped the button on her jeans and exposed a little belly flesh.

His eyes darted straight for it. The hunger in his gaze made her breath catch. It made him look so feral, but he blinked and it faded.

"No, I was promised a date, a formal one, with you in a dress." He stepped into the room and offered her a hand to stand.

She took it. Her man not only read romance, he wanted it in his life. Maybe she should have read one his books to get an idea of what he expected. She bit her bottom lip.

"You're nervous?" He chuckled and pushed a stray curl behind her ear.

"It's been a long time since someone asked me on a date. I'm not sure how to behave." The heat of her blush burned her cheeks. "I don't want to disappoint you."

He lifted her chin with his finger. "I made you blush." The awe in his voice made it deeper, sexier and the innocence of his words made her love him so much more. "Nothing you do would ever disappoint me. I'm still thrilled you want to spend any time with me."

There were two sides to this man, the hungry beast who peeked from his eyes like when she popped her button, and the sweet gentleman who saved his virginity for someone special.

She'd be that person, no matter what it took.

* * * *

The fireworks ended over the Chicago River. Spice and Eric watched them from the Signature Room on top of the John Hancock Center. The city sparkled below them. A busboy removed their empty dinner plates from the table, then refilled the wine glasses.

Spice's smile lit up his evening. "How did you ever get such a great table on such short notice?"

"I know the cook." Being an Alpha had some perks. Loyalty to pack members still ran deep, even in his large antisocial pack. It was something he tried to nurture. The head cook, being a member, offered him an open reservation as an incentive to find a mate.

"A man with connections." She reached across the table and took his hand. Live piano music drifted through the room while she gazed at him across the candle-lit table.

This night couldn't get more perfect. She wore a small, slinky black dress that left just enough flesh exposed to spark a man's imagination. It clung to every rounded curve with spaghetti straps baring the white creamy skin of her shoulders and back. When they entered the room earlier, he couldn't help but notice the stares she drew. His heart swelled with pride.

"You've changed so much." She squeezed his hand. The statement hit a sensitive chord within him. He had changed a lot; he wasn't even human anymore. How the heck would he tell her without her running away?

He'd always wanted her but never imagined he would get a chance to have and keep her. The fear of losing her grew each day. He swallowed around the lump in his throat and squeezed her hand back. "I'm not the only one. Two years ago you wouldn't have given me the time of day."

A wounded look came to her eyes. "I didn't mean to hurt you, but you're right. I learned some hard lessons while away." She brought the wine glass to her lips and drank the dark red liquid until she emptied the vessel, then lifted the bottle to fill it once more.

"Where did you go?"

"I'm a firm believer that the past is behind me, and I don't care to dwell on it." She raised her glass again, but he placed a finger on the rim and stopped it before it reached her lips.

"I'll let you keep your secrets if you let me keep mine." He quirked an eyebrow at her and waited. They needed honesty for a relationship to work. If she couldn't confide in him, then he wasn't ready to take any more steps, no matter how much he wanted to fuck her.

"You have a secret?" She set her glass down.

"Yup."

"Let's hear it."

He laughed and leaned back in his chair. "Ladies first."

"Nobody's ever accused me of being a lady." She tapped a long, manicured, red painted nail on the glass's rim. "Fine, I'll go first but your secret better be worth it." The wine made her cheeks rosy and her smile a little lopsided.

He grinned. Maybe he should let her finish the bottle. It could prove to be interesting.

She took a sip. "I went to Las Vegas and tried to make it as a dancer."

He remembered Sugar mentioning something about Spice taking dance classes and getting a scholarship to a school.

"I bombed. The competition was too much. I ran out of money and met this guy..." She ran her finger around the rim of her glass and stared at the contents as if lost in the memory. "He made me feel special." She smiled with a touch of sorrow. "I was a fool. He talked me into doing things I'm not proud of to make money." She glanced at Eric as if waiting for him to prompt her for details. He didn't need them. "Six months ago he introduced me to a vampire and I started to ah—work for him."

Now he understood where her hostility toward Daedalus came from. The shame in her voice made him regret pushing her to confess. "Spice, I'm sorry. You don't have to continue if you don't want to."

She sighed, then drained the glass of wine. "I need to finish now that I've started. I was his pet, something pretty to keep around and show off and use. Once I came to my senses, I realized there were two possible outcomes to living with a vampire, eventually getting killed by him or becoming one. I didn't like my life and hated my future, so I ran." She reached for the bottle with a shaky hand.

He took it and kissed her fingers. "Here's to new beginnings."

The trembles stopped and she met his gaze. Light from the candle reflected off the unshed tears in her eyes.

"I bet you're a beautiful dancer." He stood and came around to her chair, then offered his hand. "Show me." They had the rest of their lifetime to get to know each other. He didn't need to press for more info. Now, she would confide in him without worrying about judgment.

Her face transformed as she beamed up at him and took his hand. He led her onto the dance floor and hoped he wouldn't make a huge fool of himself.

She twirled around him to the slow blues song and faced him with her hands on his chest. Her stiletto heels gave her more height and brought her rosebud mouth closer to his. He only had to bend at the neck and—

With a playful glint in her eyes, she stepped back and placed his hands on her waist, then rested her hands on his shoulders.

The waltz was the only dance he knew. It may have seemed odd with the music, but she never complained. She moved with grace in his hands, light as a feather and smooth as silk. She made a few adjustments to their steps and made it look easy and fresh.

He could have danced with her all night, but the song ended and she stepped into his arms and whispered, "I have a present for you at home. Let's make it an early night."

The instant cock salute those words produced made him a little dizzy, and he closed his eyes for a moment. He used her body as a shield as he shifted it to the side.

Her gaze followed his hand. She grinned at him and slid past him as she brushed her fingers over the bulge in his pants.

Mortified, he glanced at the tables but caught only a few stares. Most were envious ones. He rushed their waiter and paid the bill while she strolled by the windows, waiting for him. His beast wanted to scoop her up and have her as dessert right on the table. He needed to take a few deep, cleansing breaths and concentrate on making his beast sleep. If she meant what he hoped for, to consummate their relationship, then he didn't want the creature to be part of tonight. The loss of his virginity was for him and Spice alone.

CHAPTER 5

Spice squirmed the whole way home. Sharing her past with Eric was like a weight lifted from her shoulders. Suddenly she didn't feel so alone. The meal, the talk, and the dance were perfect. Now the best part of the date could begin. Just the thought made her wet with anticipation.

Eric fumbled the keys as he tried to unlock the front door. A feral growl escaped him and made her jump. He glanced at her with alarm. "Sorry, I didn't mean to frighten you."

"No problem." She stepped closer to him and took the keys from his hands. "Just promise to save it for bed, I liked it."

She turned her back on him to unlock the door. The light poured out as she went inside the house. She looked over her shoulder and caught the glimpse of amber in his eyes. *Weren't they a chocolate brown?*

He blinked and stared at her. The color she remembered returned.

The house sat quiet for once. No board game shouts from the living room or sports from Daedalus's man-cave. Somehow everyone knew what she planned for tonight and apparently approved since they had given them some privacy.

They hung up their coats and their eyes met. Her courage crashed. What if she overdid things in bed and freaked him out? It never worried her when they fooled around because he set limits. Tonight was no holds barred.

He planted a soft kiss on her mouth. "It'll be fine. I want to do this."

Her insecurities must have shown on her face. "That's the problem. I don't want it to be *fine*. I want to blow your mind away."

A large grin spread his   lips. "You can blow me all you want."

She rolled her eyes. They'd be all right, she'd just let him have the reins. "Then follow me, baby. I want you to show me your dark secret."

His eyebrows shot up and his eyes widened as if she'd slapped him instead of inviting him to drop his trousers. Then it dawned on her, his secret, he hadn't told her yet. She'd meant his cock when she spoke. Kicking herself in the ass for wrecking the moment, she pulled him down to her lips and kissed him with enough heat to make him forget his name. With an expert's ease, she slipped her tongue inside his mouth.

He returned her every move with as much passion.

They shuffled to the bedroom in each other's arms. At the door she pulled away. "Make yourself comfy. I'll be right back." She retreated to his bathroom and yanked off the dress. Under it she wore a matching set of black strapless bra and panties. She plumped the girls up and pulled the edges of her underwear to show a little more ass. Reaching for her heels she hesitated. He mentioned he liked them, so she left them on.

Candle-lit shadows filled the bedroom when she returned. The blankets sat in a pile on the floor, only a white sheet and pillows remained on the bed. Her breath caught when she saw Eric. He lay on his back with arms behind his head, wearing nothing but his suntan. Light played along the lines of his muscles, making them more defined.

Nothing would please her more than to touch and massage every inch of his long legs and torso. She'd seen her fair share of buff bodies and knew the difference between beach muscles and working muscles. This was a body of a fighter, sleek and lean, ready to snap into action. Odd, how an image of a predator came to mind when she looked at her gentle, loving boyfriend.

"Are you going to stand there all night?" He grinned at her.

"Let me enjoy the moment. I've never seen you completely naked in this kind of light before." She strolled to the dresser and lifted the wrapped present, then brought it to the bed.

Eric rolled to his side and leaned on an elbow to sit up. "What's this?"

"The present I told you about." She sat on the edge of the mattress. Offering him the gift made her a little queasy. What if he didn't like it? She could stand on a stage without any clothes in front of a bunch of strangers and not feel a bit insecure, but one selfless act made her squirm.

He chuckled. "When you said you had a present for me at the house, I thought you meant…sex."

"That's *your* present to *me*, silly." She placed the gift in front of him. "Open it."

He did as she asked and stared at the book, then flipped the cover. "It's signed? You met her?" He touched the signature. "Wow, this is nice of you, Spice. You didn't have to though."

"I know, but I wanted to." She ran her fingers through his thick hair. "I like making you happy." Truth rang in her words, and she hoped he heard it. Everyone worried she'd break his heart, but no one considered how frail her own heart had become. She was about to lay her hopes and dreams on this man and if he failed her, she didn't think she'd survive. "I love you, Eric."

His head snapped up from examining the book. "What?" He set the gift onto the floor, then gathered her into his arms. "Really?" The question was softly asked.

She scooted closer to him so they sat touching, and nodded, afraid she'd say the wrong thing.

He buried his hands into her curls and drew her mouth to his. The demand of his lips as they consumed hers ignited the fire that had dwindled down to simmering coals. She didn't need to hear the words, he already told her with his   actions.

The firm muscles under her hands flexed as he pulled her onto his lap. His hard, full cock pressed against her panties, and he rocked his hips.

She dug her nails into his shoulders. At this pace, they'd both come before he entered her. With all her willpower, she shoved away from his warm embrace and sat on his thighs. "Whoa, turn down the heat."

"I want you." He gripped her ass and tried to coax her back onto his cock.

"Trust me, I can't wait to have you too, but we don't get a second chance at a first time."

The words must have reached a part of his brain not focused on entering her pussy. He stopped dragging her over his body and took a deep breath. Then a small evil smile came to his mouth. He lay on his back and placed his hands behind his head. "Please, do with me as you will then."

Originally, she wanted to give him the reins and let him have her as he needed, but this could be better. He'd last longer and the experience would be mutually beneficial, a moment to remember.

Her eyes traced from his face to his chest, running along his abdomen to his thick, erect cock. It looked ready to explode. She could see it pulse with his heartbeat. If she indulged in what she wanted to do by stroking and sucking it, then it would be over. She wanted him to climax with her.

This night was for him.

He definitely didn't need any more foreplay but she did. Stretching herself along his body, she pulled one of his hands from behind his head and guided it inside her panties. She entwined her fingers with his and pinched her clit as he stroked her pussy.

The brush of his fingers at her entrance sent a shiver down her spine. He entered with a slow slide and she joined her finger with his, showing him what she needed.

A groan came from deep inside his chest. His free hand slipped into the cup of her bra and released her breast from its confines.

She leaned forward and offered her hard nub to his mouth. Elation electrified her as he sucked on it and sent a thrill of pleasure through her nipple. She ground on their entwined hands and pumped their fingers deeper inside.

"You're overdressed, Spice." He spoke in a voice thick with desire as he removed his hands from her body and tugged on her lingerie.

The withdrawal of his touch almost made her cry out. Her bra snapped open and slipped off her shoulders.

His hands cupped her breasts and squeezed before flipping her onto her back with a feral growl. She squeaked with surprise, but the passionate handling only stoked her sinful desires.

He yanked her panties down her legs and tossed them to the floor, then spread her thighs far apart as he pressed his mouth to her pussy.

She could have sworn she heard him whisper, "Mine," before plunging his tongue inside her, sucking with a carnivorous hunger. Writhing under the onslaught, she dug her hands into his hair and wrapped her legs over his shoulders to rest her stiletto heels on his back.

Pressure built between her legs, she moaned and raised her hips to open them more for him. He slipped a finger inside her as he stared up her body to meet her gaze. The candlelight reflected off the deep amber of his eyes. Untamed fever burned in his stare.

It excited her. She inhaled a shaky breath and released her hold on him.

With an unnatural grace he crawled up her body, lifted her hips to his, and thrust his cock into her pussy. Each succinct lunge went deeper and deeper inside.

She cried out, astounded at his fervor and loving every moment of it. Her quiet gentleman turned animal in bed. She'd died and gone to heaven.

His breaths came in gasps and sharp little growls joined in time with his thrusts until he arched his back and drove himself as deep as he could go. The heat of his seed filled her, and she cried out with him as the pressure exploded, replaced with ecstasy.

* * * *

Eric lay in their bed with Spice cradled in his arms and pressed against his body. In the dead of night, he couldn't sleep. How could he? A self-satisfied grin spread across his face. He really made her scream on their second round. She'd even left a few scratches on his back. Too bad they'd be healed by morning.

He never told her his secret. Guilt threaded itself around his heart. First thing tomorrow, he'd confess. She did say nothing would drive her away from him. God, he hoped she really meant those words.

He pulled her closer and buried his nose in her hair.

The scent soothed him and his beast. She smelled like his. No other way to describe it. So much for keeping his beast under wraps, it liked Spice as much as he did. For once, they agreed on something.

His cellphone went off. In the silence of the house, it made him jump as if struck by a cow prod.

Spice murmured in her sleep while he untangled himself from her body.

Scrambling in the dark, he found his trousers and answered before it woke her. "What!" He tried to whisper.

"Get dressed, we have a problem." With that, Daedalus hung up on him.

CHAPTER 6

"Have you told her about your being an Alpha of a werewolf pack yet? Lovers should know these kinds of things." Daedalus shifted his black Jaguar XJ into second gear while Eric attached his seatbelt. The vehicle fit the vampire's personality, big, sleek, and fast. Every time Eric rode in it, he realized how little he owned.

No car and no house; his job paid well, but he didn't have the time to make a home. If Spice stayed maybe some of it could change. He sighed. "You know I slept with Spice?"

"Subtle is not your middle name, Alpha. You still carry her smell." Daedalus stopped at a red light.

"I wish you wouldn't call me that." He fiddled with the belt across his chest. Maybe if he started calling Daedalus "Prime," then he'd get the point on how annoying it was to hear his title repeatedly. "I guess the other Omegas must suspect since they deserted the house. What does Sugar think?" He should stop considering his friends as the only Omegas. They needed to be one pack.

"You haven't spoken to her about shagging her sister?" The light turned green, and he continued toward the abandoned warehouses.

"No, she knows I carry a torch for her twin. It feels odd confiding in her while Spice might be doing the same."

Daedalus laughed out loud. "So you're going to use me instead."

Eric crossed his arms over his chest, the muscles made it more difficult, he still wasn't used to them. Twenty-five years as a skin-and-bones weakling was hard to forget. "Why not? I'm worried she might be using me."

"For what? Sex?" His voice rose with incredulity. "Oh, wait a minute. You want her to fall in love with you?"

"Is that so unbelievable? I know you're not crazy about her, but she's a great person. Someone just needs to give her a chance. She's vulnerable right now, and she might *think* she loves me but really I'll turn out to be a crutch."

Even though Sugar and Spice grew up in the same horrid home, it was Spice who took the brunt of the abuse to protect her little sister. The others didn't know this, but he and Sugar did. He remembered finding Spice hiding in the apartment building's shed one afternoon. She had a black eye and split lip. When he barged in she threatened him. *Don't you go running off and telling Sugar, you little dweeb, or I'll pound your ass.* Most would have been insulted, but he'd heard her parents yelling through the thin walls of the building and knew she'd pretended to be her twin. She's taken that beating and others for Sugar. In an odd way, he thought of her as a hero.

Daedalus took the corner at a sharp angle, making Eric's seatbelt strain. "You're a dumbass, worrying about love when we're on our way to break up a room full of women who are competing to be your pack mate. You need to man-up and take care of your pack. Not moan about a human girl."

"I'm here, aren't I? We'll stop this nonsense tonight. I'm going to it make illegal to challenge without my permission."

"You can't do that, Eric. Haven't you read the copy of the Accords I gave you?" Silence filled the car as Daedalus sped to the on-ramp of the interstate. "Look, challenges are pertinent to werewolf packs. It sets the hierarchy. The strongest female should lead the pack at your side."

Eric looked out the window at the other cars as they passed them. No one would convince him to take a stranger as his mate. He needed to find a way out this mess. "You're telling me to back off from Spice."

"I'm telling you if you fall in love, it will only end with heartbreak. Arranged marriages still exist and they work…mostly. This is almost the same thing. You can agree to have lovers if you insist on keeping the girl."

He shook his head before facing Daedalus. "It's too late. She smells like mine. I can't touch another woman."

"Damn it, you being a romantic drives me nuts." Daedalus hit the steering wheel with the palm of his hand. They came up to their exit and cut across two lanes to catch it.

"Holy crap, you're going to have a wreck and kill me."

"It wouldn't be any worse of a disaster than what you're doing to your own life." He made a right turn and screeched into an industrial park, then slammed on his brake and popped the shift stick into neutral. At this time of the night the place was deserted. "You inherited a sick pack, and you need to nurse them back to health."

Anger boiled in Eric's gut. He undid his seatbelt so he could face the vampire-turned-asshole. "I didn't ask for this responsibility." Then he grabbed Daedalus by the shirt and shoved him against the car door. "I don't care about these Ayumu mongrels."

"They're Omegas now." Daedalus's cool, calm voice reached the reasoning part of Eric's brain. "If she means so much to you, then make her wolf. Take her as your mate."

The suggestion slapped him across the face. "I'd never turn anyone on purpose." He let go of his friend and sat back in his seat.

Daedalus straightened his shirt. "Why not? Ask her first, I'm not telling you to do it against her will."

"I-I…" Eric stared out the windshield at the buildings. "How do you tell someone you're a werewolf?" Sure, the law considered them legal citizens, just like vampires, but people didn't accept them. Where was the romance in turning into a hairy monster? He quirked an eyebrow at his companion. Or a bloodsucker. "This isn't about me, is it? You must have asked Sugar to become a vampire."

For a moment, Eric didn't think Daedalus would answer him but it made sense. The vampire   sat   still, like stone, as only the dead could.

"I did."

"And?" He couldn't guess Sugar's decision. A year ago she'd run from all of them, too freaked out by their differences. Now, they lived happily under one roof. She'd even joined them a few times on full moon celebrations in the forest to watch them change. Maybe Spice could accept him.

"She's thinking about it. To be honest, I thought she'd turn me down, so I'm happy she's at least giving the idea a chance." He shrugged. "If she says 'no' I'll be forced to watch her age and die, and I don't want to. Is it selfish of me?"

"Is it selfish of me to want to be with the woman I love and not take some stranger as a mate?" He gave a silent prayer of thanks for getting this opportunity to make his point to his thickheaded mentor. Daedalus was a true friend and had a lot of experience for them to fall back on, but he thought and lived like a warrior.

Eric was a lover.

"No, it's not. Point made, but I'm not the one you truly have to convince. There's a warehouse full of female werewolves duking it out as we speak. What are you going to do, Alpha?"

"Shit if I know. Let's go before someone gets seriously hurt."

Daedalus shifted the car back into motion and drove to the warehouse where Eric had killed Michael, the old Ayumu alpha. Forest surrounded the building as it tried to reclaim this abandoned area. It was ideal for the pack to use.

Eric hated the place. Not just because it held bad memories but it symbolized the way the pack lived their lives. Hidden and abandoned by humanity. Things needed to change and as alpha it became his responsibility.

Ten cars sat in the parking lot by the entrance. A low growl rumbled in his throat. Daedalus heard through the grapevine some of the females were forming challenge rounds tonight, but Eric hoped the rumor to be false. When he took control of the pack, he'd asked them for a year before he picked a mate. His one year anniversary passed a month ago. Since then, the women with ambition to lead next to him had been challenging each other to obtain dominance. The one who wins gets the prize. Him.

They parked next to the cars. "What next, Alpha?"

"If I break this challenge up, they'll start another one tomorrow. I'm getting tired of these games."

Daedalus leaned his seat back and placed his hands behind his head. "If you need me, holler. I'll come running."

To add to Eric's stress, over the last few weeks Daedalus had stopped being a physical presence at his side. *Time to cut the apron strings,* he'd said.

"Sure you will."

The vampire grinned and flashed his fangs.

Eric opened the car door and climbed out. He stretched since his six-foot frame felt cramped after being folded into the sports car. A faint cry of cheering came from the warehouse. He rolled his eyes. How was he going to deal with this?

He walked to the door and entered the building. Two werewolves fought inside a cacophonous ring of crazed women and snarling beasts. The larger of the fighters smashed her opponent to the ground, then pinned her with a clawed foot. She howled her win.

At least these fights weren't to the death.

After she gloated, the female beast looked in his direction. From her scent, he recognized her as Clair, the most dominant of the challengers so far. She changed back to her female form, her fur melted to smooth skin and her bones slid into place without a single pop. Her long brown hair fell to her hips but instead of using it to cover her nudity, she flung it over her   shoulders.

The others turned to stare at him.

Show no fear. I'm bigger and stronger than them. He swallowed. "Time to go home everyone. Fun's over." With a gesture of his arms to scatter, he approached the group. A few whimpered and crawled away but most stood their ground. They were competing to be the alpha female after all. "I said it's time to leave." He glared at each one.

Four others walked away, which left three facing him. Clair crossed her arms under her bare breasts. "If you won't choose a mate then the *Accords* state we're entitled to fight for it."

She used the Accords against him. The very thing he'd done to get Michael into the challenge ring. Most paranormal races still followed the general laws set down centuries ago. Vampires, merpeople, selkies, and other Were races, but the werewolf population had forgotten them. Eric suspected on purpose but couldn't figure out why. He brought the Accords back to the Ayumu—the Omegas, he needed to stop thinking of them as separate.

"I'm very aware of your rights, Clair, but I've found a potential mate. These challenges are over until I've courted her."

"You can't do that now! We gave you a year." Clair howled and changed back to beast form. It took strength and stamina to transform twice in a short period of time. Eric had no doubt who would win those challenges and didn't care for Clair one bit.

She and the other two females stalked toward him.

His beast roared and tore from his body. He was going to kick their disobedient, mangy asses.

Clair crouched low to the ground and stalked on all fours while her two companions circled him on either side. The woman on his right started to change into her beast form but couldn't complete the act. She crumpled to the ground in an exhausted heap.

He sighed at the sight. It was irresponsible of Clair to encourage acts of stupidity from her pack mates. A Were could die if caught in such a state. What kind of leader would she be? His pack would wither and die if she became their heart.

Without further contemplation, Eric pounced on the woman to his left, who remained in her human form. He threw her against the wall. Her head banged against the hard surface, and she fell to her knees. She was lucky he restrained his beast. It wanted her unconscious.

A snarl warned him of Clair's attack. He spun and caught her neck in his grip mid-leap. Her confident demeanor evaporated into a whine.

"Did you really think the three of you could take me on?" He sent his thought to her mind but could sense her beast had more control over her than it should. Disgusted, he tossed her toward the exit, then changed back to his human form. Naked, he faced her beast, crossed his arms over his chest, and glared at her. "Get out."

If she didn't fear him, she would have followed suit and changed back as well, but she stayed in her beast form. When she started to crawl away, he turned his back on her.

Big mistake.

The treacherous bitch lashed out and gouged his back with her claws. Not a fatal wound but it hurt him.

If he'd called for Daedalus's help it would make him look weak. With a growl born of frustration, he spun around to watch Clair run out the exit with her tail between her legs, abandoning her accomplices.

He turned to the woman slumped against the wall who rubbed the back of her head. "This is what you want in a leader?"

She didn't respond or meet his gaze, merely laid herself prone on the ground.

When Eric stumbled out of the warehouse, naked and injured, the vampire jumped out of the car and offered a shoulder to lean on. "You sure have a way with women. Remind me to never take any of your advice."

Eric chuckled.

Daedalus pulled a gym bag from the trunk of the car, opened it, and offered Eric his workout clothes.

"They stink."

"Don't be a wuss. Dawn's approaching, hurry and dress." He got into the driver's side and started the vehicle.

On the trip back, an overturned vehicle caused a traffic jam on the interstate. Daedalus shouted at the windshield. "Eleven hundred years old and I'm going to fry in the sun because humans can't drive."

"Leave the car with me and find a hiding spot until nightfall." Eric grimaced as he turned in his seat. He could feel the blood trickling down his back from Clair's claw marks.

Daedalus's pupils dilated as he stared at him. "You're bleeding quite a bit." He ran his tongue over a fang.

"Snap out of it, buddy. The cars are moving again."

His friend blinked and turned his attention back to the road.

They raced against time to get home and lost as they pulled up to the house.

Daedalus's exposed head burst into flames as he stepped out of the car and the first rays of sunlight peeked over the horizon. Shrill shrieks accompanied it.

Eric scooped his friend into his arms, not thinking of burns, and ran for the house. Kicking in the door, he found Sugar inside, the source of those screeches as she watched her lover burn from the living room window.

CHAPTER 7

The sound of the front door being kicked in and Sugar's distressed high-pitched voice startled Spice from a deep sleep. She jumped out of bed and reached to wake Eric only to find him already gone. Grabbing a dirty t-shirt and jeans from the floor, she got dressed while stumbling down the hall to investigate the noise.

Sugar's voice came from the basement and Spice ran by the front door, which hung from one hinge. Oh God, someone had broken in and was attacking her twin.

She glimpsed sunlight peaking over the horizon. Thin smoke wafted in the air and made her cough. What the fuck? "Sugar!"

Taking the stairs two at time, she ran past Sam and Tyler's empty bedrooms to the open door of Daedalus's man-cave. She saw Sugar ahead as she ran through the doorway following someone. If this was some sort of sex game she'd kick both their asses. Then the time dawned on her half-asleep brain, what was a vampire doing up during the day?

A smoke trail led to Daedalus's room, and anger boiled in her chest as she heard her little sister's sob. Someone had hurt *her* twin. She stomped the rest of the way into the room, then stopped in stunned silence.

Eric placed a limp Daedalus in his coffin and allowed Sugar to give him a quick kiss before closing the lid. "He'll be all right. We just got the timing wrong." He chuckled. "Maybe he'll have a tan after this."

Sugar smacked his arm. "It's not funny."

Crossing her arms over her chest, Spice fumed. "Can someone explain to me what the hell is going on?"

Her sister twisted around, tears stained her cheeks and soot smudged her nose. She wiped it on the sleeve of her housecoat. "The sunlight caught Daedalus on the way in the house. I freaked when I saw his head burst into flames." She glanced at the coffin. "He'll heal in his sleep. We just needed to get him inside."

"That explains the smoke." A flaming head? *Cool.* "Is it always this exciting around here?" The adrenaline still coursed in her bloodstream which made her shout the last question. Everything seemed under control. No one had broken in, Sugar appeared physically fine, and Eric was accounted for. She took a few deep breaths, and her heart rate slowed.

Blood drops on the floor led to the shiny black coffin. "Why is he bleeding?" She pointed to the trail.

"What?" Sugar spun around and reached for the lid, but Eric took her hands.

"It's from me." He glanced at Spice.

In three steps, she was at his side and examining his body. A large blood stain spread across the back of his shirt. She grabbed the bottom of it. "Off," she ordered as she pulled it over his head.

He groaned when he lifted his arms. Four deep lacerations crossed his back from the right shoulder to left hip, one next to the other.

"Oh my God, something attacked you!" She leaned in for a closer look. "I can't see in this light. You might need stitches."

"I'll be fine, Spice."

"My ass, you'll be fine. You probably got rabies from whatever clawed you. Up to the bathroom where I can see your wounds better." She smacked him on the bottom. "Now."

Sugar glanced at the coffin, then back at them.

"I'll take care of Eric. You can stay here if you want." Not like her twin could do anything for Daedalus, but if she needed to be close to the coffin for her own sanity, so be it.

Spice followed Eric up the stairs. Blood oozed from the jagged wounds in slow drips and seeped into his gray track pants. Not as much bleeding as she'd expect though.

In the bathroom, he stood in front of the large vanity over the sink and looked at his back. "It will heal, Spice. Don't worry about me."

Upon closer examination, she saw that some of the gouges went to muscle. Her stomach rolled over. "You need to see a doctor. We'll use Daedalus's car, it probably has blood all over it anyway."

Eric moaned. "He's going to kill me when he sees the passenger seat."

"Screw him." She opened the cabinets looking for disinfectant and bandages. The least she could do was clean the wounds and prevent infection from setting in. "What kind of dog attacked you anyway? A Rottweiler?"

She heard him shuffle his feet, then sit on the covered toilet. "It was a werewolf."

The bottle of peroxide slipped from her hands and she blinked while it tumbled to the floor. She heard the words, but it didn't want to register.

"Spice?"

She lifted her chin and stared into his brown eyes, then the adrenaline kicked in again. "Jesus H. Christ, Eric. Th-that's contagious, right? We need to get you to the hospital. Do they have a vaccine or something?" She gasped. "I better call nine-one-one." She spun around and ran out of the bathroom to the kitchen where a phone hung on the wall.

Things had been going too well. She *knew* it. A black cloud of bad luck followed her wherever she went, and now she'd passed it on to Eric.

In her frenzy to reach the phone, she didn't hear him follow her. As she picked up the receiver, he placed a finger on the button to disconnect the line before she dialed.

"Don't," he whispered. "I never told you my secret."

She slowly hung up the receiver. Her heart dropped and rolled with her stomach. Deep down inside she knew what he'd tell her.

"I won't catch it, Spice. I am already a werewolf."

Her knees weakened and she sank to the floor. "When did you plan on telling me?" His eyes, she'd seen them change color but let it go. It explained the changes that had occurred since the last time she'd seen him, not only the physical aspects but the more feral edge she glimpsed on occasion.

From the corner of her vision, she saw him wince as he crouched next to her. "Last night, this morning, as soon as I could get the courage."

Turning her head to stare at him, she noticed how he braced himself as if waiting for a physical blow. His shaggy, long hair fell over his bent head like a veil. The strong line of his muscled shoulders sagged as he balanced himself on the balls of his feet and used one hand on the floor to steady his stance. His fingers lay splayed by her hip.

Did it matter?

Werewolves were considered legal citizens. Hell, Sugar shacked up with a vampire. Eric made her world a brighter, better place. No man had ever done that for her. This week they'd been together gave her more joy than any other time in her life. She brushed her fingers over his hand.

His head lifted, and he met her gaze. The pain etched on his face aged him. It wrung her heart like nothing ever had. She'd caused it, not his wounds, and she never wanted to see this expression again. Reaching out, she touched his chin and came to her knees to draw closer to him. "*What* you are doesn't matter, only *who* you are does."

Such simple words, yet it carried

the heavy weight of how much he meant to her. He rewarded her with a huge smile. The one she loved. The one he'd given her when he first realized who she was. Comfort and warmth radiated from that smile.

It lifted her soul.

"You're not going to leave me?" He sat next to her.

"Never."

He wrapped her in his arms but grimaced with the fast movement.

"We should treat those wounds."

"No, trust me. They'll be healed by nightfall. Injuries don't last long with werewolves. These haven't healed yet because I got them in my human form, so they take a little more time. The ones I got as a beast are already gone."

Beast? She swallowed, not sure if the dryness came from fear or an odd sense of curiosity. "What were you and Daedalus doing?"

"I was stopping a challenge, but they—"

"Challenge?"

"I-they-I." He blew out a frustrated breath. "Maybe I should start at the beginning."

She nodded. "Did you volunteer to become one?"

"No! Never. When I was in college I got attacked while walking across the campus. I don't think whoever did it planned on my surviving. They tore me apart pretty much."

"Why?"

It looked like he stared at a faraway place. "There's something about the smell of fear that can be intoxicating. If you don't restrain your beast, take control of it instead of the other way around, it can lead you down a dark path." He sat in silence for a moment, then shivered with a deep sigh. "It left me to die. I awoke in the hospital with Sugar at my side. I lived with her as I recovered until the local werewolf pack, the Ayumu, took responsibility of me. I went to live with some of them." He shook his head. "Some were no better than animals. Dominance is very important to pack hierarchy, and I didn't understand that concept at the time."

"How could you? You were dealing with a huge life change." She stroked his hair as he leaned his head against hers.

"I can't express how good it feels to tell you." He kissed her forehead. "But there's more."

She snuggled to his chest and listened to the pounding of his heart. What a sight they'd be if someone were to walk in at this moment. Eric half naked with bleeding claw marks across his back with her dressed in dirty laundry sitting on his lap in the middle of the kitchen floor. She snorted.

Eric seemed to take it as a sign to continue. "I left the pack as soon as they deemed it safe. I couldn't wait to get away from them. The apartment next to Sugar became vacant, and I took it. Your little sister was my rock during all this. She helped me find the others, Sam, Robert, Tyler and Katrina."

"They're werewolves too?" She sat up straighter in his lap and knocked his chin on her head.

He laughed while he rubbed it. "Yes."

"Sugar's the only human?"

"And you." His grin was infectious. "But you need to let me finish."

She listened as he told her how Daedalus came into their lives and the Omegas absorbed the larger pack of Ayumus.

"An alpha of a pack."

"Trying to be. I don't think I'm doing a very good job. They insist I need a mate. The old alpha, Michael, never took one, and they blame that for making them such a male dominant pack with little morals. The male alpha is the soul of the pack, but the female is the heart."

"Mate? As in they want you to fuck someone else besides me?" She crossed her arms. "I'm not into sharing."

"I wouldn't expect you to. That's what caused the fight tonight. Some of the females were conducting challenges for dominance at an abandoned warehouse we keep for such things. I stopped them. Then I announced I wanted courting rights since I found a potential mate. Three of them turned on me. I had to put them in their place, otherwise the males would view me as weak and start challenging me as well."

"You want me as a mate? To become a werewolf?"

"No, no. I'd never ask anyone to do that. I'm still not sure what to do now, but this will give me some time to think and plan. Don't worry, I'll figure it out." He ran his thumb along her cheek and heat flooded her body. "I just want us to be together."

"You fought werewolves to be with me." She grinned at him and winked. "I think I'm a little turned on."

With a display of speed she'd never witnessed from him, he dumped her on the floor and crawled on top. His eyes faded to the golden amber she'd glimpsed before, but this time he didn't try to hide it. "Then you don't hate me?"

"I meant what I said last night. I'm here for keeps, babe." She ran her fingers into his thick mane. "It's nice to know you're not perfect. Everyone should have a flaw."

He laughed. "I'm far from perfect."

"I don't know. From here you're looking pretty damn fine." She pulled him down to her lips and slid her hands around to his back.

He flinched.

"Shit."

"I'm okay, really."

She laughed. "Go to bed. I'm going to make some breakfast. After I take a plate to Sugar, I'll bring you one."

"Naked. Serve it to me naked."

She laughed. "Definitely not perfect."

CHAPTER 8

Daedalus strolled into the living room, the tip of his right ear a little less pointy since his head caught on fire two days ago. Eric tried to hide his amusement behind Spice's wild, short curls. The vampire turned out to be sensitive about the small loss.

The memories of their crazy car ride home were still vivid. When Clair and her cronies jumped him in the warehouse, he freed his beast and kicked their mangy asses. The fact they thought he could be taken down so easily ate at him. He still needed to prove himself to his pack.

Behavior like Clair's needed to be stomped out of the pack. Dishonorable, untrustworthy, and disgraceful could be used to describe many of them, but over the last year he'd chased away the worst and nurtured the best. Now he needed to figure out how to unite the old pack with the new.

His first step sat in his arms. Beautiful lush curves pressed to his body. Spice may not be wolf and could never be the pack's heart but she owned his, and with her support he could accomplish anything.

Spice, forever her little sister's champion, came to her rescue when she heard the screams only to find they'd been keeping secrets from her.

Forced to reveal the truth, he couldn't believe his luck when she accepted everything without much question. Unlike her twin, who had run, needing time to come to terms with the paranormal, Spice knew what she wanted. Him.

He kissed the back of her neck as she rolled the dice. They played Monopoly tonight with everyone in the house, and she dominated.

"No distracting the master, honey." She waved him off.

Daedalus stopped by the table with a letter in his hand. "This was pinned to the front door. It has your name on it." He offered it to Eric.

"Somebody made a hole in my brand new wooden door with a pin?" Sugar rose from the floor by the gaming table and went to inspect the damage.

"It's just a door." Daedalus followed her.

Their chatter faded into the background as Eric looked at the envelope. His name was scrawled on the front in pen. He slid his finger under the edge and tore it open, then pulled out a folded piece of paper.

His breath caught in his chest as he read it.

Spice leaned closer and read it as well. "Can she do this?"

"No." He smacked the note with his hand, wishing it was Clair's head instead, and re-read it out loud.

Eric,

Did you think I wouldn't find out she's human? Accord law states a mate has to be of the same species. Courting time denied and challenges have continued until this evening.

I've won.

Keep the girl as a pet, I don't care, but I will rule at your side.

Clair

The paper crinkled as he crushed it in his hand. "Can't I get a break?" he shouted at no one in particular.

Sugar and Daedalus returned to the room, he quirked an eyebrow at Eric, never approving of outbursts from him. *Leaders must maintain a calm exterior at all times, to reassure his people, no matter how angry or frightened they might be inside.*

Offering the note to the vampire, Eric started to pace the room with slow, steady strides. How was he going to take care of that bitch?

"They didn't know Spice is human?" Sam asked as he rose from his seat next to Katrina. His eyes darted between Daedalus and him.

"Of course not, I wouldn't be able to stall them if they did." He glared at Sam and smelled his fear from across the room.

Sweat beaded on the smaller muscular werewolf's forehead as he edged around the table.

"What did you do, Sam? Why are you suddenly afraid?"

He stopped, his breathing a little heavier, and stood behind Tyler. "I-I didn't know, man. If someone would have told me I wouldn't have said anything."

"To who?" The question came out as snarl. For a moment, a red haze blinded him. He hadn't been this angry since his confrontation with Michael.

Sam fell to all fours and crawled to his Alpha's feet. "Last night, I met a girl at a pack party. You-you asked me to go to them to feel the pulse of the pack. She took me home, and we had a good time. Her questions sounded so innocent, like curiosity about her aloof Alpha."

Eric took a few deep breaths and blew some steam off. He didn't want to hurt Sam. His anger was at Clair. "She asked about my prospective mate?"

"She seemed excited about it. I couldn't help but brag and say what a great match you guys made. It never occurred to me you couldn't mate a human."

"Didn't you ever read the copy of the Accords that I gave to everyone in the pack?"

Sam stared at the floor and shook his head.

Each of the original Omegas pack was in the room. Eric turned and looked at them. Katrina pressed herself against Tyler, who didn't have anything funny to say for once. Robert sat on the floor with his arms crossed over his chest and glared at their groveling friend.

"Did any of you read it?" Eric tried not to sound disappointed.

"I have trouble with English, but Tyler read them to me. I admit to not understanding much of it though." Katrina rested her head on her boyfriend's shoulder.

He smoothed her long black hair with his hand. "Same here, dude. I grew up with English. It's like Shakespeare wrote it or something."

Eric sighed and rubbed his temples.

"Maybe I should get a modern translation of the Accords made," Daedalus offered.

"We'll figure this out, Eric. You're not alone." Robert's declaration didn't ease his worry.

Every week something new came up, and every week he had to find a solution for the problem. The burden of the pack would eventually break him. He needed help. He needed a mate.

Spice stayed quiet, sitting on the couch, the dice still clutched in her hand. He could almost hear the wheels turning in her head. It made him nervous. She'd want to do something, but Clair would tear her apart, literally.

"Game night is over. Get off the ground, Sam. We've got work to do." He extended his hand to the smaller werewolf at his feet. Sam might not be able to keep his dick in his pants and could be careless, but he was loyal and true. Eric couldn't buy those last two qualities in a person.

Sam took Eric's hand and pulled himself to his feet. "Sorry," he mumbled, then looked around Eric to Spice. "I'm a bonehead, if you haven't figured it out yet."

"I have," she responded.

He cleared his throat and stared at his shuffling feet.

Eric glanced at her over his shoulder and winked. He didn't want his girl to carry a grudge against Sam. If memory served him right, Spice could carry one with a vengeance. "I want the four of you to split up in two groups. Find the pack and see where they stand on Clair. I'm going to see if I can find and confront her myself." He turned to Daedalus. "I'd like you to stay here and protect them." He nodded to the twins.

The Ayumu had attacked his home after he won the challenge against Michael. It wouldn't surprise him if Clair tried to kill Spice. Daedalus, a Nosferatu Prime, could easily take on whatever she planned.

"You also know the Accords better than any of us. Can you see if there's a loophole out of this?"

The vampire shook his head. "We've been down that road. The Accords clearly state—"

Eric touched his shoulder. "Look again."

"Too bad Spice's not pack."

Eric squeezed Daedalus's shoulder when he spoke those words. He didn't like the hint contained in them. Sometimes the vampire couldn't stop from meddling.

"I'll go over them now. Send someone to relieve me before dawn." He left with Sugar in tow.

The Omegas got their jackets and left the house. Eric stood by the door as Spice wrapped a scarf around his neck.

She came to her tiptoes to give him a tender, short kiss. "You do what you have to do and deal with her, Eric."

He took her face between his hands, not too surprised to hear such a comment from his fierce love. "I'm not killer, Spice."

"She sounds conniving, selfish and untrustworthy. It will poison those around her. Only the strong survive, your pack deserves someone with the strength and conviction to kill for it. If you need to take a mate besides me, I can understand, but choose one with the right qualities. I've been a mistress before, I can be one again."

He swallowed around the lump in his throat. Over his dead body.

CHAPTER 9

"Tyler's right, this stuff is difficult to read. Legalese is hard enough in modern English let alone in ancient English." Sugar passed Spice a copy of the Accords. If her smart sister couldn't read this, then she wouldn't be able to. She sighed and set it back on the table. *Piece of crap paper.*

Dawn arrived as they spent the night searching for a solution. Daedalus slept in his coffin, and Katrina crashed on the couch in the living room. The others were still out searching the city for Clair.

It drove Spice nuts to be so helpless. "I need to know more about werewolves. Do you have access to the internet?"

"Sure, there are computers in Robert and Eric's office upstairs." Spice had been there once or twice in the last two weeks but only at the doorway. "They're password protected but I have them." Sugar grabbed her sister's hand and led her.

They huddled around one of the computers, side by side. "What do you want to know?"

"How to fight a werewolf."

Sugar twisted in her seat. "Really? Have you ever seen a werewolf in its beast form? Watched them fight?"

"No, but I'm starting to think I don't have a choice. Everything you and Daedalus told me last night points to one solution. I have to challenge Clair and beat her before she claims Eric. Let's see if they have any weaknesses."

"There is another solution." Katrina's accented voice startled both sisters. She stood in the doorway, her thin, narrow face solemn and her hands clasped in front of her.

"What?" They spoke in unison. Spice screwed her lips in annoyance. Twenty-five years and they still managed to sound like the

Doublemint twins.

Katrina came into the room and sank onto Robert's thinking couch. "I will challenge Clair on your behalf. If I win, I will be Eric's mate in name only and represent you in the pack."

Spice opened her mouth but nothing came out. She turned to Sugar, who looked just as speechless. What could she possibly say? Honesty always worked best when lost for words. "Uh...do think you can win?"

"Spice." Sugar smacked her upper arm.

"Hey, she offered. I don't mean any offense, Katrina, but you're tiny. Is Clair small too?" Maybe they could make this work.

Katrina smiled. "My human size is irrelevant. What matters is how strong my beast form has become. I lived a long time as a werewolf in China before escaping to America. Over there one needs to learn to fight to live."

Sugar leaned forward. "Really? How long have you been a werewolf?"

"Longer than your age." Her smile turned secretive.

"You never told me any of this." Sugar waved her hands, confusion drawing her brow down.

"Like you advised me, I built barriers between me and the past, then focused on my friends and future. If Clair takes over as the female Alpha our pack will wilt, not grow. My future begins to appear bleak." She shrugged. "I don't know if I can win. I haven't fought a challenge in decades."

"Decades?" they both said together. Spice glared at her little sister. "Stop that."

Katrina giggled. "You two are so cute."

Spice aimed her stare at Katrina. "This doesn't sit well with me." She left her chair and paced the room between the two computer desks.

Her fingers caught in the tangles of her short curls as she ran them over her head. "Eric belongs to *me*. I should be the one fighting." Daedalus's words floated back to her memory. *Too bad she's not wolf.*

Her heart skipped a beat. It would solve all their problems. Did she have the guts? She stopped her pacing and stared at her sister, who faced a similar problem, just not as urgent.

"What if I became a werewolf?"

Sugar got to her feet. "No, Eric would be furious. He never wanted this from you."

"I know, but maybe it's what I want. I came home to find a fresh start, and I found him. He's everything I need and more than I deserve. The least I could do in return is become what he and the pack needs." She shifted her gaze to Katrina. "Is it that much of a sacrifice?"

The petite woman didn't answer. She fixed her stare on the floor.

Sugar shook her head. "It doesn't matter, there's not enough time to change you. Eric's body took weeks to transform the first time. I doubt Clair will wait."

"Sugar's right, once the pack accepts her as Eric's mate the only way you will be able to take your place by his side is a challenge to the death. We need to act now while the challenges are only to dominate." Katrina still didn't meet their mutual stares as she spoke. She fiddled with a button on her red sweater instead. "I know another way."

"And…"

Katrina leaned forward, resting her elbows on her knees, and faced them. "A human's body needs time to assimilate the werewolf contaminant. It needs to be a certain—what is the word I need?" She looked at them as if searching for the answer in their faces. "Concentration, yes? When something gets strong like coffee?"

They both nodded.

"Once at the right level, it will trigger the first change on the full moon. It is where the myth came from. Eric took time to change because he fought it. He didn't want to be werewolf. It's different for those who choose the change."

"Since I want to become one then I should be able to change sooner." Spice grinned and hugged her sister. "This might work."

"But first you need a high concentration of contaminant in your blood. I saw it happen in Beijing to a young prince, who needed to be changed quickly so he could inherit the pack from his deceased father. His choices were much as yours. If he waited for the natural change then he would have had to fight the new Alpha to regain the pack. If he became werewolf that night, then the challenges would only be to dominance. It is very dangerous what they did."

"Wasn't he born a werewolf?" Sugar asked. She came and sat next to Katrina to grasp her hand.

"No, none are. The world would be overrun with us." She chuckled. "The placenta keeps the baby human. Once they reach maturity they can choose their own destiny."

"So if I have ch-children they'll be human." Spice shook her ice cold hands, trying to get the blood to flow into them again. "What do we have to do?"

Katrina released Sugar's hold on her hand and rose from her seat to face Spice, then smoothed the wrinkles from her black slacks. "I have to get a concentrated amount of Werewolf contaminant into your heart. If your body rejects it, you'll die."

She felt her eyes almost pop from their sockets. "You gotta' *what*?"

"No!" The command in Sugar's voice made them both spin in her direction. "I won't allow that. We'll let Katrina fight. Once she wins if you want to become werewolf the old fashion way, then go ahead."

"If Katrina wins then I have to kill her to be Eric's mate, Sugar."

"Then stay human, be   his mistress and Tyler could be Katrina's lover." She jerked her head and sighted on Katrina. "You did tell Tyler, right?"

"Of course not, he would never allow me to fight."

"Great." Spice crossed her arms and tapped her foot. Eric would be elated if they managed to find a solution to stay together. If she tried to become werewolf she could die. Tyler might kill her anyway if Katrina got hurt challenging Clair in her stead. What if Katrina didn't win?

Clair would own Eric. The crunch of her teeth as they ground together snapped her out of her reverie.

She'd have to become a werewolf and fight Clair as an Alpha. Either way she'd have to face death. Sweat trickled down her back. She had more faith in the tiny oriental werewolf's knowledge than in her own fighting skill. Her best chance at survival probably lay in Katrina's hand. When she faced Clair as a beast they would fight for dominance, not death. If she lost, then she had no one to blame but herself.

She glanced at her little sister sitting on the couch, worry etched into her face. "Will you still love me if I became pack?" It was the only thing left that would stop her.

"Spicy, nothing could ever change how I feel. You're my twin, a piece of me." Tears trickled from her eyes.

"Then let's do this. That stray humping bitch won't get her claws into my man if I have anything to do with it." She knew squat about werewolves and less about the Omegas but once she won this challenge they would be hers as well. "What do I have to do?" She rubbed her hands together and stared at Katrina.

"Fight to survive." She removed her clothes and folded them into a neat pile on the couch. Naked, Katrina kissed Sugar on the forehead, who cried in silence with her legs drawn to her chest just like when they were little girls and their father yelled at them.

Spice was an expert at the art of surviving. Abusive parents, scum-sucking boyfriends, drugs, alcohol, none of them kept their hold on her. She fought back and won. This wouldn't beat her either.

Silky black fur grew from Katrina's skin. Her face elongated, bones cracked, and joints snapped as the tiny woman grew into a magnificent, huge bipedal beast.

Spice's heart fled to hide in her shoes, and her courage followed.

The beast swung its head in her direction.

She stepped back but realized she had nowhere to run. It blocked the only exit from the room. She changed her mind. This wasn't such a good plan. She opened her mouth to tell her to stop, but Katrina drew her thick muscled arm back and stabbed her long, sharp claws into Spice's heart in one smooth motion.

Sugar's ear-piercing scream filled the room so her sister couldn't tell if she screamed as well. The pain spread across her chest and stole her breath as she coughed up a splatter of blood. She raised her chin to stare at the beast. It had Katrina's eyes and sorrow poured from them. If she could speak, Spice knew she'd say *sorry*.

She wanted to tell her that everything would be all right, there was nothing to apologize for, but the room tilted and she grabbed onto Katrina's furry arm. Her claws remained embedded in Spice's body.

The beast guided her to the ground and shredded her shirt open with the other claws. She stared with tunneling vision as it leaned its muzzle close to her chest and tore her wound wider.

She cried out. It sounded weak even to her own ears. Blood pumped from her chest.

Katrina opened her mouth and drool oozed from her canines to mix in with the blood. A steady stream of the clear slime came from her mouth until it coated the wound and the bleeding stopped.

Concentration? She pondered to herself as the darkness closed in. Katrina spoke of it. Maybe werewolf drool contained more contaminant.

"What the hell is going on here?" Spice recognized Tyler's voice as he hollered. "Katrina, oh my God, what have you done?"

"She's changing Spice." Sugar's tear-filled words answered him.

"Tyler, I know what I am doing." Katrina must have returned to her human form to speak to him.

They sounded farther away. Spice wanted to shout, to tell them she was still there, but her vocal cords wouldn't work.

"You must keep Eric away from here. Take him on a wild goose chase if you have to. If she survives this wound and if I mixed in enough of my saliva with her heart's blood, she should change with the full moon tonight."

"That's a lot of *if's* Katrina," he shouted.

"I know."

CHAPTER 10

Spice cracked open an eyelid and peeked around. A computer desk faced her. She was in Eric's office on Robert's thinking couch. Someone had placed a pillow under her head and a blanket over her body.

How did she get here?

The last thing she recalled, they'd been playing Monopoly, she'd been winning, and the dice were in her hands. Daedalus gave Eric a letter.

Clair. The werewolf bitch wanted to steal Eric from her. With a swift kick of her legs, she flung the blanket off and sat up. Her feet landed on a sleeping Sugar who squeaked when stepped on.

"What are you doing on the floor?"

"What are you doing trying to leave?" Her little sister scrambled to her knees and proceeded to open Spice's shirt. A bandage covered the area over her heart.

She thought back to Katrina and the beast she'd grown into. Their plan. She touched the bloody bandage and expected to wince but no pain jarred her. Pulling on the edges, she gasped as she exposed healed new flesh. "How is that possible? I had a huge hole."

Sugar cupped her mouth with her hand and shouted, "Katrina, she's awake."

"How long have I been out?" She rotated her left shoulder and arm. Nothing hurt, this was a definite perk.

"All day. The sun's setting, and Daedalus should be awake soon."

"The sun has set, and Daedalus is already here." The vampire stormed into the room wearing a pair of black silk boxers. "What have you three brainless twits been doing? I could smell Spice's blood from my coffin."

Spice had never seen him undressed before. His skin, so pale it seemed almost translucent, covered hard, sculpted muscles over his chest, arms, and abdomen. Her sister sure had a keen eye for scrumptious male flesh. She met Sugar's gaze and gave her a mental high five.

Katrina made her way around the vampire, carrying a tray of food, which she set in front of Spice.

The smell made her stomach growl. She could discern the scent of beef and ham from the cheese and bread. Each little particle differed from the other. She passed her nose over the sandwich on the plate and inhaled deeply. Her mouth watered.

"Spice?" Sugar quirked an eyebrow at her. "Are you going to eat it or inhale it?"

She grinned. "Thank you, Katrina. I'm starved."

"That is normal." Katrina eased onto the couch next to her.

"Normal for what exactly?" Daedalus asked.

The sandwich called her name and she took a huge bite from it. Layers upon layers of meat assaulted her taste buds, and she growled in tune with her stomach as she tore into another bite.

"You might want to feed your sister more often." Daedalus stepped closer to the couch, his eyes narrowing as he observed her eating.

"Leave her be. We must deal with a greater hunger. Controlling it controls the beast within." Katrina offered her a drink. "Try not to choke though."

"Beast?" He gasped. "You made her a werewolf?" He examined her while she gobbled her food. "I must be getting old because I sense she's almost complete. How is this possible?"

Spice swallowed a half-chewed lump. "What does he mean

almost complete?"

"You still need to make your first physical transformation." The tiny oriental woman swiveled to face the vampire. "I made Spice part of the pack this morning. It was a dangerous risk, but neither of us could figure a different solution."

"Thank you for not killing me, by the way," Spice mumbled around another bite of sandwich.

"Amazing, but how?" Daedalus crouched on the balls of his feet and watched her like a spectator at the zoo.

Spice narrowed her eyes at him, and a rumble came from her chest. It stopped short as her sandwich fell onto the plate and she looked down at her body. "What the hell?" Something inside of her shifted as if trying to get comfortable. "Katrina?" She didn't mind the note of panic in her voice, it was honest. What had she done?

She gave up her humanity for the man she loved.

When did Spice Monroe start making sacrifices?

She sighed. The day Eric spit water on her and set her soul at ease.

"Your beast responded to your emotions. It will take time for you to master these skills. You won't be allowed to be by yourself for the next few weeks."

"And you plan to set a novice werewolf against a dominant alpha?" Daedalus gaped at the three of them. "This should have been set in motion weeks ago. Not tonight."

"Some people were kept in the dark." Spice shoved the last of her meal in her mouth. He made a good point. She knew how to street fight but this took it to another level. Teeth and claw versus fist and feet, she pondered for moment and concluded maybe she could use it to her advantage. "Daedalus, if you're not on board with the project, then bail. I don't need anyone knocking my confidence right now. I'm more than capable of doing that on my   own, thank you very much."

He studied her, then nodded. "I'm on board this crazy train."

She laughed and Sugar joined her. The skin under her sister's eyes looked bruised. A twinge of guilt ran through Spice. Did she ever once consider what she was putting her little sister through? She remembered her tears. Sugar had sat on this couch and watched her best friend stab her twin in the heart. After that Spice passed out but her sister stayed by her side and cared for her.

Gathering Sugar into a hug she whispered, "I love you." She was about to put her sister through hell again by trying to fight for Eric.

"Sister's stick together." Sugar patted her shoulder and they parted.

Spice glanced at Katrina. "What do I do now?"

"Is the moon out yet?"

Daedalus moved to the window. "I don't see it."

"Usually, we wait for the full moon. It helps draw out the beast."

"Great, I get to add getting furry once a month as well as getting my—"

"Hey, hey, old-fashion vampire in the room. I don't need to hear it." Daedalus left the window and crossed the room to the door. "I'm going to get dressed."

Sugar rose to follow him. "You need to feed."

He stopped her. "You're exhausted. I can wait. Sounds like tonight might provide some sport. I wouldn't mind you washing my back though."

They left Spice alone with Katrina. She twisted to face the small woman.

"We should discuss controlling your beast before you transform. Otherwise you will be seduced into allowing it to take over, to give up responsibility of your actions and ultimately part of your humanity.

This happened to many of the Ayumu, some no better than beasts even in their human forms. We've cleared out those who didn't wish to change, and taught better control to those who wanted to remain. But once you've crossed over that line it is almost impossible to regain those pieces of yourself."

"So the moral of the story is don't cross over to the dark side."

Katrina leaned forward until their noses almost touched.

"No, it is not to let the beast get control. Ever."

"You keep speaking like I have a creature living inside of me. Am I not the beast?"

"Yes, you are but the animalistic side of your nature will be more prevalent. Instinctual urges will want to dominate, but you need to be in charge of them."

"Like what?"

"Hunger, territory, sex, and pack will affect you."

Spice cleared her dry throat. "When you changed I could still see you in the beast's eyes. How do you keep it under control?"

"I always stay in the forefront of its mind. Never succumbing to the lure of oblivion."

"Oblivion? Why would you want that?"

"You have to remember, most werewolves did not choose this path. They were made against their will. The fact you volunteered for it will give you a greater advantage since you will have less inner turmoil and a purpose to your existence." Katrina took her hands. "Let us do an exercise."

She nodded. The noise in the shower, far below them in the basement, distracted her. Her new and improved hearing made it possible for her to hear that Sugar was doing more than just washing Daedalus's back. She smirked until Katrina squeezed her hands.

"I want you to close your eyes and focus inward. Try

to…introduce yourself."

Crossing her legs, Spice tried to get comfortable. Meditation wasn't on the list of things she liked to do. She closed her eyes. How did someone look inward? Roll their eyes back? Her parents always told her to quiet her mind and stop thinking, but there was no "off" button so how did—

Something prowled in the darkness.

Her eyes sprung open. "Oh, crap."

"Don't be afraid. Remember it's part of you."

"It's a lot freakin' bigger than me." Her heart pitter-pattered at the thought of becoming that creature. *Arnold Schwarzenegger, watch out.* She took a deep breath. Nobody made her cringe without a fight. Did she always win? No, but boy did she try.

Closing her eyes, she tried to remember what she did to get past the guard dogs to escape her last place of "employment" in Vegas. She pulled out a piece of imaginary meat and set it in front of her. Not a moment later the beast appeared and sniffed at the offering, then swallowed it in one bite. Covered in pure white fur, it eyed her with her own emerald green eyes. "Cool." It approached and rubbed against her shoulder. She ran her fingers through its soft fur before it disappeared.

The phone rang.

Her eyes snapped open again. Katrina stood, then walked to the desk and answered it. "Where?" She nodded. "We'll be there soon. Stall them, Tyler." With a grim expression, Katrina considered her and hung up the phone. "It's time. I know you're not ready. It may still be best if I challenge Clair first."

Spice took a shaky breath. "No. It ends tonight."

CHAPTER 11

If Eric ever saved enough money, he'd buy this abandoned warehouse and tear it down. Empty and worn, it symbolized *his* pack. The Alpha was the soul of his werewolves, but this pack didn't reflect him. He sighed. They needed him to have a mate. She would be the heart, and then the real healing could begin.

His people, *his* pack.

He observed the large group as they gathered inside. Every lifestyle and race was represented in the mix of the people who mingled in front of him. They owned Chicago after all. Some chose to attend in their beast form, which he accepted. Not everyone wanted their human form to be known.

After searching throughout the night and day for Clair so that he could confront and deny her, he'd decided to draw her out instead. She wouldn't be able to resist the opportunity to try and claim him in front of everyone. If he succumbed to her, then they'd be mated in the eyes of the pack for life. His stomach rolled at the idea. It could never happen, not with Spice in his life, but the pack would remain damaged.

Raising his arm as he stood on a dais constructed for such meetings, the room became silent. All eyes turned his way. It used to make him nervous to speak publicly. Not anymore, practice made perfect, and boy did Daedalus make him practice. He recalled his advice each time he needed to make a speech. *A good leader must know how to sway his people to his way of thinking. Words are power.*

"My people," he cried out. "My pack, some concerns have been burning in my mind. The foremost is the way I keep thinking of *us*." He rested his hands on his hips as he took a relaxed stance on the stage. "I don't know if any of you do this, but I keep thinking of this pack as divided. There's the original Ayumu, the Omegas..." He gestured to his friends standing on the dais with him, except Katrina who should be arriving soon. "And those who recently joined us in the past year."

Most in the group nodded their heads.

"This is wrong. We should be united. A family, that's what a pack is. When one of us falls down, we lift and support them. Do we fall upon them and rip out their throats? Are we Jackals?"

A few cries of "no" answered him. Good, at least someone listened.

"Of course not, our souls have been mixed with those of wolves. Strong predators who hunt together. Honesty, honor, and heart describe the wolf. Do they describe our pack?"

A low mumble developed among his people. It was about time he made them think.

Pacing the length of the dais, he waited a moment. "No, they don't. Some may say those aren't the true traits of a wolf, that wolves in their essence are vicious animals."

Someone shouted, "Yeah." He made note of who and would deal with them personally later.

"These characteristics come from us." He gestured to himself. "The human part of the equation. Every time you allow your beast to consume your humanity, the less control you have over it."

Silence blanketed the room, and his people watched him expectantly.

"As your Alpha I have decided we will no longer be known as the Omegas or as the Ayumu. We're one pack." He shouted the last sentence and paused as he waited for the echo of his voice to subside. "We're Vasi. Guardians of the streets of Chicago, our territory."

Cheers began before he finished his announcement. It warmed his heart to hear them support his idea. For a year, he wracked his brain trying to figure out what to do with his pack. Spice inspired the protector in him and brought forth this concept. They would defend the city instead of prey on it.

As the noise died down someone clapped loud three times. "Very nice, Alpha." Clair slinked through the crowd. She wore a short red dress and a pair of matching stilettos. Her long, brown hair swayed as she made her way to the dais. "As your mate, I agree with the name change. Omegas made us sound weak, but giving us a role in what…crime fighting? I don't think this would be a profitable venture."

"I don't accept you as my mate, Clair." He crossed his arms. If he didn't make a stand against her now, in front of everyone, then she'd slowly gain power.

"Your year is up, and I've won the challenges. You need a dominant female at your side. One of your own kind, not some floozy."

His lips parted to respond, but the side door burst open and the most beautiful creature he'd ever laid eyes on stalked into the warehouse.

* * * *

Spice had listened to Eric's speech through the crack of the door with Katrina. She crouched on the ground so they could both watch. Pride swelled inside of her with each point he made to the pack.

"Eric has so much potential," Daedalus commented from behind them.

They swiveled around and found him with Sugar under his protective arm.

Spice leapt to her feet. "It's not safe for you here. You should have stayed at home."

"And miss your shining moment? Never. Daedalus will stay with me. This isn't my first werewolf challenge." She grinned but wrapped her arms around the vampire's waist and squeezed.

He met Spice's glare and a silent agreement was made. Sugar's safety would be his priority.

"I'm glad you're here." The new werewolf nodded to them.

The cheering started and Katrina tugged on her elbow. "Clair is hiding in the back. I think she's waiting for the right moment to make her claim. You'd better transform."

Muscles in her shoulders tensed at the idea. *Easier said than done.* "What do I do?"

"Strip and stand in the moonlight, then do the exercise I showed you at the house. Meet your beast and invite her out."

Turning her back on the vampire, she undressed. She could hear Sugar order Daedalus to not look.

"Not like I haven't seen it before. You're identical."

"That's my point." She heard a thump.

Once naked, Spice shut her eyes and called to her beast. It perched on the edge of her awareness but wouldn't approach. She ground her teeth and urged it to take her, but it yawned. "Katrina, it's mocking me."

She heard Sugar snort and whisper to her bloodsucking boyfriend, "Sounds just like Spice."

The sound of a person clapping silenced them.

Katrina peeked back in the door's crack. "It's Clair. She's trying to claim Eric."

A snarl escaped Spice, and when she closed her eyes her beast raced to her. The collision snapped her bones and popped her joints. She tried to scream but only a howl came out.

Looking at the gravel on the ground, she raised her head. The light from the street cast her shadow onto the building. *Holy cow, I'm huge. All right!*

Without a second thought, she smashed through the door and stalked across the floor. Clair's scent filled her nose, and the beast declared her prey. Baring teeth, she paced through the crowd toward the bitch.

Clair spun around. "Who the fuck are you?" Without removing her dress, she transformed into her brown furred beast. Shredded red material fluttered at her feet and the shoes exploded.

Like I can answer, you stupid bitch.

"You can, whore."

She blinked. The voice came within her mind, not via her ears. Katrina could have mentioned that ability. *"Get away from my mate. I'm here to challenge you."*

"Not until you tell me who you are."

"Spice, his girlfriend." She glanced at Eric, waiting for his reaction at her announcement.

"We can only hear each other in beast form. You're new to this and you expect to win a challenge against me, cub?" She thwacked an open paw across Spice's muzzle and raked her claws over her eyes.

Reflex saved her sight as she ducked her chin and rolled. The crazy woman had tried to blind her. If Clair wanted to play dirty, Spice would bring the mud. She sprang onto Clair's back and bit into her neck. Fur rubbed against her tongue and tickled her nose. She shook her head like she'd seen dogs do when playing with toys and hoped to rattle Clair's brain.

"Is that all you got?" The mangy cur flipped onto her back and crushed Spice under her weight, then twisted out of her grasp.

The crowd made noise but it wasn't clear for whom. They didn't know anything about her. Heck, Eric didn't know the white werewolf was his girlfriend and soon to be mate.

Clair's teeth reached for her throat.

With a swing of her large paw, Spice batted the Jezebel away. *"Are you trying to kill me?"*

"*Never, but accidents do happen.*" She lunged and pinned Spice to the floor, then kept snapping her jaw.

Only with luck did Spice keep her from biting anything vital, but Clair landed a few painful bites around Spice's collarbone. A growl built deep in her chest. The beast wanted to hurt the one who dared try to take their mate away. It knew how to move on an instinctual level, and Spice understood how to hit.

In one of the moments where she jerked away from Clair's maw, she glimpsed Eric. Concern painted his face.

She did what Katrina warned against, she allowed the beast a little control, a partnership for just this one time. It leaped forward mentally and pried Clair from her. With supernatural speed the white wolf pierced her back claws into the opposition's abdomen and tossed her with a kick.

The brown werewolf flew off and landed on the hard concrete floor, but the pale beast didn't let her have a reprieve. Bite after bite landed on Clair's head. Blood splattered from lacerations and made the beast thirst for more. Spice tried to restrain it and needed all her strength to keep it from killing. *Don't do it.*

With a roar, Spice regained control. She grabbed Clair, lifted her high and drove her headfirst into the solid ground. Staggering back, she prepared for another assault, but the brown beast's body remained limp. It melted back into its human form.

Eric ran past her and checked Clair's pulse. "She's knocked out." He pointed to two pack members. "Take her away." Then he turned to the white werewolf. "Who are you?"

Her beast retreated, and she felt herself reform into a human. She watched Eric's eyes widen as he saw who he addressed. Elation filled her.

"Spice, what have you done?"

"I've won the challenge." Standing naked in front of strangers didn't bother her. If anything it made her more empowered. This was her pack, and they needed her. The man before her would be her mate, and they needed each other.

Her future became apparent and it made her happy.

She smiled and let the things she felt shine through. Her beast preened inside and urged her to finish. Facing the pack, she shouted, "I lay claim on Eric as my mate. Does anyone dare challenge me?"

Stunned silence answered her.

Traversing the small space between her and Eric, Spice ran her fingers through his hair and yanked a handful to expose his neck.

He gasped when she jerked his head back but didn't resist as she bent her mouth to his skin and bit down until she tasted blood. Katrina had told her how to mark her mate. She licked the wound and left some saliva so it would leave a faint scar. Her mark on his skin was a better symbol than any wedding ring. She let him go.

"You did this for me?" His hands rested on her shoulders.

"For us. If I stayed human I'd only be sharing half your life, and I want it all."

His gaze wandered from her face to her breasts, then back up with more heat in his expression. "My white wolf." He pulled her into his arms and lifted her to his mouth, then returned the bite. It burned, and she held back a yelp but couldn't stop the reflexive squirming in his arms. Her thigh brushed along the hard bulge in his pants, and her pussy moistened in response.

The light touch of his tongue on the mark cooled the pain. "I want you," he whispered against her skin.

She wrapped her legs around his hips and ground against him. He felt so solid and strong as his hands cupped her bare ass. "Take me."

"Here?" It made her glad to hear excitement in his voice and not horror. They were a sick pack and needed reassurance they'd be taken care of by their alphas, who loved one another and didn't mind expressing it.

The pack seemed to settle down for the show. No one called out or jeered. She glanced over his shoulder. Most gathered in clusters to watch, some already started to enjoy themselves with fellow pack mates.

A brush of lips on her nipple startled her and elicited a moan. Eric suckled on her, drawing harder and harder on her flesh. His fingers dug into her as he pressed his confined length against her pussy.

He shuffled to the dais and laid her upon it.

She undid his pants as he removed his shirt. The jeans slid to the floor, and she shoved her hands into his boxers to stroke his hard cock. It pulsed.

Nothing seemed more right at the moment. He removed his underwear and kicked his legs free. Twisting her around to face the dais, he ran his cock between her ass cheeks while caressing the tender flesh.

She glanced at him over her shoulder and saw his eyes fade to amber just before he leaned her forward to gain access to her entrance.

His gaze locked with hers. "Your eyes, they've changed to blue."

The white wolf came to the surface, sensing her mate close and wanting him as much as she did. She pressed her rear against him in invitation.

It was all Eric needed, and he shoved his cock all the way into her, growling the word, "Mine."

It didn't hurt since she was already wet, but the sudden sensation and pleasure made her groan out loud.

He snarled as he began to pump in a quickening rhythm. His hand reached around and fondled her breast.

The delicate touch, such a contrast to the brutal, yet intoxicating thrusting from behind, sent chills down her spine which made her clench even tighter around him.

"Oh, yes... Spice...oh, yes." He released her nipple and grabbed her hips. His strokes grew desperate.

The cry of her name on his lips made her curl her back to give him better access to her core. Aching ecstasy grew inside, she couldn't hold it back anymore. Her orgasm shook her body as she met him thrust for thrust until his cries of release joined hers.

He collapsed next to her and gathered her to his sweat-soaked chest. "I love you, Spice."

She drew his face to hers and placed a gentle kiss on his lips. "I love you too."

A massive cheer filled the warehouse as hope filled a united pack. From this day forward, their pack would be strong and proud, they would be Vasi.

THE BETA

BOOK THREE

CHAPTER 1

Competent leadership went hand-in-hand with confidence. Tonight, Robert couldn't find either. The alpha of the Vasi werewolf pack had left Chicago on his honeymoon, which placed Robert, his beta, in charge.

The weight of responsibility crushed him like a big, fat elephant. His goal to keep the pack intact seemed jinxed.

He folded his eyeglasses and placed them in a case, tucking it in his back pocket. If they broke it wouldn't be a big deal. They weren't prescription anymore. Becoming a werewolf cured his eyesight. He just wore them out of habit, like a safety blanket.

Before knocking on the apartment door, he took a deep, shaky breath, and prayed it wouldn't be his last. Burgundy paint cracked and flaked when his knuckles rapped the door.

"What?" a deep voice barked from the other side.

He hated this part of his duties to the pack. It blowed. Why Eric, his alpha, insisted on making him beta was beyond him. Even Daedalus, their vampire trainer, appeared doubtful about the decision. Robert agreed with him. He sucked at confrontation, didn't like people in general, and preferred computer linguistics over speaking.

Glaring at the door, he restrained his beast who didn't like being pushed into this situation anymore than he did. "Let me in, Talon." A thug's name suited him.

The door cracked open, and a set of dark brown eyes challenged him through a veil of unwashed hair. Talon's beast had too much control over him. Shifters like him gave their race a bad name. "What's the problem, Bob?"

A growl rumbled in Robert's chest at the jibe. "It's Robert, or do you want me to start addressing you by your given name, Timothy?"

Pulling the door open, Talon loomed over him. "You can address me any way you want, asshole, but I ain't responsible for my actions."

This type of macho posturing was why Robert left his old pack before finding the Vasi. He didn't have time to waste on pieces of shit like Talon and couldn't care less about werewolf hierarchy. "Actually, that's why I'm here."

Robert's teeth elongated just enough to indicate deadly intent, then he jumped the brute, going straight for the idiot's jugular. He bit Talon's flesh hard, not piercing the skin, and they landed on the apartment's carpeted floor. The scent of stale cigarette smoke permeated from its fibers, making Robert want to gag.

Preferring to remain mostly in his human form, Robert had learned, with a ton of painful practice, to allow his beast's development in concentrated parts of his body instead of all at once. Now he could grow his claws, teeth, or other things at will. It took concentration and exquisite control to accomplish it. As far as he knew, no other Vasi had this ability.

"So." He let the word roll in his chest as he spoke around a mouthful of Talon's flesh.

His prey didn't struggle, which surprised the hell out of him. He expected…more. But despite the lack of resistance, the smell of fury poured from Talon.

Placing a knee on the thug's sternum, Robert pressed his one hundred and sixty pound frame on him as he allowed his claws to grow and rest under Talon's eye. He released his grip on the idiot's throat. "Rumors are racing through the pack. I thought I'd get the truth from the source."

Three more days, he only had to keep things together for three more freaking days before Eric and Spice got home.

When Eric won the alpha's challenge two years ago, Robert thought their problems were over, but they'd only just begun. Thank God, Spice showed up at their doorstep and mated with Eric. The pack needed a strong alpha couple to pull it out of the depravity it had fallen into with the old alpha.

Chicago's werewolves had grown and matured under their nurturing guidance. They'd chased off most of the troublemakers and supported the weak, but a few issues remained, like Talon.

"Some concerned pack mates called me." Sweat trickled down Robert's back as he ground his knee into Talon's chest. The jerk might be playing nice now, but Robert expected to leave here with quite a few bruises if not worse. "They're worried you're going to try something stupid."

Movement in the window across the room caught Robert's attention.

Daedalus stood outside on the ledge of the third-story apartment. He gave Robert a thumbs-up then leaned against the frame as if watching a show.

Talon shifted under Robert's weight and threw him off balance. Landing on his side, he rolled with the force and got to his feet. Years of training with Daedalus, the Nosferatu vampire warrior who surveyed the fight, kicked in.

As his opponent charged, Robert's heart raced with anticipation. When Talon's hands reached for him, he twisted out of his way, grabbed his adversary's head and used the momentum to slam it in the wall.

The plaster cracked and dented inward. Sliding to the floor, Talon lay still.

Robert stumbled back, waiting for retaliation, but his assailant didn't move. Talon's chest rose as Robert flipped him over, but his eyes remained rolled back in his head. Robert blinked. Talon was unconscious? He'd won that easily?

Yes! He pumped his arm in victory. All those antacids he'd popped this afternoon were for nothing. His first unofficial challenge, and he ruled.

A tap at the window reminded him of his audience. Heat rose in his cheeks, and he dragged his gaze to his vampire trainer.

Daedalus gestured to open the window, so he scurried over to comply.

"Did you kill him?"

"No." Robert glanced at Talon's supine body.

"You're within your rights. Your pack mates heard him say he was going to attack you." Daedalus squeezed his six-foot frame through the opening into the apartment. "What a dump."

"Killing won't solve my problems. I need to earn the pack's respect so no one will think to challenge me again, but not this way. Not to mention, killing is illegal." The idea of murder turned his stomach, though it appealed to his beast. Good thing he always maintained strict control and not the other way around. Too bad he couldn't say the same for Talon.

Some pack members held poor dominance over their inner beast, losing too much of their humanity as the animal took more and more control of their personality. Some poor souls lost it all and became nothing but animals needing to be put down. The old alpha allowed terrible things like this to happen, which had left the pack a mess.

"In some instances killing is necessary." Daedalus crossed the room, baring his fangs as he   crouched next to Talon.

Robert's soul shriveled at the sight. "Don't." Could he fight the vampire and defend his helpless, yet stupid, pack mate? Sure, but he'd lose.

Daedalus was a gazillion-year-old vampire warrior who thought tossing him around the practice mat taught good fighting skills. After the way Robert just defeated Talon maybe the vampire really knew how to teach. Didn't mean Robert could defeat his instructor.

Daedalus paused. "It's a mistake to let him live. He'll come after you again. Creatures like Talon always do."

Hanging his head, Robert played with the temptation. Only three more days, then these kinds of decisions went back on his alpha's shoulders. "Let him be. I'll deal with it if he didn't learn his lesson tonight."

Disappointment passed over Daedalus's face. Robert hoped it was because of a missed meal and not his decision. He and the vampire were far from best friends, but he did respect the bastard's opinion.

"Let's go," Robert said. "I'm sure there's still time to find a nice juicy evil-doer before sunrise for you to snack on." He left the apartment and heard Daedalus close the door as he followed.

"You did well tonight." Daedalus slapped his back so hard it rattled his molars. "There's an alpha in you. I knew it. We'll schedule more sparing time together. Hone your reflexes and increase the speed of your attacks." The Nosferatu eyed Robert's shoulders and arms. "Maybe add some bulk with more weight training."

"I don't think—"

Daedalus waved and ran ahead. "I'll see you tomorrow night, buddy."

"—that's necessary." God, they were buddies now? He sighed. Crap and a truckload of it. He had no desire to get molded into an alpha. He wasn't thrilled at   being the

Vasi's beta. More sparring time meant more bruises.

He descended the stairs out of Talon's apartment building and exited onto the sidewalk. At this time of the night, traffic trickled one car at a time. The neighborhood left much to be desired, and he had parked his car blocks from here to avoid any theft. Muggers were welcomed to try him though. If he had to, he'd bust out his beast in an emergency.

Paranormal races were legal citizens, after all, but they still needed to be discreet. Occasionally a pitchfork-and-torch-wielding mob formed, so the Vasi tried to stay low-key. They didn't need bad publicity.

* * * *

Esther Longfellow watched her mark climb through the third-story window of the red brick apartment building across the street. The vampire had used his fingertips placed in the mortar joints to scale the wall. He did it with such ease, her stomach went queasy. After sitting on the sill for a few minutes, Daedalus crawled inside. His friend had entered the building by the fucking door earlier. What were they doing?

She'd hunted vampires for years, but never from the Nosferatu clan. No one ever had until this contract came out. The payment offered too many zeros to ignore. But she wasn't stupid enough to sign anything until she'd assessed the situation. The dead couldn't spend money.

Her heart had seized earlier when out of nowhere the vampire had passed her on the street after she'd parked her car. What a lucky break. She'd followed him and his friend from a distance to a decrepit apartment building, then ducked into the alley across the street.

The Nosferatu didn't even try to hide his origins. Bald head, exposed pointed ears curling on each side, and a flash of fang as he'd spoken to the thin young man next to him. It had to be Daedalus. She doubted Chicago could house more than one Nosferatu vampire. They were very territorial.

Crouching in the alley across from the apartments, she aimed her digital camera and zoomed the night vision on the vampire as he exited through the front door. No doubt about it, he matched the pictures in her file. Why did he go in through a window and out the door? What evil deed was he up to?

She took a deep, calming breath, squashing her excitement. Now wasn't the time to attack. Her bag of tricks sat in the trunk of her car and she couldn't focus after being mentally shaken from the lucky encounter. She respected what she hunted. A fan of the paranormal, her secret obsession made her a formidable slayer. She didn't want them all destroyed, only the troublemakers, the evil-doers, the murderers.

And Daedalus liked to kill.

This takedown would need a lot of preparation, two of them being a quick getaway and a comfortable hole to hide in for the remainder of her life. The Nosferatu clan was a vengeful lot.

If she succeeded in slaying a Prime from this clan, they'd write her name in the slayer's history book. She grinned. Legally, what she did for a living was considered murder but in her book she served justice.

Watching him disappear down the block, she leaned against the alley wall. She couldn't risk following him anymore. Lacking information, she needed to do some more research like finding out where he rested during the day. She hadn't become successful by being unprepared. The challenge of this contract got her blood pumping.

Another man exited the building not long after. He wore a rumpled button-down, short-sleeved shirt tucked into loose jeans. His mouse brown hair cried for a cut and a comb.

He pushed his glasses up his nose and bent to tie his running shoes.

Recognizing him as the person who had accompanied Daedalus

earlier, Esther heard opportunity knocking. He didn't look like a threat being thin and weak. She crossed the street and approached him from behind. "Excuse me. Do you have the time?"

Glancing over his shoulder, his gaze traveled along her bare legs, to her knee length loose skirt, and finally met her stare. Her breath caught in her throat. The irises of his eyes reflected a non-existent light and shone pale amber. He blinked and it vanished, must have been the glasses that gave such a strange effect.

He rose in a single fluid motion that set her predator alarm off. Checking his cellphone, he gave her a shy smile. "It's ten after two." He scanned the area around them. "This is a dangerous part of town, ma'am. You shouldn't walk around alone. Trouble is going to find you."

Or maybe find him. She eyed his wiry arms and changed her assessment of him. Lean, tight muscles slid under his skin as he moved. He wasn't weak, more like a cross between a martial artist and a geek.

"Are you offering to walk me home?" Flashing him her most flirtatious smile, she toyed with a piece of her hair.

He swallowed. "S-sure." Shuffling to her side, he fell in next to her, eyes darting around them.

Men were so easy to manipulate, but this one actually wanted to protect her. So cute, she could have pinched him. Trying to be discreet, she took quick peeks at him. Nice strong chin and straight nose. Maybe a hint of freckles? It was difficult to tell in the dark.

"I'm Esther." She held out her hand. What the hell prompted her to use her real name?

Wrapping a firm hand around hers, he shook it. "I'm Robert."

His touch sent tingles along her arm. The name seemed too mature for him. "What are you doing out so late, Rob?" How did such a polite man like him get involved with a Nosferatu? She checked his neck for bites and didn't see anything, but there were more places on the body to feed from besides the neck. It would be a shame if he was a blood slave.

"Robert is fine. I was checking on a…friend." He stuffed his hands in his pockets. "And you, Esther?"

She laughed. "I'm up to no good." And she winked at him.

A rosy blush surfaced on his cheeks as he stumbled.

Something in this man attracted the devil inside of her. She entangled her arm around his and leaned into his hard body. The strength hidden under the geeky exterior sent a pleasant shiver through her body. Not all things were as they appeared. She hated surprises but not this one. If this was an act then he deserved an Emmy. She glanced at him, pleased that she needed to arch her neck back slightly to meet his sharp green gaze. She liked them tall, and she prayed he was the real deal.

God, what was she doing? She assessed him like a potential lover instead of a possible avenue to get her mark. *Stupid, focus.* Once Daedalus was out of the picture she'd come back for Rob if she still wanted him. Until then…she stopped in front of a duplex. "This is my place." She lied with the ease of an expert.

"All right." He shoved his hands deeper in his front pockets as if not sure what to do with them. "It was nice meeting you, Esther." His gaze flickered to hers, and he cleared his throat. "Would you like to have dinner sometime?"

The innocent anxiety of his request melted her to the spot. In her profession the men she got acquainted with were arrogant sons of bitches. "I'd like that." The answer came out before she knew it, but at least it rung with honesty. Something she didn't hear often enough.

He grinned, relief awash on his expression, and took out his cellphone. "Give me your number and I'll call you to make plans."

Torn, her heart fluttered in a small flight of frenzy. She wanted to see him again, but knew she could never offer what he deserved.

Smiling, she gave him a fake number. Better for him if he never got to know her, but she wanted one more thing before they parted. She stepped closer. "Won't you kiss me goodbye?"

Returning his phone to his pocket, Rob ran his hands along her arms as he bent forward. The light, chaste brush of lips on hers sparked a craving for more.

As he withdrew, she followed and threw her arms around his neck, closing the distance between their bodies.

His shoulders tensed, but she didn't release him as she licked his bottom lip, asking to enter. He opened his mouth, getting braver when she moaned and pressed harder against him. Strong arms engulfed her, fingers threading through her hair, as Rob bent into her body.

She wished she could say she didn't enjoy it, but the fire behind his kiss almost had her ready to pull him into a dark corner and undo those loose jeans of his. Oh, how she'd make him beg to never stop. Running her hands down his back, she took slow pleasure in the lean power under his clothes. Every defined muscle traced a delicious image in her mind. Arousal bloomed between her thighs. She continued down until she grabbed his ass.

This time the moan that tore from her throat came involuntarily. Damn, she wanted him, bad, but she did what she had to and finished the kiss by softly nipping his delectable bottom lip.

His eyes widened, and he touched the spot where she'd bitten him.

"Too much?"

He raised an eyebrow. "I liked it. I'm just surprised that I did."

Waving with her right hand, she tucked the left one behind her back. "Goodbye, Rob. I'll talk with you soon."

He grinned and strutted down the block, turning at the corner.

Releasing the breath she held, she examined the content of her hand. A worn brown leather wallet the size of her palm with the info she needed from Rob to find her mark.

CHAPTER 2

The building blocked Robert's view of Esther as he turned the corner. His car wasn't in this direction, but he didn't want her to witness his jump and heel click. The werewolf blood running in his veins enhanced the excited leap, making it higher than a human's. He bent his knees to absorb the impact of landing. Tonight, he'd kicked ass and kissed a dark-haired beauty. Her smell still lingered on his hands with the memory of how her thick, mahogany hair felt curled around his fingers.

He couldn't believe his ears when she asked him for the time. Tall, she had long legs with a nice curve to her hips and breasts, intelligent blue eyes and a personality playful enough to draw him out his shell. She'd taken control of the conversation, no hesitation in asking him to accompany her home or in kissing him. He loved smart, confident women but one had never liked him back.

Grinning like a fool, he jogged to his car, burning off the extra energy her kiss produced. He'd wanted to do so much more with her, like push her against the wall so she could wrap her legs around his hips and allow him to grind against her core. Maybe tomorrow night, he'd get what he fantasized.

Approaching the car, he pulled out the keys. The gas gage was on empty on his way here. He needed to fill the tank, but he couldn't recall how much cash he'd brought with him. After working for banks and credit card companies for the last few years, he never liked using either, not trusting the system. His right back pocket, where he usually placed his wallet, was empty. Checking the left pocket, his heart sank into his gut as it turned out empty as well. He patted the front ones and only found his cell. Maybe he'd dropped it while wrestling with Talon?

Deep down inside, he knew the truth. Esther.

He was such a fool. Beautiful women didn't ask geeks like him for a kiss. Grinding his teeth, he pictured her laughing at him as she flipped through his wallet, counting what little cash he carried.

The hole in his gut grew wider. Crap, he didn't have anything to buy gas and no way to get home but his own two feet. The last thing he wanted to do was call Daedalus or anyone from the pack for a lift. He'd never hear the end of it.

Respect was something you earned, and how would he ever obtain any if he fell for obvious scams?

Clenching his fists, Robert turned around and marched back to where he'd left Esther. His beast stretched inside him, frustrated that he wouldn't release it. Control over one's inner monster sounded easy, but the struggle became an hourly routine. Shifters dealt with this all the time, day or night, in sickness or in health. The first rule of the Vasi pack was human dominance over animal instinct, because once the beast started calling the shots the shifter began to forget right versus wrong and listened to the laws of the jungle instead.

Robert crouched by the spot where Esther had stood as she'd kissed him. Sometimes animal instincts came in handy. Her scent left a trail. He wanted his wallet back, and his pride.

Creeping into the nearby alley, he undressed, folded his clothes into a neat pile, and hid them behind a trash can. Naked, he called to his beast and allowed the full change. Pain built in his body as his limbs grew and bone molded into new shapes. He used to scream or howl as he transformed, but after three years of making the shift, he'd learned how to absorb the discomfort. It only took a few seconds, then he saw the world through his beast's eyes.

As a powerful, efficient killing machine he needed restraint. He took a deep breath, taking in the surrounding scents, then shook to settle his fur. Bi-pedal, he stood over six feet tall, but the elongated arms and increased flexibility meant he could run on all four when needed, topping speeds of forty miles an hour on a flat stretch.

Esther didn't stand a chance.

Licking his muzzle, he bent low to inhale her delicious scent, not surprised to find it led away from the duplex she claimed was her home. He followed her heady smell farther up the street where she'd crossed and entered another alley. The muscles in his back bunched, wanting to spring into action, to run howling into the night, sending fear in all who dared cross his path. He stopped in the alley and forced a calm over his beast. Nothing good would come from rampaging through this neighborhood. They needed to focus, take their time, and find their prey.

Fury at how the female had manipulated him boiled in his stomach. A growl rose in his throat as he stalked along the narrow alley. Filthy water lay in scattered puddles, and the faint scent of urine almost masked Esther's trail. He swung his head back and forth in a slow arc, not wanting to miss it.

The alley opened to a quiet street, not far from where he'd met Daedalus. No one should be around to witness a werewolf out for a stroll this late at night. He hoped. Even as a legal citizen, his size and form still freaked people out. Dead was dead when lynched by an illegal mob. Prosecution needed evidence, witnesses, and a compassionate jury to convict for murder. Those things tended to disappear when paranormal beings were the victims. Better to keep a low profile.

Scrambling over the cement, he raced along the sidewalk from shadow to shadow, just like Daedalus taught him. His heart pounded as her scent grew stronger, fresher. Around the corner, he spotted her not fifty yards away, wallet in hand as she rifled through his stuff.

The snarl escaped him before he could control the beast.

* * * *

The address on Rob's driver's license was located in a wealthier part of the city, according to the GPS app on her phone. Esther saved it and rubbed her chest. For some reason, it felt hollow.

The wallet contained very little—some cash, ID, and an ATM card. No credit cards, gym memberships, business cards. Hell, it looked like her wallet, except her ID was fake. She gasped. Could his be? Who *was* Robert McKay?

Someone who lived in a rich area should have more. Nothing about Rob fit her expectations. Investigating him interested her far more than her ticket-to-wealth Nosferatu.

A snarl from the pits of hell tore through the night air. Her heart leaped straight into her throat. She dived toward the building, rolling to get momentum, and sprung onto her feet.

Approaching from the end of the street was a huge, dark werewolf. Amber eyes glowed as it stalked closer.

She shoved Rob's wallet in her bra and palmed the thirty-eight special from her waistband. Some believed that women should carry small caliber handguns like a twenty-two or even a thirty-two, but that shit wouldn't stop a two hundred pound man, let alone a vampire or shifter. Just piss them off enough to want to take their time tearing you limb from limb. So a large caliber gun was a necessity in her profession. Her easy-to-conceal gun packed power.

Standing with her legs braced apart, she aimed. "Don't try it, fucker. This ain't no pop toy."

It didn't listen, just kept pacing forward. Her breaths became ragged. Stupid idiot probably lost control of his beast and now she'd have to wound him. She squeezed off a warning shot next to his clawed foot. She didn't kill for free.

The werewolf leaped from the ricochet of cement, rebounding off the building next to him with his feet, and sprung forward with incredible agility. This wasn't the run-of-the-mill shifter out of control, he was a trained warrior.

Shit!

She twisted and ran, knees pumping to her chest with every ounce of speed she could gather while wearing heels. People would be amazed at how fast a terrified woman could move on stilettos. She'd had enough practice to be a gold medalist. Killing werewolves was easy, it was the not getting scratched or bitten part that made her run like a coward. She didn't stand a chance at hand-to-hand combat with the thing, let alone outracing it. Her only chance lay with her car and her gun.

If that monster scratched her, then she'd be joining the pack. She didn't play well with others. The irony of a slayer turned monster wasn't lost on her. Actually, it happened more often than not, but she owned a special bullet to take care of herself if that ever occurred, and she'd take her destroyer on that last journey as well.

Heavy panting drew nearer as it closed the distance between them. She should have shot it dead when she had him in her sights. Jumping onto the hood of her silver gray sedan, Esther slid across it and landed on her feet. She swung around, aiming her thirty-eight special at her assailant's chest, but nothing followed her.

She choked on her fear. Where'd it go? Crouching low behind the car, she kept the gun ready, scanning the area. Nothing. How could something that big vanish?

The thumping of her heart drowned out her hearing. She tried to take a deep breath, to find the calm void she escaped to while hunting monsters, but damn it, she was the prey this time. A chill ran down her spine.

Taking one hand off her weapon, she reached in her pocket for her car keys. She tugged at them, but they snagged on something. She yanked and yanked, but it wouldn't budge. Her stomach cramped as the street remained quiet, almost as if it held its breath.

She glanced at the tangle of loose threads wrapped around the key ring and gave it another yank, but it only tightened the knot.

Hot breath blew on the back of her neck. She jumped in a lithe motion, landing on her feet, and spun around with her gun ready.

The creature plucked the thirty-eight special from her hands before she could pull the trigger. He discarded it over his shoulder like it was a toy. Towering two feet above her head, he glared with his iridescent amber eyes. His shoulders spanned at least twice her width.

"You are one big mother fucker," she whispered, awe apparent in her voice.

He bared his teeth and lunged.

She pressed against the car as her body froze, then pried her eyes open when the end didn't come.

The werewolf melted before her eyes as it transformed back to his human form. His fur shrank into pale white skin covering wiry muscles that slid back into place. The color of his irises darkened until she gazed into a set of sharp green eyes.

"You!" She placed her hands on Rob's bare chest and tried to shove.

He didn't budge an inch.

Rob was a werewolf? It took a moment for her thoughts to collect into something coherent, then she realized he was naked. Her prior imagination didn't do his body justice. Fine sculpted muscles covered his torso, arms, and legs. She stared—no, she might as well be honest—she gawked.

His cock swelled under her observation.

She swallowed around a hard lump in her throat.

"You have something I want." Rob placed a finger under her chin and dragged her gaze back to his face. He had something she wanted too.

With his hands, he patted her body. He yanked her car keys out of her pocket, tearing the tangle of threads, and dropped them to the ground. A growl rumbled deep in his chest. He spun her around, pressing her to the car.

Wetness pooled between her thighs. She wanted him to take her. Now. She didn't care if the whole neighborhood watched.

He used his hip against her lower back to pin her as he continued to search for his wallet.

Pickpocketing the thing was the best decision she'd ever made. She squirmed under his hips until she felt his erect cock against her ass and leaned into it. Hearing his sharp intake of breath drove her devilish side crazy. She rubbed against him, inviting more than a little pat and tickle.

Rob propped his forehead against her hair. "Esther, what are you doing?"

"What do you think?" She rested her body along his. "I never would have guessed in a million years that you were a shifter."

His hand slid over her abdomen. "Where's my wallet?"

"In my bra."

"Of course it is." He sighed and held out his hand. "Can you give it to me?"

Still a gentleman. She knew he wanted her, and she offered herself on a freaking silver platter. The men she knew would have torn off her panties and been balls deep inside of her by now. "Come and get it."

His grip on her tightened as he ground his cock against her. Slowly, he slipped his hand down her V-neck shirt. "Which side?"

She laughed, it sounded deep and sultry. "Guess."

Going deeper, he cupped her left breast inside her bra, taking his time to search.

Her nipples hardened at the brush of his hand. She arched her back, craving more.

"Nothing here." He switched hands and searched her right cup. "A-ha." He pulled out his belonging then quickly returned his hand inside her bra. He pinched her nipple and rolled it between his fingers until she cried out. Then he retreated from her. "You're beautiful, Esther, but I don't bed women I can't trust."

She clung to the car and caught her breath.

As Rob strolled away from her he changed back to his beast form. She'd never watched the transformation before. The fluid way he changed and grew must have hurt like hell, but he didn't utter a sound, just kept walking with his wallet in hand.

"Rob?"

The werewolf glanced over his shoulder.

"I'd let you tie me up if that would make you feel safer."

CHAPTER 3

Esther dozed with one eye open. All afternoon she sat in her car, parked a few houses from Rob's, and watched nothing happen. As the place stayed quiet her thoughts drifted to neutral ground.

Or at least, they tried to. Rob left her in a bad way last night. Her vibrator finished the job, but she didn't get the kind of satisfaction he could have provided. What the hell was going on? A man never drew this kind of attention from her, she didn't believe in lust at first sight, but Rob proved her wrong. He wasn't a man though, but a full-blown werewolf, a warrior werewolf.

Fanning herself with her hand, she cracked open the car window. She should have dragged him into the alley when she'd kissed him. They would both be happier, and maybe she would have had a dinner date tonight instead of being crammed in her sedan with the remains of Taco Hell on her passenger seat.

She sat in front of his beautiful brownstone with a lovely granite staircase, hoping to follow Rob to Daedalus's lair. That's how she explained this stakeout slash stalker thing to herself for the hundredth time. *Focus on the Nosferatu, not the hottie werewolf.*

A pretty blonde walked by her car, wavy hair hung past her shoulders, heels clicking on the pavement as she hurried in the evening's fading light. If Esther had curves like that Rob would never have walked away.

The blonde climbed the steps to Rob's home.

No fucking way. Esther's heart took a nosedive as she sat up in her seat, clutching the steering wheel as if it were the edge of a cliff. Double-crossing bastard made a pass at her when he already had a nice piece of ass at home. The door to the house opened, and a gorgeous Asian woman with silky black hair past her waist stepped out. They exchanged a few words before continuing in opposite directions.

Esther checked her GPS. The address was correct. Could she have saved it wrong? She watched the Asian woman climb into a car, imaging Rob caressing her slim body as he'd done to her last night. She had the right place. Rob had a harem, and he'd played her like a finely tuned instrument with his geeky, innocent act. She knew he'd been too good to be true.

Her mind raced over all the painful things she would inflict on him once she caught his mangy werewolf ass. Contract or not, this trip just became personal.

* * * *

Twisting in his bed, Robert tossed the sheet off. He dragged his fingers through his hair and didn't need to look to know his cock tented his boxers. All afternoon he'd tried to sleep, but Esther kept intruding on his dreams.

Glaring at the bulge, he palmed it as he recalled the way her soft breast fit in his hand. Stroking his cock, he pictured her arching her back at his touch and releasing a little moan. She'd offered to be tied as he deserted her last night. A drop of dew spilled from his tip. He imagined her strapped to his bed, oiled, and really pissed off. His breaths quickened as he watched her writhe in his mind. He curled onto his side, pumping hard as he pictured climbing between her thighs and thrusting deep inside her wet pussy. In hot jets, he came into his sheets and moaned her name.

He rolled onto his back and stared at the ceiling. How pathetic, he jacked off to a woman he'd turned down. She didn't react like he'd expected when he found her with his wallet. Most women would have run screaming. She'd gotten intense and pulled out a gun, then shot at him.

What shocked him the most was the desire in her gaze as she assessed his body with a possessive eye. Her fear scent had faded and the smell of her arousal took over. She couldn't fake that. He turned her on, and that fact set him on fire. Grinning, Robert rose from his bed and pulled the sheets off, tossing them in the laundry basket.

All things considering, he'd had an excellent night. Maybe next time he'd get to keep the girl. Esther was beautiful on the outside, but her deceitful nature left him cold. How could he trust a woman like that? His gaze passed over his wallet. She hadn't taken anything from it.

Not like she had enough time to spend what little he carried. Still, she gave it back easy enough. He turned on the shower and stepped into the stinging spray.

The beast wanted a mate, or maybe he should say *to mate*. Every day, like clockwork, he woke to a hard-on. The other Vasi males in the house had admitted to similar problems, but they had access to release.

Eric had Spice, Tyler was with Katrina, and Sam took anyone willing to keep his bed warm. Robert needed a female in his life, someone to hang out with and give him direction. The pickings in the pack were slim though. Those who interested him were already taken, and getting involved with a human could be tricky. When did he confess to being a werewolf? On the first date?

After rinsing the soap from his body, he towel dried, dressed in jeans and a t-shirt, then put his glasses on. Too bad shifters didn't have an online dating service. Pack politics would make that difficult though. Alphas were territorial about females, they wouldn't let anyone stroll into their area and take one. Even Eric, who Robert considered pretty sane for an alpha, wouldn't let that happen.

Racing down the steps, he almost trampled Katrina as she crossed his path at the bottom of the staircase. She was on her way to the front door. "Oops, sorry." He smiled at her. "Didn't see you coming."

She straightened his glasses and returned his smile. "I heard you did a good job with Talon last night. Have a fun evening." She wore a black dress and heels with her hair loose down her back. Her outfit accentuated her Asian beauty.

"Date with Tyler tonight?"

"Yes, I am meeting him downtown for dinner." She paused at the door. "Do you want to come?"

He shook his head. "I've got plans." Lying was better than being a third wheel. He'd almost had a dinner date. Retreating to the kitchen before his pack mate asked any questions, Robert tossed a bagel in the toaster while he listened to the front door open and close. The click of heels in the hallway made him glance out the kitchen entrance. "Sugar, you're home late."

The petite blonde set her purse on the counter.

Sugar owned the brownstone they all lived in, the original Omegas pack—Eric, Tyler, Sam, Katrina, and himself—paid her rent. They'd been neighbors at first in an apartment complex. Then they started having troubles with the old pack of Chicago, the Ayumu. That was when they hired Daedalus, a badass Nosferatu vampire, to teach them how to fight. He and Sugar had fallen crazy in love. When Eric defeated the old alpha of the Ayumu, the Omegas absorbed them. Then Eric changed their name to Vasi, which meant Vanguards in the old language.

"I missed my bus. Is Daedalus awake yet?" Sugar straightened her skirt.

"I haven't seen him, but I've only been awake a few minutes myself."

Her smile turned sad as she examined his face. "You look exhausted. Don't let him work you so hard, Robert."

The *him* she referred to was the pack's Nosferatu vampire warrior and her true love. "He's only doing what's best for us. Don't worry, I can take it." He slathered the bagel with peanut butter and poured a tall glass of milk.

Once Daedalus was ready they'd go running before hitting the all night gym. Yay.

"He told me you refused to kill Talon."

Rob nodded while chewing on his meal.

"I'm glad. He wouldn't agree with me—"

"Damn right, I don't agree." Daedalus stormed into the kitchen and blocked the entrance with his six-foot-two frame and crossed his arms over his chest. "Sugar, we discussed you placing ideas in their heads. I can't have the boys hesitating on the field of battle."

She confronted him with her five foot nothing, barely a hundred and ten pound body. "Field of battle? This is Chicago in the twenty-first century."

If Rob had someone to place a bet with he'd put his money on Sugar winning. The little librarian had grown a backbone in the last year.

"Babe, Dark Ages or not, the pack needs warriors to protect their territory."

"From what? They've chased off all the scum. The Vasi are coming together as one. No more factions. This should be a time of peace and you're acting like—like—"

"Something bad is about to happen. Don't talk military strategy with me. If I wanted to take over this city, now would be the time I'd strike. The pack is happy and their guard is down. Not to mention the alpha is out of the city."

Rob's appetite vanished. He set his bagel back on the plate and drank the rest of his milk to wash down the bite stuck in his throat. Daedalus was the life of the party.

The vampire glared at him. "Taking Talon out of the picture last night would have sent a strong message to anyone listening."

Rob swallowed. "He didn't really do anything that merited his death."

"He challenged you. *You.*" Daedalus poked him in the chest with a finger. "The beta of the pack. You're just as important as an alpha. Eric is the strength, he gathers the fold, but the beta, Robert, is the guiding hand."

"I know, I know. We've had this conversation already. I still don't see why anyone needs to die."

"I agree." Sugar took Robert's hand.

Fury flashed in Daedalus's eyes as he stared at their touch.

Rob released his hold on Sugar as if burned.

She didn't notice any of it, or at least she pretended not to as she continued to confront Daedalus. "I hate it when you kill."

"Killing is in my nature. Vampires aren't related to the Easter Bunny, Sugar."

"And this is what you want me to become? A murderer?"

If Rob could have fit in the cupboard by his feet, he would have crawled into it like he did when he was a kid and his parents fought. Trapped in a corner, they forced him to witness their on-going disagreements. Daedalus didn't want to watch Sugar grow old and die. Turning her into a vampire would prevent that, but the thought of it terrified Sugar.

Ain't love grand? And he wanted this?

"Is that how you see me? I don't always kill to feed."

She gasped and covered her throat with her hand. "I thought you stopped feeding on others period."

Like a fish out of water, the Nosferatu gaped. "I—I—"

"Who else have you been using? I haven't noticed as many bite marks on the boys." Sugar glanced at Rob's neck. He hated when it was his turn to feed the vampire, but he'd done it to prevent this kind of fight. "He doesn't even have an old mark on him."

"The boys are tired of me feeding from them. I can't keep forcing them, Sugar. It's like rape."

She cringed. "I didn't know." The color from her cheeks faded. "Then who?"

Daedalus wouldn't look at her.

"He's been using the scum off the street. Rapists, thieves, and drug dealers, the criminals police haven't caught yet." Rob couldn't stand watching them be angry. His whole childhood he'd witnessed his parents tear at each other. Sugar and Daedalus deserved better. They fought the odds trying to be together. "He's doing the city a service."

A tear spilled from her eye. "You kill them like that Ayumu asshole who tried to hurt me?"

Not the best example that Robert would have chosen. Sugar hadn't seen Daedalus shred that beast in the woods the night Eric won the alpha challenge, but she heard it from the parking lot and the event almost drove her away from all of them forever.

The vampire rolled his massive shoulders before leaning forward to face Sugar with his fangs bared. "Yes, I'm a murderer. It's what I've always been." He pushed past her and grabbed his black leather coat off the hook by the back sliding glass door, then left.

Sugar ran to the door and stared at the night. "He's gone. Shit, I keep screwing things up, Robert."

He'd never heard her swear before. "He'll be back. Let him cool off."

"How long have you known he's been feeding off others?" She pressed her forehead against the glass.

"A while." Feeling two inches tall, he placed his hands on her shoulders. "Sugar, you've been through this before. You can't expect him to change. He's been a vampire for centuries."

"But it's okay for everyone to expect me to change for him?" She touched his hand and squeezed. "I know you guys don't understand why I won't become a vampire. I'm not stupid, Robert. How would I feed?"

"You can use us or at least me. It's not the feeding part the wigs me out. It's the guy-on-guy thing that makes me uncomfortable."

She chuckled. "Daedalus could barely contain himself when I touched your hand. He'd rip your throat out if I fed on you."

"Good point. There's Katrina and Spice. We'll figure out a way."

"I'm tired and I don't... Killing is just wrong." She turned around and hugged him. "I'm glad you kept him from killing Talon last night. I don't know what to do."

He hugged her back. Two more days before Eric and Spice got back. He needed to keep the pack and their household together *two more days.* "Don't do anything. Let me talk to Daedalus." He pushed away to make eye contact with her. "I promise, things will work out. Okay?"

She nodded and wiped a tear from her eye.

His cellphone rang. It sat on the entrance table where he'd dropped it last night. He needed to answer, all pack members knew to call him this week and not to bother Eric.

Sugar gestured for him to go.

The caller ID showed it came from a Vasi member. Crap. He should have stayed in bed.

"Hello?" Listening to his pack mate, he watched Sugar make a cup of tea, then curl up on the couch with a well-worn paperback book. "I'll be there as soon as I can." He closed the connection.

All bad things came in threes. First Sugar and Daedalus's argument, now Talon was stirring up trouble at a bar on the other side of town. Someone in the pack tried to intervene, but got his ass beat for the effort. Robert would have to deal with Talon again. What would be the third issue?

He shoved his phone and car keys in his pockets. Two more days. At least he didn't have to work out tonight since Daedalus pulled a *Houdini.*

"I have to go, Sugar. Are you going to be okay?"

She glanced at him with a brave smile. "Sure."

His heart wrung for her, so he ran to the basement and barged into Sam's bedroom.

The short werewolf was pulling a muscle shirt over his overly developed torso. "Don't you know how to knock? I could have had a guest in here."

"Doesn't matter. I need to go take care of a problem."

"Is this problem named Talon?"

Robert nodded.

"Need some back-up?"

His stomach clenched at the thought of having to face Talon alone. "Probably, but I need you to stay home with Sugar instead."

Sam came to attention at the mention of their token human female. "What's wrong with her? Is she sick?"

"Big fight with Daedalus. Just keep her company until I can straighten things out."

His buddy nodded. "Sure, but keep in touch. Tyler and I are available. You don't need to take care of everything by yourself."

"Eric does."

"Bullshit, he turns to you whenever something needs to be done." Sam clapped him on the shoulder and left the room taking the stairs two at a time. "Sugar, get your sweater. I need someone to take me to the movies."

Robert followed the noise upstairs where his two friends discussed recent movie releases and exited out the front door.

CHAPTER 4

Rap music thumped loud enough to rattle Robert's teeth while he pushed his way through Molten, the crowded bar, which contained all the things he didn't care for: noise, drugs, and people. Some of the Vasi liked to party here and from the phone call he'd received Talon had paid them a visit.

In the back, he saw some familiar faces and headed their way, but as he drew closer he noticed that most of the clientele sitting at these tables were from the pack. They gathered to him as if pulled by a magnet. Instinctual pack hierarchy, and it gave him heartburn. These people looked to him for guidance in Eric's absence, and his own instincts cried to glance over his left shoulder where his alpha usually stood.

He cleared his throat. *Time to man up.* "What happened?"

Simon, one of the more dominate males of the pack, rose from the table, sporting a fresh black eye and a fat lip. "Talon showed up shit-faced and started picking on a new member." He shot a look at a young guy sitting at a corner table.

Aaron, the kid's name was Aaron. He reminded Robert of himself when he transitioned from human to werewolf. Lost, alone and weak, but at least he had the Vasi for support. Robert didn't have anyone in the beginning until he met Eric.

"You okay, Aaron?" he shouted over the din. Daedalus told him to use names whenever possible. It was suppose to reassure his pack mates that he cared. By the kid's smile and nod, Robert would have to say it worked.

"We pulled Talon off the kid, but the dude's out of control. He said something about us betraying him, that he didn't recognize your unauthorized challenge last night." Simon chuckled. "Said you beat him."

"Well, it wasn't an unauthorized challenge. It was a warning, which is why he's still breathing. I'm starting to regret that part."

The smile on Simon's face transformed to surprise. "You beat him by yourself?"

Nice, even his pack thought him a trophy beta. He nodded, not trusting his mouth to be diplomatic.

Excited glances and pointing passed through the gathering as the news spread.

"Do you know where Talon's headed?" Robert needed to get his claws on that beast and shake some sense into him. Even if Robert lost a challenge to that idiot, Eric would never accept Talon as beta. Maybe the dude had a death wish? If he kept acting like this it would leave Robert no choice. God, he'd never killed anyone before and didn't want to ever start.

"He didn't say, but he likes to hang out at a biker's bar over by the Ukrainian village. The Twisted Tire or something? It's off I-Ninety." Two other males gathered by Simon. "Do you want us to come with you?"

Robert could hear both Daedalus and Eric in his head encouraging him to say *yes*. It would be a good bonding experience for him and the pack. A social event for males, get to know your beta night and watch him kick ass. "Not yet. I need to track him first, and I'll move faster on my own." For social animals, he and his beast didn't fit in. They preferred solitude, and that's why they'd become omega in the first place.

The Vasi had their share of omegas, just like any other pack, but they were nurtured instead of abused. Like little Aaron sitting at the table nursing his beer. The pack didn't cast him out when Talon jumped him, they rallied around him. Robert really admired Eric's work with the Vasi and hoped other packs would follow his example.

When Simon and his companions appeared disappointed at his refusal, Robert sighed and dug deep. "If I need back-up, you'll be the first I call."

They grinned and nodded.

He turned to leave and faced a wall of humans. Pushing through that mass of flesh flared his proximity alarms, and his beast strained at the yoke to thrash at the people who dared come too close. An exit sign glowed above the crowd, and he released the breath he'd been holding. Skirting along the wall, he shoved the door open when he reached it.

It brought him out to a narrow alley on the side of the building. The cool air was a relief, then he caught a whiff of a familiar scent. Something sharp and clean he'd recently had his face buried in.

Esther.

The door closed behind him with a *thunk* and took what little light it gave. She stood with her legs apart in the center of the alley, silhouetted by the distant street lights.

"Are you following me, Esther?" The muscles in his back tensed as he smelled gun powder. She held a gun again. Damn it. He glanced over his shoulder for cover if she got trigger happy.

"I'm trying to figure out what kind of sick game you're playing, Rob." She stepped closer, and he could see the outline of her weapon pointed at his head. "I hate being played for a fool, but you did a great job making me feel like one."

He searched the area, however escape appeared slim. Next time, he'd take the damn front door. "I'm not the pickpocket." She wasn't either. Small-time thieves didn't follow werewolves around with guns in their pockets. He couldn't think of too many people who would. "Are you crazy? My pack is behind this door. If you shoot me they'll tear you apart."

"How many girlfriends are in there?"

"Girlfriends?   None,   I   don't have—"

She stormed toward him and pressed the gun to his chest as he retreated to the brick wall. "I saw the blonde go into your house."

"Su-Sugar?"

She laughed without mirth. "Of course, she'd have a name like that. What's the Asian woman's name, Coco?"

"Katrina. They're my roommates, not my girlfriends."

The gun wavered, then pressed harder onto his sternum. "Bullshit."

Survival should have been foremost in his mind, but the hard light in Esther's eyes as she glared into his made him realize something extraordinary. "You're jealous."

"Fuck you, Robert."

He grinned, he couldn't help it. "I like it better when you call me Rob." Taking a step from the wall, he pushed the gun aside. "Maybe I should take you up on your offer, Esther. Considering you always seem armed, tying you up may be in my best interest."

* * * *

Esther retreated across the alley from Rob, fumbling her weapon as she clicked the safety back on and shoved it into her shoulder holster. The last thing she needed to do was shoot herself. Why did he have to bring up the tying? She'd never offered such a thing to anyone before, but the idea of Rob dominating her flicked her pussy button to the *on* position.

Would she really fall for the roommate line?

Rob strolled toward her, self-confidence oozed from him, the unsure geek of last night absent. His green eyes burned with an internal light from the beast within.

Yeah, she'd fall for the line.

The brick wall stopped her progress. Should she run? She wanted to, but she also wanted him to catch her. Without another thought, she took off away from the street. She didn't want some Good Samaritan or the cops interrupting them.

A surprised growl rumbled from her werewolf as she left him in her dust. If he didn't chase her, she'd go back there and kick his ass for being a dweeb.

He didn't disappoint, though. The pounding of his running shoes followed her.

Racing around the corner, her boots slipped on loose gravel and she went down on her knees, scraping her palms as she fought for balance.

Rob caught her by the shoulders. "Are you all right?"

"Not the kind of hard chase I wanted to give you." She chuckled and sat back on her heels, eyes level with his groin. He tried to assist her to her feet, but she shook off his hands. "I'm happy here." She'd spent the afternoon regretting letting him out of her grasp last night. Robert wouldn't escape so easily this time. She reached for the fly of his jeans.

He startled at her touch. "Here? Now?" The shock in his voice only drove her more.

"Of course." She undid his button.

"Esther." Desire and uncertainty warred as he spoke her name. He glanced over his shoulder. Here was the unsure gentleman she'd met last night, the one who stirred her devilish thoughts.

"We're definitely doing this now." She unzipped his fly, happy to find him already erect.

He gasped as she kissed his tip, running her tongue in slow circles until she moistened his head, then she blew over the area. She sensed a slight shiver course through his body.

"I'm not letting you get away this time."

Slipping him into her mouth, she heard him whisper, "I'm not going anywhere."

It was hard to grin with a cock in her mouth. With a slow pace, she slid him deep in her throat and withdrew, dragging her tongue over him. After a few strokes, Rob's breaths became irregular and he moved his hips to her rhythm. She loved the power he allowed her to have over him. Not demanding anything from her and taking what she offered with enthusiasm.

Esther ran her hands under his t-shirt, over his abs, and around to his lower back. Digging her nails into his skin, she increased her speed and sucked him hard.

A groan resounded around them as he grabbed her shoulders as if needing the support.

The taste of his excitement dripped on the back of her tongue. She pushed him harder, faster until all she heard was his labored breathing.

"I'm going to come." He tried to slip out, but she only pulled him closer, deeper. "Oh God."

She felt his muscles tense as he came in hot spurts, his cries echoing in the dark alley as she swallowed him. His knees wobbled, and she steadied him with her hands as he slipped out of her mouth. "Easy." She stood and wrapped her arms around his waist, a smug smile plastered to her face.

He hugged her close and buried his face in her hair.

"Let's go back to your place." She nudged him.

"Yes, that sounds good." He placed a kiss on her neck, his hands traveling along her body. "Crap. I can't. Not yet." His warmth faded as he released his hold on her and zipped his pants. "I need to take care of a problem first."

"Maybe I can help."

"This is a pack issue. I need to take care of it myself." He touched her face. "Why are you following me, Esther?"

"I wanted to apologize for taking your wallet. I remembered your address and went there this evening. That's when I saw the women." The lie came so easily to her lips. As a mistress of deception, the pain it caused surprised her. She blinked, unsure what to do next. Confess? What good would that do? Rob would leave her, no matter when she told him the truth. Better to live with a lie for a while and have him for as long as she could. "I got angry and followed you to the bar."

"So jealous you wanted to shoot me?"

"Nothing's more dangerous than a woman scorned." She took his hand. "What's your problem?"

"I have a pack member stirring trouble. A lot of trouble, especially for me. I need to take him down a peg or two."

"I know some things about werewolf packs. Shouldn't your alpha be disciplining the troublemaker?"

"Sure, if he was in town. It's up to me while he's gone."

"You're the beta?"

He frowned at the shock in her voice. "You sure know how to make a man feel good about himself." He let her go and stuck his hands in his pockets. "I need to go."

"Wait." She grabbed his elbow. She was screwing up everything and really didn't want to lose him yet. "You always catch me off guard by not being who or what I expect." Standing in front of him, she blocked his path. With his unnatural strength, he could have knocked her out of the way, but he didn't. "I'm not good with surprises, but I like that you're different. Not like most of the men I know."

"You've known a lot men, Esther?" His tone softened.

"Yes, but none of them compare to you." She chuckled. "I've definitely never stalked any of *them*. Let me drive you. When you're done, we can continue where we left off."

"That would be nice." He placed his arm around her shoulders and drew her closer. "I hope you realize I don't have anything worth stealing at home."

She gave him a small punch in the flank. "That's not funny." How could she blame him for that joke after her pickpocket routine? Robert was going to break her heart, she just knew it, yet here she was offering it like a sacrifice.

He flinched but laughed. "Just needed to clear that up."

"Fine. We'll go to my hotel room instead."

CHAPTER 5

"You're from out of town?" Robert glanced at Esther as they walked out of the alley onto the sidewalk by the club. His strong arm gripped her shoulders, pulling her closer.

"I'm in transition." She never stayed anywhere too long, but given the right incentive, she might relocate here. "We'll take my car."

"Fine by me." He shrugged. "So, what do you do for a living then?"

"I hunt vampires."

He laughed and squeezed her shoulders. "Good thing I'm a werewolf." He totally missed the truth and thought it a joke. She swallowed her disappointment.

"Yeah." Yet, she carried silver bullets in her gun tonight. Wasn't she a bitch. "Here's my car." She unlocked the doors and got into the driver's seat. "Where to?"

"Take I-Ninety. We're going to a biker bar where my problem likes to hang out and see if he's there."

"Good, I could use a stiff drink." She started the car and pulled out. "Are you going to fight him?"

"Probably. Can you stay out of it if I do?" He twisted in his seat to face her.

"Umm...if he's going to kill you, I'll need to shoot him. Otherwise, I'll stay out of it. I understand the whole dominance games packs have to play."

"Who *are* you, Esther?"

She glanced at him as he stared at her profile as if memorizing it.

"You kiss me, steal my wallet, shoot at me, follow me, then give me a blow-job almost at gunpoint. You're either an escaped mental patient or someone really interesting."

"I'll opt for the interesting someone. And I shot because you were in beast form and I didn't know who you were. Not to mention, you scared the crap out of me."

"You weren't that scared." He tapped his nose. "Good sense of smell. What aren't you telling me? Not every girl I meet pulls a thirty-eight out of her waistband."

"You know your guns." She took the on-ramp to the interstate. "I'm not the only one with secrets, Rob. I saw the way you moved when I pulled the trigger. You're no-run-of-the-mill beta. Why does the Vasi pack need warriors?"

"You know the pack's name?" He leaned in closer and sniffed.

"What the hell are you doing?"

"Just double checking and making sure you're not a werewolf masking her scent." He cleared his throat. "Pure human."

She weaved through the scant late night traffic. Their silence stretched. "So, are you going to answer my question?" The air in the car grew warm, so she kicked on the AC.

"Let's agree to keep our own secrets for now." He played with the vent, angling the air to hit him more directly. "Esther?"

"Yeah?"

"I don't trust you."

She gripped the steering wheel tight. "I don't blame you."

God, he was getting under her skin. She wanted him to trust her. Shit, she wanted to enter that fucking bar and blow away his problem too. What a mess. She'd already decided to not take the contract on the Nosferatu. To accomplish such a task she needed to be in the game one hundred percent. Not have her head in the clouds over a werewolf and her heart dangling on a thread.

"Take this exit." His voice deepened, and his eyes shone with that inner light werewolves got when their beasts were close to the surface of shifting.

"You all right?" She took the exit. If he shifted in the car with her, she'd probably crash.

"I'm fine. I'm in control. Just getting ready." He rolled down his window and stuck his face into the wind. "Make a left at the light. It should be two blocks down. It's called the Twisted Tire."

She took the turn and made it past one block when Rob leaned his torso out the window in a sudden jerk.

"Damn, can you stop?"

"Did I miss it?" She pulled over and parked along the deserted street.

"No, I smell someone I know, and I need to talk to him too." He opened the door and leaped out, then spun around. "Wait here for me?"

"I'm not going anywhere."

He grinned and ran down a side street.

Shaking her head, she leaned it against her steering wheel. He smelled someone? What an odd thing for her to just accept, or would be if he were human…which he wasn't. *Esther, what are you doing playing chauffer for a werewolf and also not taking a contract that could take care of you for life?* She groaned. Could Rob be worth it? Something in her gut told her he would be.

* * * *

Robert jogged around the building next to where Esther parked. He watched the rooftops until he saw who he smelled.

On a four-story building a set of huge boots dangled over the roof's edge. Not too many men had feet that size, and Daedalus liked a place with a view. Even if he fell, nothing would happen to him. Was it coincidence he sat here so close to where Talon hung out? Robert didn't think so.

Climbing the fire escape, he reached the roof easy enough. "Hey." He hopped onto the surface and trotted to the vampire. Sitting next to him, he leaned on his hands. They could see Lake Michigan as a big flat, black spot dwarfing the city's edge. "Nice view."

"Yeah." Daedalus continued to stare at the city, an aura of dark foreboding surrounding him.

"You waiting on Talon?"

"I was, but I started thinking about Sugar." He shifted his shoulder, then glanced at Rob. "She okay when you left?"

"Sam took her to the movies."

He nodded. "You're good friends. She deserves the best."

"Go home, Daedalus. She should be back soon. Surprise her with something." Two more days before Eric and Spice came home. They would know what to do. He needed to keep the pack and his small family together for that short amount of time. Should be an easy task but everything wanted to fall apart.

"I've got nothing left to give her, Robert. She can't accept what I am, and I can't watch her grow old and die. No matter what, I'm headed for heartbreak. It's like watching someone cut off a piece of you. It would be better to do it quick and fast. Leave now before the pain becomes unbearable."

"That's stupid." The moment the words left his mouth he knew he was a dead shifter. He did a backward somersault and avoided a slap to his noggin. "Listen before you decide to beat me to a pulp, D."

"D?" The Nosferatu twisted.

"We're buddies now, right?" He grinned at Daedalus who only stared back at him as if he'd grown two heads. "Don't make any rash decisions."

"I'm not," he shouted. "Ever since I asked Sugar to cross over and become a vampire things have been heading this way." He turned his back on Robert. "I've never *asked* a woman to cross over. Part of me wishes I'd just gone ahead and had it done. At least, I'd have the rest of eternity to make it up to her instead of a few decades wishing I'd done it when we first met."

"She never would have forgiven you." Robert didn't want to sit on the edge of the building anymore. It would be too easy for Daedalus to shove him off. He might survive the fall, but it would hurt like hell, and the vampire was in an ugly mood.

"Time heals all wounds. Trust me on this one."

"Then why haven't you done it?"

"I don't know. Maybe that's why I'm off my game. I—I care too much. It's not a good habit, take my advice on this, Robert."

"You want her to want this." Robert ran his fingers through his hair, trying to yank a solution from his head manually. "You're both so stubborn. You remind me of my parents, believing so much in your own ideas you're willing to let it tear you apart."

Daedalus rose from the edge and faced him. Anger radiated from him in waves.

Yet Robert's mouth kept on its suicidal path. "I'd give anything to experience what you and Sugar have. There's a solution, you just need to think outside the box. Isn't there some other way for her to live longer instead of becoming vampire?"

"I don't know," Daedalus snapped. "Never thought about it." He crossed his thick arms over his chest. "When did you get so smart about women?"

Robert chuckled. "I'm not. Just ask the crazy one following me tonight."

"You've got a girl with you? And you're up here?" The vampire leaned over the side of the roof and glanced at the street, then waved. "You call *me* stupid. She's hot. Nice leather. Didn't take you for the dominatrix liking kind."

"Never mind her." He edged to the side and watched Esther rush to the car. Great, the vampire spooked her. "Sugar still has a few decades before you need to make a decision."

"You say that like it's a lot of time." A frown pulled at the corner of his mouth, increasing the darkness of his expression. "It's not fair to her either if she won't cross over, Robert. She should find herself a human mate. Maybe she could have children."

Rubbing his forehead, Robert tried to wish away the pounding in his temples. "Don't leave. It would kill her." God, he didn't want to have to live with a falling-apart Sugar. It would be like living with his mother all over again after his father left. "If you want, the three of us can sit down and discuss options."

The surprised bark of laughter drew Robert's attention from staring at the roof surface. Daedalus grinned. "You want to mediate? It's a love affair, not a contract."

"Bullshit. Love is about give and take. What are you willing to lose in return for what you want? Once both of you figure out the answer to that question, then we can negotiate."

Daedalus raised a non-existent eyebrow.

* * * *

Esther stared hard at the silhouettes on the roof. She didn't need night vision goggles to see who stood with Rob. The bald head and pointed tips of his ears were all the evidence she required. Her equipment sat in her trunk a few feet away. Temptation warred with logic.

And she knew fate had played a hand in this too. Twice in two days she'd run into Daedalus, and she believed in destiny. She'd also met Rob.

Her gut twisted as her cellphone beeped. Glancing at the message, her fate was sealed. They   doubled her fee to take the contract.

The vampire leaned over the edge of the building and waved as if daring her to take the shot.

Racing to her car, she yanked her keys out her pocket and pressed the button on the remote to open the trunk. She had minutes to do this. It would probably be her only chance. Damn Rob and his connection to the Nosferatu.

She snapped open her long flat case and pulled out her miniature crossbow, then grabbed a wooden bolt, the next best thing to a stake. She ran across the street, knelt, and aimed.

Rob stood next to Daedalus, waving his hands in the air like they were arguing. *Damn, look at him standing up to that monster.* Pride swelled in her chest. She could really use a man like that in her life, someone with enough balls to confront her when she was making a mistake, like now.

The vampire stood inside her scope mounted on the crossbow. With a steady hand, she pulled the trigger.

CHAPTER 6

"Look, you love Sugar and she loves you. That's the important part. Maybe getting an objective view point on your relationship would help." Robert extended his hands out to Daedalus.

"You want us to see a therapist? Who the hell deals with vampires, Robert?"

"Okay, not a therapist but you've got friends. Maybe Spice can help. She became a werewolf for Eric."

"Fucking rub it in, man." If looks could kill, Robert was a dead shifter walking.

"Is that it? Spice choosing to be part of the pack? Is that why you're all twisted in knots lately?"

"Wouldn't you be if you were in my shoes? Sugar won't make that kind of sacrifice for me. If I could become human, I'd do it in a heartbeat. I'm not feeling the love. She doesn't get what I am, and now she's trying to control how I feed." He shook his head. "When she came back for me, after the whole Ayumu fiasco, I thought I could take whatever she offered and be happy but not anymore."

"Fuck." A hole formed in Robert's gut as he listened to Daedalus pour his heart out. "Does anyone else know how you feel?"

"No. *I* barely understand how I feel."

"You need to tell her. Now." He pulled out his cellphone and stepped closer, offering it to the vampire. A soft twang caught his attention. He twisted to face the street and a sharp pain pierced his chest, knocking the air from his lungs.

He gasped, but it only made the pain worse. Staring at his chest, he couldn't believe what he saw. An arrow stuck out of him. An arrow? Who the fuck used arrows? The world spun, and he heard a rush of words from Daedalus but couldn't understand what he said. His knees gave out and he fell.

And kept falling. Shouldn't he have hit the roof surface by now? Seemed a long, long way down.

* * * *

Esther watched Rob fall off the roof. Her heart stalled, and she couldn't get it to start again. The world compressed around her, making it hard to breathe let alone move.

Rob clutched the bolt in his chest. The one *she'd* shot. It was meant for Daedalus, but the split second she squeezed the trigger Rob stepped forward and took the hit.

The clatter of her crossbow hitting the sidewalk shattered her nightmare state. What the fuck had she done?

Her gentleman werewolf flipped mid-air, curling around his wound, and landed on his back with a loud *thud* that she felt through her boots.

She was halfway across the street at a dead run before her brain caught up. "No, no, no…" The word skipped like a broken record. Something warm stained her cheeks. Wiping it with her hand, she found tears. She hadn't cried in years, but then she'd never killed an innocent before.

His body lay in the dented, cracked concrete. Blood formed like a big amaryllis bloom on the front of his t-shirt. Each shallow breath sent a gurgle of blood from his lungs.

Kneeling at his side, she didn't know what to do. Her hands fluttered over his chest, knowing she needed to stop the bleeding but afraid to touch him. She couldn't get past the fact she'd hurt someone she actually liked.

"Rob?" She brushed her fingertips over his cheeks, her hands trembled so much it made them difficult to control. "What have I done?"

"What do you mean?" An iron strong grip grabbed her shoulder and yanked her to her feet.

Her eyes met the black, soulless glare of Daedalus, a Prime of the Nosferatu clan. The Infernal Champion of the Brotherhood, Vile Butcher of Babylon, and Subjugator of the Accords, to name a few of his titles.

As if a bucket of ice-cold water had been dumped over her head, her terror and shock transformed at the sight of her target. She snapped back into herself and met his stare. "It was meant for you, Bearer of Ill Will." With Rob dying at her feet, she didn't deserve to live. Her only salvation was if the vampire finished her before she had to witness Rob's last breath.

The Nosferatu dropped her. "What?"

Before she could respond a clash of raw power penetrated her mental shields and entered her mind. Any human could keep a vampire from their thoughts if they bothered to learn how. Daedalus proved too strong for her to block even with her years of practice.

He raped her mind like a savage and flipped through her thoughts as if reading a book.

Frozen and helpless, she watched from a dark corner of her head until he tore her identity from her grasp. She cried out, the sound echoing down the street.

"A slayer?" The vampire stumbled from her and leaned on the brick building behind him as his gaze darted to Rob. "That bolt was meant for me." He knelt beside the werewolf. "Robert?" With a gentle shake, he repeated the question. "Come on, buddy, open your eyes. You need to shift."

Buddy? They were friends? The heavy despair in Daedalus's voice only confirmed it. She stared at the Nosferatu, a killer of thousands, as a tear slipped from the corner of his eye.

All this time she thought the vampire used her naïve Rob. It didn't appear like that at all. She took a deep shaky breath. "Shouldn't I call nine-one-one?" Her cellphone trembled in her hand as she held it out.

"No use. There's too much damage." He shook Rob harder. "Robert, let's go. Time to wake up, we've got miles to run." The snap in his command came with practiced ease.

Rob's eyelids fluttered open with a weak groan.

"Listen to me." Daedalus hovered over his face. "You need to shift. The change will heal the damage."

Her werewolf blinked. "Esther?"

She crept closer until he could see her.

"Are you all right?" he asked.

Fuck, he didn't know she'd shot him. "Yes." A sob wracked her chest. "Shift, Rob." She wiped her nose with her hand. "Please."

"Can't—" His eyelids closed and his chest shuddered with an exhale, then he didn't move again.

"Rob!" His name tore from her raw throat. "I'm so sorry." She glanced at Daedalus and regretted it.

Death stared back at her.

She shrank away and got to her feet. "It was meant for you, asshole. Why'd he have to move at the last minute?" All her stakes were in the trunk of her car, so she palmed her thirty-eight from her shoulder holster.

He mirrored her movements and moved around Rob's body. "I'm going to make you suffer, slayer, and listen to you beg for the mercy you never showed him."

This was the monster she hunted, not the one who just shed a tear. "You might have played nice vampire for him but I know who you really are."

"I am many things, but to you I am Pain." He moved so quickly she sensed his body more than saw it.

Only her keen reflexes kept her out of his grasp. She spun, aimed, and squeezed the trigger, but she may as well have used a spit ball straw for all the damage the bullets did. She knew the bullets caused vampires pain, but Daedalus didn't even grimace.

He stormed toward her and clutched her throat before slamming her into the building. Her heels tap danced against the brick as they dangled, and she tried to draw breath, but his vise-like grip wouldn't let the smallest amount of air in.

"This is just the beginning, Esther."

With the lack of oxygen, her vision faded yet she did hear a faint growl of surprise to her right. She glanced and saw the blurred outline of Rob in full beast form getting to his feet. Bipedal, he stood well over six feet tall, covered in a glossy chocolate brown fur. He flexed the long claws extending from his fingertips, and the ears on top of his wolfen head folded back.

Her heart soared, and she heard the angels sing.

He lived.

And she was about to die.

A furious cry shred the night just before Daedalus's grip was torn from her throat and she fell to the ground. Coughing up a lung and dragging in a breath thick with air, she tried to stand. Her knees didn't think it a good idea though. She leaned on her hands and blinked her vision clear.

Rob, in beast form, grappled with the Nosferatu, keeping his body between her and the vampire. The fool was defending her.

With a twist of speed, her werewolf pinned the ancient vampire under his clawed hands. Teeth bared, he snapped at his friend's head.

Daedalus held off the attack. Barely. If Rob finished her task and killed the Nosferatu, he would never forgive her once he found out the truth. A lead ball of certainty sank in her gut.

The Vanguards Books 1 – 3 | Annie Nicholas

Never.

"Rob, stop!" she shouted. "I'm the one who shot you."

He stopped mid-bite, with Daedalus's arm sandwiched between his sharp teeth. They stared at each other for a moment before the vampire nodded. Rob opened his mouth, and Daedalus slipped his arm out, then wrapped the werewolf in a bone-cracking hug.

"Dumbass, you hooked up with a slayer." The vampire released Rob and rose from the ground.

The beast swung around with a sharp glare. It almost sliced her in half.

"You stepped in my line of sight. I was aiming at him." She pointed at Daedalus, suddenly feeling like she was back in grade school.

Rob tilted his head, ears folded back as he stalked around her. A low growl emanated from his chest.

"You're either very good at what you do or very stupid for taking a contract on my kind." The Nosferatu examined his arm, bending it with ease.

"I'm not feeling very smart at the moment. I refused the initial contract." She pulled out the phone from her pocket. Both males tensed as she moved. "Take it easy, boys. I'm not deadly with a *BlackBerry*. Look at the messages. They doubled the cash out."

Daedalus pocketed the phone without reading it. "Grab her. My car is around the corner. We'll finish this at home."

Without any effort, Rob lifted her in his arms gently.

"For what it's worth, I'm really sorry." And she was. Even though he'd never believe her, she needed him to hear it. "I don't think I would have been able to live with myself if you'd had died." The emotional roller coaster of the last half hour made the truth easy to admit. She leaned her head on his shoulder, the soft fur a small comfort. Her strength disappeared and with it her desire to fight.

Rob lived.

What was wrong with her? She never made rash decisions where marks were concerned. What made her grab her crossbow without a plan? The money would have been nice, but if it were the driving force she'd have taken the contract in the first place.

It almost seemed like fate grabbed her by the ass and turned off her brain. The target so easily accessible and the shitload of payout dangling like a carrot. She'd fucked it all up though. No kill and worse, no Rob.

They approached a two door black sports car. Daedalus held open the passenger door. He folded the front seat down so Rob could squeeze into the backseat with her.

The drive didn't take long with the vampire's heavy foot on the accelerator. He parked close to Rob's brownstone. "I'll get you some clothes. We don't need to cause trouble if one of the neighbors is watching, and I don't need any more grief from Sugar." Daedalus slammed the driver's side door shut.

Rob melted back into his human form next to her, his glare never left hers as his eyes changed from bright amber to sharp green.

The transformation fascinated her. All these years in her profession, but until yesterday, she'd never been this close to a shifter as he changed.

"For fuck's sake, Esther. A slayer?" The contempt in his expression hurt. "Is this why you've been after me? Using my friendship with Daedalus to get close enough to kill him?" The car shook as he punched the front seat.

She shrank back. The moonlight gleamed on his bare skin and waves of fury emanated from his body. "I didn't know you were friends. I thought he was using you, like most of his race does."

The dark glance he shot   at   her

brooked no belief.

"When I approached you on the street, I'd hoped to follow you so I could find his lair but—but..." She swallowed with a mouth gone dry. "You kept surprising me. You never do what I expect. Like now, why am I still alive? You should have killed me by now. I'm all unbalanced around you, which is a terrible thing in my profession."

He tapped at the fresh scar on his chest. "No shit."

"I've got good aim." She glanced out the window. "You should be careful dealing with vampires, Rob."

"Not everything is what you think you see, Esther. You're a human looking in from the outside and only gazing at the surface. There's a whole ocean of stuff under the stories humans are told."

She blinked. "Like how you could heal the way you did?"

"Yeah, well, that was a surprise for me too. It's why my pack needs Daedalus. We've lost too much knowledge over the centuries." He watched the Nosferatu return with a pile of clothes. "I won't let you kill him." He directed his stare at her, making his deadly intentions clear if she crossed that line.

CHAPTER 7

"I get the message." Esther frowned at Robert.

He doubted she did. Chances were pretty good she'd take another crack at Daedalus if the opportunity arose. Then he'd have to kill her. Wouldn't it be his luck his first kill would be a woman he liked.

The car door opened and she startled. Daedalus tossed some clothes at Robert then gripped the slayer's arm, yanking her out.

Betrayal left a sour taste in Robert's mouth. "Store her in my bathroom while I gather the others." The order slipped from him. He noticed Daedalus do a double take, but he escorted Esther without question.

Nothing like being on the brink of death to give a male perspective. He'd been ready to tear the vampire's throat out for Esther. The most shocking thing was that he'd almost accomplished it. Sometime in the last twenty-four hours Esther had become his. What the hell was he going to do about that? She'd used and abused him.

His beast writhed inside. It wanted to storm up to the second floor, break into the bathroom, and mark her…or spank her…or both. Taking a deep breath, he sat back and went through the calming exercises he used to control the beast. Thankfully, it also worked on the raging erection under the pile of clothes he held in his lap.

With a shake of his head, he dismissed both beast and Esther to the back of his mind. Tonight he needed to be the pack's beta. One more day before his alpha got home. One. More. Day.

He got dressed in a pair of nylon workout pants and a green t-shirt that read *Never Moon a Werewolf.* Reflexively, he reached for his glasses, but they must have smashed on the sidewalk when he'd fallen from the roof.

He jogged over to the brownstone. No one would have guessed

he'd had an arrow in his chest and internal injuries less than an hour ago. Eric needed to know about that shifting trick. It hurt like hell to heal that fast though, and it took a lot of energy. He needed food, a truck load of it, to build back his reserve.

As he opened the door he expected to hear his roommates arguing inside but silence greeted him.

Daedalus descended the stairs. "I wedged a chair under the doorknob. She's not going anywhere."

"I'll go wake up the others if you get Sugar." Some nights they stayed awake late and hung out with the Nosferatu, but it was a weeknight. Day jobs awaited Tyler, Katrina, and Sam. Only Eric and himself made their own work hours. They tended to be night owls anyway. Maybe that's how this odd camaraderie with Daedalus developed from trainee to friend?

"Let them sleep. We'll talk first, then you can decide what to do."

He had to decide? Watching the vampire disappear into the kitchen, Robert did a little what-the-fucking before following. "So, what's going on? Why is Esther trying to turn you into ashes?"

Daedalus stood bent over, digging inside the fridge and tossing food onto the counter. "For money, it's the nature of her profession." He organized the bread, sandwich meat, cheese, and mayo next to each other.

Drool dripped from the corner of Robert's mouth, to his horror, and he quickly wiped it away.

"Vampires have been hunted by slayers since we've existed. They get better weapons and the rules shift, but nothing else changes. They try to kill us and we do the same." He glanced at Robert. "The real question is who hired her? And traditionally, I'm supposed to kill her."

"No." The word was out of his mouth before his brain registered it but there laid the truth. He'd fight Daedalus again to protect her, and maybe for the sandwich he was making. "If I'm letting Talon live, I'm keeping Esther."

Lifting his head, the vampire cocked a non-existent eyebrow, then slid the best looking double-decker sandwich Robert had ever seen toward him. "Keeping her?"

"I mean keeping her alive." He grabbed the sandwich and resisted the urge to gobble the thing straight off the plate.

"Slayers are dangerous, manipulative people. I peeked in her head. She's good at what she does."

Robert finished his snack in wolf-sized bites. "Shit." He ran his fingers through his hair. All his emotions were tangled. "My head is saying she's playing me, but my heart—beast is jerking me around. Did you see anything in her mind about me?"

"I didn't take the grand tour. You were dying at my feet." Daedalus held up the meat. "Another?"

Robert's stomach flipped and the acid rose. "No, thanks." Crossing the kitchen, he opened a cabinet and pulled out the antacids.

"You're popping a lot of those lately."

He snorted and almost choked on a damn tablet. "I wonder why?"

Tyler shuffled into the kitchen, his red curly hair sticking out at all angles. He and Katrina shared a bedroom in the basement next to Daedalus's man-cave. He rubbed the sleep from his eyes. "What are you guys doing?"

"Nothing." Robert and the vampire echoed each other like the twins, Sugar and Spice, did at times. Sugar was Daedalus's human lover, and Spice the pack's female alpha.

"I thought we're not supposed to keep secrets from each other. Isn't that some kind of unspoken law after all the crap we've been through?" They'd fought side by side as pack to protect each other. "You're both sneaking around the house like a bomb might go off. Spill it."

Tyler was right. They couldn't hide Esther in the bathroom forever, and he couldn't just let her go.

"A vampire slayer tried to kill Daedalus tonight."

The remains of sleep vanished from Tyler's eyes. "Wow. What did you do with the body?"

Shaking his head, Daedalus gestured to Robert. "He has a crush on her, so he won't let me finish the deed."

"The slayer's a woman?" He glanced at Robert. "That's kind of hot."

Robert couldn't help but chuckle. Tyler had that effect on everyone.

"I think she likes him as well. She seemed pretty distraught when she *accidently* shot him." Daedalus glanced at Robert. "Instead of escaping she stayed to help you."

"She shot you?" Tyler's voice rose.

"Shush, you'll wake everyone. He's all right now." Daedalus stood between both werewolves, glancing back and forth like at a tennis match.

Robert turned all his attention on the cornered vampire. "Which brings me to the question of how did you know I'd heal if I shifted?"

"You didn't know?" Daedalus tilted his head to the side as if surprised.

"No." Really, how would they? One didn't receive an instruction manual when they became a werewolf. Most packs, present day, believed in trial and error, something his alpha was trying to change. New recruits needed a mentor. "Never been shot before tonight. Makes me wonder what else we don't know."

Daedalus rubbed his bald head. "Me too."

"You shifted and your injuries healed?" Tyler's eyes grew wide.

"It was the coolest thing." Robert stepped forward. "I fell from four stories with an arrow in my chest. When I woke up Daedalus told me to shift and my beast took control."

"An arrow? Like in Robin Hood?" They tripped over each other's sentences.

"She used a crossbow. The bolt is like a wooden stake, and she could kill vampires without having to get close, like an assassin."

"So she's smart as well as deadly."

"Excuse me." The Nosferatu cleared his throat. "Let me interrupt your excitement from almost *dying*. She's a killer. Nothing romantic about that."

"You're a killer." Robert's retort hung in the air. "What's the difference? You kill those you think are evil, so does she."

"I don't get paid, and I do it to survive." His gaze narrowed. "And I'm not evil."

"Anyway." Tyler dragged out the word. "What do we do now?"

"Keep her until Eric and Spice get home, then we can decide."

Daedalus rolled his eyes. "She'll escape by then."

"Afraid she'll get you?" Robert shot back.

"A little, especially with you mooning over her. I didn't get this old by being careless. You're going to get me killed or worse, she'll get to one of the others in the house." He plucked her phone from his pocket and scrolled through the messages.

"What are you looking for?" Tyler leaned in.

"I want to know how much I'm worth." He stopped and hit a button.

Tyler let out a low whistle. "For that much, I'd kill you."

The vampire elbowed his skinny friend. "This means trouble. Esther is the first to try, but others might come." He scratched his chin while examining the email. "I can't tell who sent this." Tossing the phone to Robert, he stood and stretched. "Can you do something with it on your computers?"

Fumbling the phone, Robert finally got a grip on it. "I'll try. It might help to know who you've pissed off."

"The list is endless."

"What about all those security people you used to have at Pal Robi Inc.? Can't they help?" Tyler suggested. Daedalus used to run the security company when they hired him to teach them how to fight. It felt like ages ago. He'd quit when he moved in with Sugar.

"They report to my clan. If word gets out I'm being hunted they may call me home."

"Aren't you some kind of boss? Uh—the Prime?" Robert never wanted to pry in Daedalus's past. He'd rather be ignorant of the things the Nosferatu had done.

"Prime does not translate into King. There are many Primes. We're more like police. Chicago is in my jurisdiction, but eventually the council will question my absence." Daedalus shrugged. "I'm running out of excuses to remain here."

Now Robert understood another reason to Daedalus's desperation to turn Sugar. He'd have to go home one day and she might not follow as a human. His stomach clenched at the thought of gentle Sugar surrounded by vampires. He crunched another antacid and met Daedalus's stare.

"Yeah, you got it." The vampire stood and crossed the kitchen. "I'll be in the bedroom until dawn if you get any more information out of that message."

Nodding, Robert walked Tyler to the stairs. He went to the second floor and his friend to the basement. Once inside his bedroom he paused by the bathroom door with a chair jammed under the knob. He pressed his ear to the wood and listened. "Esther?"

After a moment of silence, she answered. "Yeah."

"You need anything?"

"No. Have you decided my fate?" Her voice sounded amused, but he could smell her fear. He didn't like it and leaned his head against the doorjamb.

"No." He sighed. "But I'll make sure nothing bad happens to you, okay?"

The sound of shuffling came through the wood as if she drew closer. "Why? I've been nothing but terrible to you."

He laughed, but there was no mirth to it. "I know. I guess I can't help being a schmuck."

"Are you going to let me out?"

"Not yet. I've got something to do first."

CHAPTER 8

Stars blanketed the night sky outside of Rob's bathroom window. Esther kept the light off so she'd see them better. There were worse places to be imprisoned. She had water, a toilet, and if she got bored she'd take a hot bath.

Cool air blew against her face through the open window, hinting that fall was on the way. The chill soothed the ache around her neck where Daedalus had tried to strangle her. It wouldn't take much effort to pop the screen out and climb the rainspout to the ground. Not much effort at all.

She tapped her fingernail on the sill as she considered the possibility. If she left that meant never seeing Rob again and *never* was a really long time. The thought left an empty pit in her stomach. Since when did she let her heart rule her life?

Her turning point was the moment Rob melted from his beast form to human as he pinned her to the car. Hunting her down and outthinking her had changed her perspective of him from some cute geek to someone she respected. And wanted. Bad.

Damn, he could have taken her against the car or in the alley at the club, but he always needed to be a gentleman and be dutiful to his pack. *Let's not forget the fucking vampire.*

How did Rob get mixed up with the Nosferatu? He said she only saw the surface of things. Maybe she did, but she couldn't learn to see more from in here. What was Daedalus telling him? He probably wanted to kill her. That's how things rolled between their kinds.

She should have run the moment the arrow struck Rob. Just the memory made her nauseous. He'd come so close to dying. The world would have been worse off without Rob in it. God, she loved everything about him.

Leaning her forehead on the window, she closed her eyes. She recalled the first time they'd met and how shy he'd been, acting as her protector. Silent and strong, he bore his responsibilities with such seriousness.

She banged her head on the glass and listened to the rattle. Now or never. Choose a life filled with what-ifs or take a fucking leap of faith on a werewolf who should hate her.

His possible rejection kept her at the edge of escaping. Her fingers traced the screen. Ah shit, if he broke her heart she'd just gut him.

The sound of a chair scraping against wood outside the bathroom drew her from her debate. As the door swung open, Rob stood in a halo of light cast from his bedroom lamp. "I need your help."

"And if I don't give it?" She turned from the window and faced him. The desire to help and the fear of being vulnerable twisted her stomach to the point she thought she might vomit right there in front of him.

He shrugged. "Then I close the door."

A shiver ran down her spine. The step she took toward him appeared normal but, in her reality, it was the hardest thing she'd ever done. After all her lies she needed to prove her sincerity somehow. "I'll help." Her voice sounded strained even to her own ears.

"Are you okay?"

"I…I…" *Want to tell you how sorry I am.* "I'm fine. What do you need?" She'd apologized enough.

He gestured for her to follow him. They left his sparsely decorated bedroom and crossed the hall to an office. A long table-like desk lined the wall with two computers side by side with wires running along the edges. On the closest screen was her email sign-in.

"Your account is pretty secure." Rob sat at the desk and offered her the chair next to him. "I could break in, but that would take time. I want you to sign-in."

"Why?"

He quirked an eyebrow. "Don't play coy. It doesn't suit you."

She crossed her arms over her chest. His comment stung. "You won't be able to trace the emails from this account. They come from a third party."

"Let me try."

She sighed. It was a test and one she needed to pass. Not for Rob but for herself. If she was going to give herself to him, she would go all the way.

"Fine." After typing her ID and password what remained of her resolve faded. She'd been bribed and hunted in the past for information about her contacts and never gave anything over. Apparently, kindness and trust were her Achilles heels. Not like she was giving him her contacts or anything. All he could do was read the emails, even replying didn't work.

Rob opened the email offering her twice the usual fee to kill Daedalus. He switched programs and began transferring codes. The computer ran through numbers with a counter at the bottom.

He twisted in his chair to face her. "I designed this myself. It's not your run-of-the-mill tracer." He grinned at her pointed stare. "I like computers. The numbers and codes make sense to me. Everything is black and white, there's no gray area like people seem to have." His direct stare bothered her.

Not knowing where to look, she glanced at a collection of encased *Star Trek* figures on a shelf. She smiled. "My mother was a Whovian."

"What?"

"Dr. Who. When I was young I was allowed to stay up until one AM on Saturday nights to watch it with her on PBS." She cleared her throat. "I still like to watch it. You?"

"I've seen it, but I'm not much of a fan."

"Really? Are his concepts too advanced for you?" She leaned forward and grinned as his eyes narrowed at her challenge.

"The show jumps through time, rotates characters and actors, and they interact with historical figures. You have a ship disguised as a phone box, a sonic screwdriver, and a hero who can't die. The rules of reality don't apply to Dr. Who. Where *Star Trek* is a known quantity. It's set in the future. You have the laws of physics, the crew, and Star Fleet. They visit planets and solve problems in an hour. It's linear. There really is no comparison." A satisfied smile crossed his face. "Most of the technology and gadgets we enjoy today were first seen in some form on those early Trek episodes. Cellphones, iTouch, PDAs. Not so much for Dr. Who. The technology of the TARDIS falls into 'science so advanced it is indistinguishable from magic' area." He chuckled and a blush covered his cheeks. "Is my geek showing?"

She laughed and threw back her head, wincing at the sharp pain from the bruises around her neck.

Leaning toward her, he tilted her chin to the ceiling. "Let me take a look at that in better lighting." He took her hand and guided her to his bedroom.

For a lack of a chair, she sat on the edge of his bed while he went into the bathroom.

He returned with a cool wet cloth and knelt in front of her.

The cold soothed the ache of her ligation marks. "Of course, the only real sci-fi show worth watching is *Babylon Five*." Her comment brought him up short.

"You're full of surprises. I love that show too, but don't tell my housemates. They'll start calling me a traitor."

She laughed again, and it made her feel free. Nothing about being with Rob was forced. Being with him made her act like, well, herself. Maybe that's what attracted her to him the most. He made her real.

She'd been acting most of her adult life and almost forgot who Esther was.

"You have a wonderful laugh." He smiled at her as he stood and rolled his shoulders as if working out some knots. "The computer program will take a few hours to run. We should get some sleep."

Patting his twin-sized bed, she winked at him. "Looks cozy."

"You can sleep here. I'll take the floor."

She frowned. "I'm not proposing marriage, Rob, just me to keep you warm. I'm much more comfortable than the hard floor." Lying across the comforter, she cleared her throat as it went dry.

Her werewolf stared at her with hungry eyes. The amber color of his beast had returned, and a low growl rumbled in his chest. "I bet you are." His voice had grown deeper, and she got wetter between her thighs.

Undoing her jacket, she tossed it to the floor, never taking her gaze off him. The drumming of her heart filled her ears. She scooted farther up the bed as he slowly crawled over her. Ever since they'd met, she'd wanted this. Anticipation was such a bitch.

With a tug, he hooked his fingers around the waistband of her pants and released the button, then the zipper. From under him, he appeared much bigger, stronger than she'd thought.

In a frantic move, she tugged her t-shirt over her head.

"Slow down, let me do this." He took her eager hands from her pants and placed them over her head. Peeling her leather pants from her legs an inch at a time, he followed their path with a trail of kisses. Each caress dragged her closer to the edge.

"Rob?" Her voice shook.

The leathers joined her jacket and t-shirt on the floor. "Hmm?" He ran his canines along her hip as he removed her thong.

"Oh, shit." Her breaths became desperate.

"You like that?"

"Yes."

He placed a light kiss on her bikini line, which sent a tremor down her legs. If he went any slower her bottom half would go numb from need. Rising onto his elbow, he lay on his side and unclasped the front of her bra, setting her breasts free. His gaze was so intense it almost seemed like he stroked her skin.

More, she needed a lot more. She arched her back, inviting him to touch her.

With an unsure slide, his hand traveled from her lower abdomen to her chest, then finally to her breast. The brush of his fingertips over her nipples set them on fire.

Never one to take the backseat when it came to sex, she wrapped her arms around his neck and yanked him close, pressing a frantic hard kiss to his thin mouth. He tasted of scandalous mischief and forbidden cravings.

If a rescue had busted down the door and interrupted them to set her free, she'd have found her thirty-eight special and shot them between the eyes. Nothing was taking her out of Rob's arms.

He leaned to the side and pulled something out of his back pocket. Maybe a condom? With a strong grip, he gathered her hands from his neck and placed them above her head. He pressed his clothed body on top of hers and kissed along her neck.

Something cold and metallic snapped around her wrists. She yanked reflexively at the cuffs, which he'd secured to one of the headboard's wooden slats. "What the fuck? Where did theses come from?"

"Eric, my alpha, left them in our office. I can't take any chances with you. Then again, with your history, you could probably strangle me with your thighs." He set the key on his bedside table. "I'm naive, not stupid. Fool me once..." He let the old saying fade, the meaning very clear to her.

Too bad he didn't understand she never wanted to fool him again. When she watched him fall off the roof her heart had chosen to run *to* him instead of away. She'd made her choice, and she'd stick to it until the end. "Fine, I didn't have plans on going anywhere." Relaxing into the bed, she stretched her body along its length. "I'm game, then." She writhed her body under his, grinding her hip against his hard cock.

The feral glow returned to Rob's stare, and the carnal hunger that came with it reminded her of what exactly she taunted. It only made her want him more.

His tongue flashed as he licked his lips. "I wish I could trust you." The regret in his voice broke her heart, but then he gave her mischievous grin. "I can at least return your favor."

"I don't want payback. I want—"

He scooted down between her legs, lifting one over his shoulder.

"Oh, if you insist." She gnawed at her lower lip and shifted her shoulders so she could lift her head.

Meeting her stare, a fine blush rose on his cheeks again. He cleared his throat. "If I'm doing something wrong, tell me." He gave her a devilish smile. "And if I'm doing it right, let me know."

Her breath caught in her chest. "Is this your first time?"

"No." He placed a kiss on her inner thigh, working his way north, and she'd forgotten what she'd asked. "But I'm not a player like most shifters."

He couldn't have said a more perfect thing, and she was laying claim on his werewolf ass. Nosferatu be damned. No one would chase her off.

She expected his first lick to be hesitant, but once again he surprised her.

With a sure, steady stroke between her nether lips, Rob paid back the blow-job she'd given him. She never considered it a favor. She'd wanted to taste him and to let him know her desires.

Resting his lean body on the bed, Rob looked like a man settling in for a good long time. Each lap got deeper and longer as he began to explore her inner secrets.

God help her, she moaned and leaned her head back on the pillow, resting her cuffed wrists on the bed. He took his time and brought her back to the edge of ecstasy. Her breaths became ragged as she fought against her release.

Running his tongue around her clit sent a jolt of pleasure straight to her brain.

"Rob!"

He latched on the area, sucking as he thrust his fingers into her pussy.

She clung to the edge, not wanting to go over just yet, needing this moment to last as long as it could. It might be the last time he ever touched her.

CHAPTER 9

The bright, late afternoon sunlight drilled its way into Robert's consciousness through his eyelids and woke him. Its warmth spread over his body, but as he stretched he realized the heat didn't come from the sun but from the body pressed alongside him. He cracked open an eye.

Esther lay plastered across his chest, one leg thrown over his and her only free arm around his neck. Her face was turned up toward his with her lips parted. A sweet temptation. Her taste still lingered in his mouth. She'd cried out his name as she orgasmed last night over and over.

He'd released one wrist from the metal cuffs afterward so she could sleep more comfortably and was relieved she didn't pressure him for more than he was willing to offer her. When it came to Esther, he walked a tightrope of indecision. Part of him wanted to believe her sincerity, the other part thought he should have handed her over to Daedalus.

Any threat to the pack should be dealt with swiftly and without mercy. He ran a fingertip over her lush bottom lip. But was she a threat? She could be, but she could also be an asset. These last few days without Eric at his side showed him the pack lacked enough warriors.

His beast stirred. All she needed was one little bite or a nice deep scratch from him in his beast form and she could be his forever. The pack instinct would keep her from being a threat.

She moaned and pulled him closer, rubbing her face into his t-shirt.

It was nice fantasy, but he'd never do it on purpose. His conscience would eat him alive if he did. If she stayed at his side, he wanted it to be her choice.

The sharp ring of the pack cellphone startled both of them upright in bed.

Esther yanked at her restraint. "What the hell?" Brushing the hair from her face, she blinked and watched him crawl off the bed and answer the call.

He glanced at the caller ID and stifled a growl. "What do you want, Talon?" Robert sat on the edge of the bed with a very naked and soft Esther laying down in a daze next to him.

"We need to talk. Can you meet with me?" Talon replied.

"Yeah, I'll be at the pack's gathering hall in an hour."

"Fine." Talon disconnected the call.

The delicate touch of Esther's fingers searching under Robert's wrinkled shirt made him jump.

"Why such a serious face?" She inched closer, hooking her fingers in his jeans. She looked perfect in his bed. Sleep tossed hair formed a dark halo around her face and the thin sheet gathered around her waist, her exposed breasts drawing his gaze. Her heated blue stare was full of come-hither-and-ravish-me. Nothing would have pleased him more than to spend the day buried inside her.

But—there was always a *but* with Esther—he couldn't trust her. Not with something as fragile as his heart. A woman like her probably ate men like him for breakfast. He rubbed at the dull ache in his chest.

The action caused her gaze to drop, and she released her grip on his clothes. "Is there anything I can do to make things right between us?"

"Probably not. I'll always wonder if you're being sincere or just playing a part to get what you want."

She pulled her cuffed arm, and the metal rattled against the wooden headboard. "I want *you*. Fuck, I screwed things up so bad. I wish—I wish…" She turned her face away.

Those heartfelt words almost tore apart his resolve. But—he sighed and got a fresh set of clothes. There wasn't time to shower.

"Where are you going?"

"I never finished last night's mission. My troublemaking pack mate needs to be taught a lesson."

"You're not going alone."

He chuckled at the command in her tone. Naked and cuffed to a bed yet still thought she was in control. He could really fall in love with a woman like Esther. "I don't have much of a choice. It's too early for Daedalus to rise, and most of my roommates are at work."

"Most. Who's home? Take them." She pleaded with her eyes. "Hell, take me. Cuff me to your wrist if you have to. I can still use a gun with one hand."

He changed clothes in the same room. She'd seen him naked before. He felt her gaze roam over his body. "My friend, Sam, is still here. He'll watch over you." He pinned her with a glare. "I'll be very upset if anything happens to him while I'm gone."

The handcuff clanked as she tried to cross her arms over her chest. "Damn it." She flung her hands to her sides. "I'm not going to hurt anyone."

He raised his eyebrow and wished he could believe her.

"You should take me along. Don't go by yourself." She slid to the edge of the bed. "Please."

Lifting the key from the bedside table, he approached her.

She grinned and offered her restraint.

After unlocking the cuff, he grabbed hold of her waist and carried her to the bathroom.

"Wait! What are you doing?" Strong and agile, she squirmed in his grasp.

Dumping her on the cold tile floor, he pointed at her. "You want to earn my trust. You. Stay. Here." He ran his fingers through his hair. His thoughts flickered to the antacids in the kitchen cupboard. "I have enough problems, Esther. Do me a favor and don't add to them."

He gathered her clothes and tossed them in with her. Closing the door, he heard her grumbling under her breath, using his name in vain. With a shake of his head, he jammed the chair under the doorknob using his supernatural strength to ensure it stayed there. Bathrooms were meant to lock people out, not in.

Cutting across the hallway, he checked on the computer tracker's progress. It had finished tracing the email from Esther's account to a third party's account, but the kicker in his programming tracked it to the original sender.

The results made him slump onto his chair. What the fuck? It had to be wrong. He re-typed in the codes again then re-ran the program. It should be finished by the time he got home. The results didn't make sense.

Taking the stairs two at a time he descended to the basement, hoping Sam didn't have someone sharing his bed. It would be difficult discussing a prisoner in front of a stranger. He knocked on the bedroom door and it swung open.

Sam stood in only a pair of workout shorts. A set of free weights lay scattered around the room, and the buff werewolf pulled out his earbuds as he turned off the MP3 player at his hip. "Hey there, Sleeping Beauty. Get some action last night?" His voice dripped in sarcasm.

Robert barked out a laugh. "Why would you think that?"

"Tyler told me everything about the slayer you're hiding. I peeked in on both of you when no one showed up for breakfast. I needed to make sure she didn't try to off you again." He winked. "You both looked nice and cozy in that narrow bed of yours. Too bad she's a killer." He reached over and smacked Robert across the head. "What are you doing? She should be locked in the bathroom."

"Hey." Robert ducked the next swat and grabbed Sam's wrist. "I need you to keep an eye on her, dickhead. She's locked in the bathroom now." Releasing his well-meaning friend, he sighed. "And for the record, she shot me by accident and I haven't fucked her. Okay?" He glanced down the hallway at the vampire's man-cave where Daedalus slept during the day. "Make sure that's locked. I can't promise she won't try to kill Daedalus again."

"Sure." Sam's brow furrowed. "Where are you going?"

"I need to get—something from the corporate office. I'm falling behind on work."

"All right, I'll keep things tight here." Sam offered up his knuckles that Robert bumped with his own.

"I'll call and check in." Robert sprinted up the stairs, grabbed his keys and ran out the front door. On the stoop outside, he hesitated. The door had been unlocked. They always kept it secured. He glanced around, locked it, and then shook his head.

* * * *

Esther yanked on her leather pants and shoved her feet into her boots. What did Rob have against accepting help? She bet he didn't tell anyone from his pack what he was doing, let alone take one of them along.

Stomping to the window, she popped out the screen with an expert's ease and set it on the floor. She didn't have much time before he got to his car and drove off. The drainpipe held her weight as she shimmied down to a well-manicured garden.

How could he think she'd sit quietly in that bathroom all day while his life was in danger? Dread squeezed her heart with its sharp claws. He probably thought she *didn't* care.

No matter what happened she needed to make sure Rob was all right.

The   brownstones   all   shared their side walls. There wasn't any way to the front except through the house or around the back alley.

She snuck to the sliding glass door on the stone porch. Pressing her body to the wall, she glanced into a large kitchen. The coast looked clear. She scanned the yard and ran to the toolshed. After finding two flat head screwdrivers, she returned to the glass door panel and popped it off the track enough to stress the latch lock mechanism. She shoved it open and squeezed inside, then shut it.

Taking one silent step at a time, she crept to the front. When Daedalus brought her into the brownstone last night he'd tossed his keys on the front entrance table. She spotted and grabbed them. Two male voices carried from the basement. Her heart skipped a beat and froze for a second before she unlocked the front door. Hurrying to Daedalus's sports car, she opened the door and got inside before Rob saw her.

She got behind the steering wheel and watched Rob hesitate at the front door before locking it. He jogged to a sedan, pulling out a few minutes later.

Following at a discreet distance, Esther kept the car within sight. They traveled to the interstate, then to an industrial park. The area appeared deserted, making it difficult to follow him. She needed to pull off the road before he recognized the vampire's car.

The move made her lose him. She drove around the park trying to figure out where the fuck he disappeared to. Hitting the steering wheel, she began to circle the warehouses hoping he parked in back of one.

At the third building, she found the car next to a blue Jeep but both were empty. She parked and jumped out, automatically reaching for her thirty-eight special, but the Nosferatu had disarmed her last night. Popping the trunk open, she prayed to find a tool chest filled with weapons but only found a tire iron.

Rob was around here somewhere, however, so was Talon.

CHAPTER 10

The warehouse door swung closed behind Robert. It echoed inside the empty building and shut out the fading sunlight, leaving him entombed in darkness. He flipped the switch, and the neon lighting came on.

The Vasi used to gather as a pack here. Now, they met at a bar owned by a member in the downtown district. The warehouse held too many bad memories. When the Ayumu held Chicago the place was utilized for challenges and punishment. Frequently.

Those things didn't happen often anymore. Robert paced around the empty floor where Eric, his best friend, had taken a huge risk by facing the old alpha in combat. Eric had killed him. Continuing his tour down Nightmare Avenue, Robert passed the empty bleachers. He'd accompanied Eric that night into the arena as his beta, but he didn't know what that responsibility had entailed at the time.

Tonight, he finally got it. He needed to do the things to protect the pack no matter how it affected his conscience.

Talon wasn't leaving Chicago, and Robert needed to take care of this problem before Eric got home, for the pack, for himself, and for his best friend.

Glancing at his phone, he considered checking on Sam and reminding him to offer Esther a meal. When he got home later this evening he'd probably need to wear some armor before confronting her. She'd been pretty pissed when he dumped her in the bathroom, and she didn't like him meeting Talon alone or at least, she acted like it. Who knew with Esther? She may have been looking for an escape when she offered to accompany him.

The sound of a click made Robert spin around. Talon stepped into the warehouse holding his hands out to his side. "Hey, Bob."

Robert sighed at the name. So Talon would choose the hard way of dealing with him. No truce would be found tonight. "What problem do you have with me, Talon?"

"Not you specifically, runt, but the whole damn pack is turning into a bunch of pansies because of you and the Omegas. How long before some other pack comes in and takes over this city?"

"Only if you consider law abiding as weak."

"We're not human, Bob." Talon crossed the room and confronted him. "Why should we follow their rules?"

Robert hated the skip of his heartbeat as he met Talon's glare. Fear had a distinct smell, and if his pack mate caught a whiff of it he'd think he won.

According to Daedalus, a healthy dose of fear kept most warriors honorable, especially if doing wrong made them afraid. The fearless needed to be watched since they corrupted easily.

Talon never carried the scent of fear.

"I never said human laws. We follow the Accords like our ancestors did."

A sneer emerged on Talon's face, a werewolf of few intelligent words.

"If you called me out here for a challenge, then we'll need some witnesses to make it official. I beat you once, I can do it again." Robert kicked off his shoes and removed his t-shirt. Clothes became expensive when his beast tore through them every time.

"I brought witnesses." Talon whistled. The warehouse door opened, and two werewolves Robert recognized stepped in. They'd been chased out of Chicago last year for not conforming to the new laws and alpha.

"Hey, Joshua and Charles. Long time no see." Robert eased away, trying to assess the area for an escape.

They spread out, blocking the only unlocked door. Each began to strip, a bad sign.

His gut clenched. Three against one seemed like old-fashioned Ayumu strategy. "Eric would never consider you as a beta by using these tactics. Stop being a coward and challenge me properly."

Laughing, Talon removed his clothes as his companions transformed to beasts. "This isn't about becoming a pack beta, Bob." He grinned. "This is a message to the Vasi. The Ayumu didn't die with Michael. We're gathering." With this statement Talon transformed.

Robert didn't wait for an invitation. He allowed his beast free reign and it exploded forth, tearing out of his body. This fight required speed and agility, not controlled change like he was used to. The pain of the sudden transformation almost blinded him.

Someone tackled his legs from the side, and he hit the concrete floor like a sack of potatoes. His head rebounded off the hard surface and Tweety Bird paid him a visit before he got twisted into a pretzel on his back.

A set of teeth tried to clamp around his neck, but his reflexes saved him by tucking in his chin and rolling. With teeth and claw, they attacked him as a group.

All those sparing sessions with Daedalus beating the crap out of him finally made sense.

He never heard or saw the door open, not a footstep, or even a shadow. The first Robert knew of Esther's presence was the sound of a skull getting cracked.

Movement in the room stopped for a split second as the males counted heads and stared at one mean looking slayer wielding what looked like a—tire rod?

She didn't hesitate as she hit Joshua on the back swing with cold professionalism.

Speechless   by   her

appearance and inspired by her courage, Robert found the strength to heel kick the swaying Joshua, then roll onto Talon. Blood oozed from a multitude of wounds on Robert's hide. He'd already lost a great deal when Esther wounded him and the healing had taken a lot of energy. One good night's sleep and a sandwich hadn't replenished his reserve, yet he still pinned the mangy mutt to the floor.

All of Robert's reluctance about killing disappeared as he watched Esther defend herself against the two other werewolves who'd recovered from her attack. He needed to keep her safe. With a roar, he launched himself, placing his body between them and Esther. He couldn't bear it if she got hurt, and every instinct in his DNA cried to protect her.

As their opponents circled them she placed herself at his back. "Stay close," she whispered.

They fought, attacked, and defended as if they'd been partners for years. Her speed and aim complimented his strength and agility. Together they weaved through their lethal dance, her with a tire rod and him with claws. Swing, thrust, block, and pierce. Their bodies knew each other, sensing the other's next move until only Talon remained.

Joshua and Charles had deserted him and Talon turned to follow.

Robert watched his female block the door with her slim, fragile human body. Pressure squeezed his chest as his heart stopped.

Legs apart, Esther took a swing at Talon's head as he sped toward her.

With unnatural grace he managed to duck and caught her around the waist. Twisting, he pressed her back to his chest, pinning her arms to the side. The clang of the tire rod hitting the cement echoed. Heavy breathing became the only sound to fill the silence as Talon glared at him. The fiend bent slowly until his intentions became clear.

Esther screamed and struggled, unable to break free. Their eyes met, and for the first time Robert saw terror in them.

No amount of speed or magic could have gotten Robert there in time, but he tried. Damn, he tried.

Talon bit her shoulder.

The scent of blood filled his nose and her cries of, "No, no, no—" filled his ears.

It made his soul cringe knowing that pain didn't cause her shouts but her awareness of the infection Talon gave her. Robert reached them before Talon could make the kill, grabbed his jaw, and pried it from her flesh.

Wrestling to the floor, Talon's claws dug into Robert's back, a spur of force driving him as he pinned Robert. Suddenly Talon slumped against his body, a dead weight crushing him.

He shoved the beast off and saw Esther looming above them, a bloody tire rod back in her hands. Robert shifted to his human form and scrambled to his feet, then removed the blunt weapon from her clenched fingers. "Esther?"

"The—the bastard bit me." She kicked the unconscious Talon. "Rabies filled cocksucker."

"I'll take you to the hospital. I heard that General is offering an experimental vaccine to treat the infection." He dressed in his discarded clothes.

* * * *

Watching Rob pull his shirt on inside-out and cram his feet into his shoes, Esther's distress eased. Things like this happened. Getting turned into a monster was one of the many risks slayers faced, but most died when it happened, some at their own hand. She owned a special bullet to use in this type of emergency, but watching Rob made her doubt she'd need it.

She removed her jacket and glanced at the wound on her shoulder. Blood seeped into her black shirt, leaving a dark wet spot. No way would she avoid being infected.

The punctures were too deep.

Crap.

"Let's go." Rob picked her jacket off the ground, wrapped her in it, and lifted her in his arms. Worry lines creased his forehead.

"He bit my shoulder, not my legs. I *can* walk." If he got any sweeter she'd get a cavity.

He shoved the door open using his elbows and knees.

"We're just going to leave Talon here?" She tried to get a glimpse of the inert werewolf on the floor before the door closed.

Rob stomped toward his sedan when he did a double take. "Did you take Daedalus's car?"

"Yes."

"Better not take you home after the hospital. He's going to skin you alive."

"No, he's not." A familiar male voice spoke from behind them. "You've both been busy bees while I slept. Theft, assault, breaking and entering… Anything I'm missing?"

The vampire looked less than pleased, and Rob only clutched her tighter.

"Oh yeah, I forgot stupidity. What the hell is going on?" Daedalus planted his feet firmly on the pavement and crossed his arms over his chest. His pupils dilated, making them appear black. "I smell blood."

"She's injured. I'm taking her to the hospital."

The vampire stared at her, and for a split second she feared she'd be getting a second bite. He shook his head as if coming out of a dream.

"You're hungry." Rob made it a statement, not doubting what they'd both witnessed.

"Robert?" Esther used his full name for the first time and finally got his attention. "I'm not going to any hospital."

"Esther, you're in shock. You're going to at least get—"

"I'm not getting used as some lab rat." She raised her voice. "Put me down."

He blinked, then set her feet on the ground as if she were made of glass. "What about the virus?"

Her gut clenched. She pictured the special bullet she kept just for this occasion, then stared into Rob's concerned gaze. "I'll deal with it."

He frowned yet nodded. "Okay." Rubbing his chin, he glanced from her to Daedalus and back. "How did you both find me?"

Daedalus shrugged. "Easy. I have a tracer on my car. What I'd like to know is how Esther stole it. I have every security device known to man on it."

Quirking an eyebrow at him, she couldn't help but be impressed. Not many vamps his age converted to modern tech. "I took your keys."

"Well, I'll be damned." He grinned, flashing fang.

"Last I checked you already are." She faced Rob. "I do this for a living, remember?" Then she poked him in the chest with her finger at each word. "You always take back-up." She dropped her hand. "They would have killed you."

He stared at her, his expression softening. "You could have left the city or gone after him." He gestured to Daedalus.

"I know." She cleared her throat. "But I already watched you almost die once. Couldn't stand the idea of Talon finishing the job." Her gaze roved the ground going from discarded gum to pebble to crack until she felt a set of strong arms wrap around her. She lifted her face to find Rob close, his piercing green gaze boring into hers, then she winced as he tightened his grip. Searing pain shot through her shoulder.

"Sorry." He loosened his hold.

She touched under her jacket, and her fingers came out covered in blood.

"Fuck." Daedalus's fangs extended and he spun away, pacing as if caged. "Take her home already."

The door to the warehouse opened and Talon in beast form filled the space. A growl rumbled from him as he rubbed his head.

Rob shoved her behind him. "Talon, I'd like to introduce you to my buddy, Daedalus." He gestured to the hungry vampire. "Daedalus, I'd like you to meet dinner."

The Nosferatu's ears perked up. "Really? What happened to no killing?"

"I changed my mind." Rob turned to face her. "Let's go home."

CHAPTER 11

The hot water from the shower stung as it cascaded over Esther's head and trickled into the bite mark on her shoulder. She stood still with the bar of soap grasped in her hand and her eyes closed.

She was a werewolf.

Losing her humanity had never seemed an option before today. She'd always kept a spare bullet to put through her head if she got infected. Rob changed everything. Now she had something to live for.

Who was Esther if not a slayer?

Daedalus had better take his time draining Talon dry and make him suffer for what he'd done to her. She tossed the bar of soap against the tiled wall.

The bathroom door creaked open. "I brought some fresh towels." Her uncertain future tied her soul in knots, but Rob's voice, filled with promises, melted something tight inside her chest.

Alone most of her life, Esther never understood how forlorn she'd been until meeting Rob. Even her dreams held a seat for one. How empty her life appeared, a big void of violence, money, and casual sex, which never touched her heart or her soul.

"Esther?" The shower curtain slid over. Rob held a folded thick, white towel and still wore his fucking shirt inside-out.

God, he was the most precious thing in the world. With a sudden sob, she hid her face in her hands, unable to stop the emotional onslaught that shook her shoulders and back.

"Oh no, Esther— Please, no." He shut the water off and wrapped her in the towel. Carrying her in his arms, he spoke gentle words that didn't penetrate the dark cloud of despair around her.

She didn't make much noise as the tears burned her cheeks. Her throat was out of practice when it came to crying and it got sore from the effort. She wiped her cheeks while the sobs faded and realized she sat on Rob's lap as he leaned against the sink cabinet.

"This is all my fault." He stroked her wet hair.

Pulling the towel tighter around her chest, she rested her head on his shoulder. "I don't remember you biting me."

"No, but I had the chance to kill Talon the night we met and I chickened out."

She lifted her chin to gaze at his face.

His thin lips frowned, regret filling his eyes.

"Well, if we're going to play this silly game, then I can be at fault too. I didn't need to follow you or try and block the door." She turned his face toward hers and placed a chaste kiss on his mouth. "Your turn."

He rewarded her with a small, crooked smile.

She grinned back. "What now? I mean, how long does it take for me to—to change?"

"Everyone is different. It all depends on how much virus transferred into your system. Usually, it takes a week to a month before you can shift shape." He looked at the floor and cleared his throat. "There'll be nightmares. It's how the beast develops, and you'll be on probation for a year, living with a mentor so you stay in control."

She blinked at him, her mind gone blank. A mentor? Live somewhere else? What about her apartment in New York?

"If your beast takes over completely and you kill someone, no jury in the world will have mercy. They'll destroy you. Having a mentor is important and non-negotiable with the Vasi."

Overwhelmed, Esther nodded and stared at him, unable to ask the thousands of questions racing through her mind.

He must have sensed something, because he looked up from the floor at her. "If you want to be part of a different pack I'm sure my alpha can make arrangements. Don't feel like you have to— I mean, I'd—we'd never force you to stay."

Stay? Rob kept her safe, he understood her. Why would she go anywhere? "Can I stay?"

Relief flooded his expression. "Yes, of course." He hugged her. "You've got time to adjust. It's a big change, but we've all been through the same process. You're not alone." He squeezed her. "I'll be there for you."

Those five words were the nicest things anyone had ever said to her. She threw her arms around his neck and hugged him back. "Can you be my mentor?"

Stroking her hair, he leaned away and gave her a shy smile. The same one he'd given her the night they met. "I hoped you would ask. You'll have to live here with us. I can move into the office across the hall, and you can have my room."

"Your room? But I want…" She couldn't finish her sentence. No matter what she did he wouldn't ever trust her.

"What do you want?" Pushing some loose strands of hair behind her ear, he gazed into her eyes.

"You."

* * * *

Robert released the breath he'd been holding. The drumming of his heart was the only thing he could hear. It made him lightheaded. "You say and do all the right things but…" There was always a *but* with Esther. Could he live with *buts* complicating his life?

Vulnerable, she clung to him, pleading with her eyes, not even trying to defend her actions. He didn't think many people ever saw this side of Esther, his hardcore slayer.

He didn't want a difficult relationship. "Are you going to break my heart, Esther?"

"What?" The shock on her face appeared genuine.

"I could fall in love with you." He cupped her beautiful face within the palms of his hands. "I'm willing to take that leap and place my faith in you. Just—answer my question honestly."

She placed her hands on his. "I'd never hurt you. Not on purpose, not even if *you* broke *my* heart."

She was going to become a werewolf. Her life would change, which meant no more slaying. She'd come to his aid when it was a three-to-one fight. Maybe he should trust her now.

He tossed his doubts out of his heart and mind. Esther belonged to him and he to her. As she developed into a werewolf their bond would grow and he'd have a true mate. Something he never considered possible. He grinned as he drew her mouth to his.

Dropping her towel, she draped her limbs around him.

The sharp flavor of mint greeted his tongue as he slipped it between her lips. A thousand pounds of responsibilities, anxiety, and stress dissipated with her taste.

With an aggression born of her nature, Esther tore at the buttons of his jeans.

Groaning as his erection strained in their confines, he removed her hands, not wanting their first time having sex to be on the bathroom floor. In a few hours Eric would be home and nothing short of the end of the world would take Robert from Esther's side.

When he stood, she clung to his hips and ground her pussy to his hard, needy cock. It pulsed. Damn, he would so fuck her senseless.

She squirmed in his arms while he hurried to the unmade bed, her soft, warm flesh inviting his hands to explore. With his knees, he hit the edge of the bed and he set her down.

Lying back, she stretched along the mattress in all her glorious nudity.

Robert stared. Words didn't exist for the gratitude he felt toward the odd series of events that led them to this moment. He undressed, then crept over her body.

Skin slid over skin. Her hard nipples traced along his chest, and she arched her back with a low moan.

He loved the way she reacted to his touch. It nurtured his confidence and hell, boosted his ego. She'd climaxed for him last night and called out his name. Tonight he would make her beg for it to never stop. Although, with the way she stared at him at the moment, it was possible he might end up being the one on his knees begging.

Cupping her breast in his palm, he brought her tight nub to his mouth and sucked in hard draws.

She grasped his shoulders, digging her nails into him. Her breaths came quickly.

The sharp pain aroused him more. It called to his beast who recognized the act as possessive. He growled his approval and worked her other firm mound. The scent of her arousal grew stronger. Dipping his hand between her thighs to her wet pussy, he slipped his fingers into her hot velvet.

Her moans grew louder, more desperate, while he thrust his digits inside. With his thumb, he searched for that special spot, the elusive clitoris. Her sharp cry signaled his discovery and he massaged the spot, taking it for a test drive.

Her hips rolled in an inviting manner. Rotating and grinding, she helped him stimulate her pleasure point.

The beast and human side of Robert shared his body equally, both wanting Esther. Instinct became logic as her new scent carried the innate flavor of pack, and more importantly, she smelled like his. He nipped the bud he suckled with his teeth, experimenting with the fine edge of pain and pleasure.

The muscles in her pussy clenched around his fingers, wetness soaking his hand. Her moans became higher in pitch as she achieved her climax. The first of many, he hoped.

As if melting, Esther's body molded to the mattress and pillows. Pride swelled his chest as a lazy smile graced her face.

He finally understood why some wars were fought over women. Nothing would take her from him without a fight. His cock pressed against his abdomen, demanding attention.

Esther spread her knees. Glistening and slick, her nether lips were flushed the same shade of pink as her cheeks. "Do you need a written invitation?"

"Anxious?"

She gave a deep laugh. "Damn right I am. I've wanted you since the day we met." Reaching between his thighs, she stroked him with a feathery touch.

A shiver shook his body. He closed his eyes, resting his forehead on her shoulder while he growled his approval.

"Three days is a long time to wait, Rob." Esther's advances grew more aggressive. Stroking with both hands, she showed no mercy and milked his cock.

Of their own accord, his hips thrust in time. He gripped the bedding and tried to catch his breath. By some miracle he kept from coming, even though her hands felt so fucking great. After a few more strokes he noticed his erratic breathing, and he sat back between her bent legs and removed her hands.

She was perfect for him, driving and challenging him in life and in bed. He grabbed her ass and lifted her pussy to meet his cock. The heat of her cream slipped over his tip and he rubbed his stiff rod at her entrance, barely penetrating.

It drove *her* wild.

And she drove *him* over the edge. He shoved inside of her to his balls.

His name left her lips and she dug her nails into his ass, pulling him even deeper.

Everyone in the house must have heard her. He grinned and thrust harder, faster, so she'd do it again. Once he started pounding inside her, he didn't care if she shouted out the alphabet backward. Secret muscles squeezed him like no hands ever could. Smooth and soft, her pussy enveloped him as he burrowed deeper.

He wanted more, needed to spread his scent all over her so every male would know she belonged to him. His momentum drove Esther to the headboard.

To avoid getting a concussion she sat and grabbed his shoulders. She wrapped her legs around his waist.

Unbelievably, he sank even deeper. From the shocked expression on her face he knew his eyes had changed color again. She always seemed taken when they became his beast's amber. The transformation was close, only a fraction of will kept him and the beast from merging, but he'd been this close before and knew how to control his change.

Esther's gasp rewarded his efforts as he channeled the beast's size into his cock.

"Oh shit, Rob." She flung her head back, exposing her graceful neck.

Bracing her back to the wall by his bed, he bit her shoulder. Thrust after hard thrust, sweat beaded on her smooth skin and some trickled down his back. The springs of his bed squealed, and his wall creaked from the abuse.

Esther's cries of encouragement kept him going. They changed in pitch all of a sudden. Her pussy grabbed hold of his cock as if made of iron, leaving him at her mercy until his seed poured into her. A howl tore from his throat.

Silence blanketed the room after his declaration. Robert kneeled and gathered his Esther into his arms. The next year would be tough on both of them. He'd just witnessed Spice's adaptation with Eric as her mentor and he knew what to expect—a lot of chaos.

Esther's blue eyes met his.

He'd love every second of it.

The front door closed and Eric's voice shouted, "We're home. What'd we miss?"

Robert glanced at the pack cellphone on his bedside table. He'd keep it and give his alphas one more day of rest. There wasn't a problem out there he couldn't handle.

ABOUT ANNIE NICHOLAS

http://www.lyricalpress.com/annie_nicholas

From my Vermont home, I create paranormals with a twist. Finding the right kind of twist for each story proves to be a challenge, especially in a series.

I struggled to find the right woman for Robert. All the month of August 2010, I wrote and wrote from his point of view trying to find the core of what I wanted. Ten thousand words later, I hit delete and erased it all. With a new start, I met Esther. Hard-ass killer, confident, and competent, the total opposite of my hero. A perfect match. A perfect twist.

Annie's Website:
www.annienicholas.webs.com
Reader eMail:
annienicholas@ymail.com

ABOUT THE VANGUARDS SERIES

Book 1: *The Omegas*
Available in ebook from Lyrical Press

Book 2: *The Alpha*
Available in ebook from Lyrical Press

Book 3: *The Beta*
Available in ebook from Lyrical Press

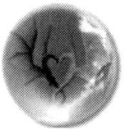

CPSIA information can be obtained at www.ICGtesting.com
Printed in the USA
BVOW012339020212

281891BV00001B/6/P